D1062771

Praise for The Country Club Murders

GUARANTEED TO BLEED (#2)

"Set in Kansas City, Missouri, in 1974, this cozy mystery effectively recreates the era through the details of down-to-earth Ellison's everyday life."

– *Booklist*

"Mulhern's lively, witty sequel to *The Deep End* finds Kansas City, Mo., socialite Ellison Russell reluctantly attending a high school football game...There she stumbles on a dying teenage boy covered in blood, who asks that she tell his girlfriend that he loves her. Ellison determines to learn the girlfriend's identity and deliver the message, plus find the boy's killer...If that's not enough for one day, an unknown man turns up shot to death in her garden. Cozy fans will eagerly await Ellison's further adventures."

– *Publishers Weekly*

"In this excellent follow-up to her debut *The Deep End*, author Mulhern continues to depict the trappings of a privileged community...Readers who enjoy the novels of Susan Isaacs will love this series that blends a strong mystery with the demands of living in an exclusive society. Watching Ellison develop the strength of character to break through both her own and her society's expectations is a sheer delight."

– *Kings River Life Magazine*

"Written sincerely, with unforgettable one-liners including: "Kizzi lived behind a curtain sewn from dry martinis." There are many more to list, but I do not want to spoil the pleasure of unexpectedly encountering such gems tucked throughout the book. Thoroughly enjoyable."

– Librarian, Jefferson-Madison Regional Library System

THE DEEP END (#1)

"Part mystery, part women's fiction, part poetry, Mulhern's debut, *The Deep End*, will draw you in with the first sentence and entrance you until the last. An engaging whodunit that kept me guessing until the end!"

– Tracy Weber,
Author of the Downward Dog Mysteries

"What truly stands out is the development of Ellison as a very realistic and very likable character...Not to be overlooked is the humor and wit that entertains throughout the novel as readers enjoy following an intelligent heroine completely coming into her own as a compelling, funny, and very intelligent woman."

– *Kings River Life Magazine*

"What a fun read! Murder in the days before cell phones, the internet, DNA and AFIS."

– *Books for Avid Readers*

"Intriguing plots, fascinating characters. From the first page to the last, Julie's mysteries grab the reader and don't let up. When all is resolved and I read the last page, I wanted to read more."

– Sally Berneathy,
USA Today Bestselling Author

"Ms. Mulhern weaves a tidy tale of murder, blackmail, and life behind the scenes in the Country Club set of the 70s...an excellent mystery, highly recommended, and I eagerly await the next in the series."

– *Any Good Book*

GUARANTEED TO BLEED

The Country Club Murders
by Julie Mulhern

THE DEEP END (#1)
GUARANTEED TO BLEED (#2)

GUARANTEED TO BLEED

THE COUNTRY CLUB MURDERS

HENERY PRESS

GUARANTEED TO BLEED
The Country Club Murders
Part of the Henery Press Mystery Collection

First Edition
Hardcover edition | October 2015

Henery Press
www.henerypress.com

Cover art by Stephanie Chontos

ISBN-13: 978-1-943390-08-3

Printed in the United States of America

To Matt with love, you know what you did.

ACKNOWLEDGMENTS

Thank you to my agent, Margaret Bail, for loading me on the plane. Thank you to Sally Berneathy, Madonna Bock and Jan Leyh for taking this journey with me. And, thank you to Anna, Art, Erin, Kendel, Rachel, and Stephanie for picking me up at the airport. I couldn't do this without you!

ONE

September 1974
Kansas City, Missouri

My second mistake was dropping my lipstick.

It clanged against the metal riser, spun for a tantalizing second just beyond my fingers' reach, then dropped to the nether regions below.

My first mistake was buying the damned thing. Purchased from a terrifyingly chic salesgirl at Galérie Lafayette in Paris, it was the perfect shade of red. A hue, she told me, so sublime the French manufacturer declined to sell it in the United States. Then she looked down her slightly hooked, Parisian nose as if she was Marie Antoinette and I was a peasant who dared ask for bread. Who wouldn't be intimidated by that level of chic? I handed over a ridiculous number of francs and bought the transformative, perfection-filled gold tube.

What was I thinking? *Rouge Chaud* had no business on my lips. I wasn't chic or sophisticated or Continental. I was a mother, an artist, a daughter. I wore soft pinks and delicate corals, not red, not *Rouge Chaud.* Lesson learned—when making major life changes, don't start with red lipstick. The stranger in the mirror looks so odd it's disheartening.

My third mistake was going after the silly thing.

"What are you doing?" Libba asked when I stood.

"I dropped my lipstick."

She nodded but I doubt she really heard me. She seemed quite intent on the line of boys in blue jerseys. Libba actually likes football, and her nephew was somewhere on the field. Maybe. Telling the difference between one boy and another was only possible when their numbers were visible.

Personally, I'd rather be audited by the IRS than sit through a game. If my daughter, Grace, wasn't cheering, I'd have skipped the whole evening—the stands, the noise, and the sight of boys knocking each other flat while their parents urged them to hit harder.

Obviously not everyone shared my opinions. The combination of a cool fall evening and a cross-state rival had packed the stands. The Suncrest fans wore phthalo blue—cadmium yellow being nearly unwearable. Across the field sat a healthy contingent of traveling Burroughs fans clad in Brunswick green.

I eased my way past the first few people seated in the crowded row, murmured apologies, avoided stepping on drinks but not toes or handbags, and blocked the views of eager parents. Something happened on the field. A collective second of held breath, then a collective gasp.

The man whose view I blocked leaned around me. "Go, baby!" He yelled loud enough to render me deaf in one ear.

Just a taste of the roar to come. Everyone cheered. They stood and yelled and stomped their feet on the risers until the stands shook.

I turned and looked. Who wouldn't?

A boy in blue with a ball tucked deep in the crook of his elbow ran down the field.

On the sidelines, Grace and her fellow cheerleaders jumped impossibly high, shook their pom-poms and encouraged more yelling.

He reached the end zone and the stands erupted.

The crackling PA system announced a defensive touchdown. High fives abounded.

I pushed my way to the end of the row, descended the stairs, and walked down the sidelines to the exit.

Space. Air. Not silence—but at least the decibels didn't threaten permanent hearing loss.

I circled around to the back of the stands.

In the stands, with lights and sounds and the distraction of determining who had the ball, I'd failed to notice the purple velvet of night pushing the last rays of sun over the western skyline. I hadn't counted on dark. Damn.

Worse, a chain-link fence enclosed the area beneath the stands. How had I never noticed it before? My quick rescue trip was fraught with complications.

Where was the blasted gate? I walked the length of the fence with my hand plunged into the bottom of my purse. A penlight lived in its depths. I was sure of it. I needed light. I didn't like my chances of finding my lipstick on the unlit ground.

I found the gate—unlocked, thank heavens—but the light still eluded me. I opened my purse wider and peered into its depths.

The gate whooshed open and hit me on the head. Hard. A galaxy's worth of stars surrounded me. Someone pushed past me, finishing the job the gate started. I fell on my ass. Thudded. The impact shuddered up my spine. Whoever it was didn't stop, didn't apologize, nothing. What the hell were they doing under there? An argument with a girl? A rendezvous with a boy? The quick trade of a fistful of crumpled ones for a small bag of pot? Far more important was the likelihood of grass stains on my new skirt.

I stood, brushed the grass off my backside, and entered the dim world beneath the stands. The beams supporting the stands above left me only one path and what little light there was had to filter past ankles and pants legs and the odd handbag. I dug again for my penlight. I found a travel pack of Kleenex, my wallet, keys, a pack of Doublemint gum, a pencil bag and a small drawing pad. Of course, no flashlight. I'd find it tomorrow when the sun shone brightly.

At least the narrow spaces between the risers that denied me light kept some of the cigarette butts and empty cups from falling. The ground was cleaner than I expected. I stopped looking where I was walking. Instead I looked up and gauged where I'd been sitting.

That's how I tripped over Bobby Lowell. Of course, when I tripped, I didn't know it was Bobby Lowell. I didn't even know it was a person. Not until he moaned.

I heard that moan and my heart tripped along with my feet. It tumbled to my knees, leaving them weak. Then the damned thing raced back to my chest so fast it left me breathless.

Alone in the uneven darkness, the last thing I'd expected was a person on the ground. I knelt. "Are you all right? What happened?"

The fickle light showed me a man. No. Too young. A boy. A boy with a stained shirt.

Someone in the stands shifted and for a half-second, the boy was caught in a shaft of light.

I saw him clearly.

Blood.

Blood had seeped through his t-shirt. Soaked it.

I gasped. "What happened?"

He didn't answer. I didn't blame him. It was a stupid question and totally irrelevant to the problem at hand—getting him help.

I yelled but my voice was lost in the cacophony of screaming football fans. What was it Daddy said about whistling in the wind?

Meanwhile the boy bled into the dirt. How much blood could a person lose?

My fumbling hands covered the wound, applied pressure. So much blood. It welled between my fingers. Warm. Gut-twisting. Horrifying. Its smell, somehow metallic, made bile rise in my throat.

"Help!"

I hardly heard my own voice. There was no way anyone in the stands would hear me. The poor kid would bleed to death listening to people cheer and the ineffectual shouts of a woman in search of a lipstick.

I yanked off my white cotton button-down, bunched it together, and pressed it against the hole in his chest. Within seconds the shirt was soaked in blood.

Damn!

"Hold on. Don't die." I struggled to my feet, flattened my hand and slid my fingers through the narrow space in the stands. I closed my hand around the first ankle I found—a narrow one. The owner of the ankle kicked—viciously—and freed herself from my grasp. My wrist scraped against the riser.

If the woman's hysterical screams were any indication, I'd ruined football games for her for all eternity.

It was worth it if she sent help. Surely someone would come investigate the bloody hand from beneath the stands.

I pulled my hand back through the slat and resumed applying pressure to the boy's chest. His breath was shallow and, impossibly, seemed louder than the sounds from the stands.

His fingers scrabbled around my fingers.

I leaned forward. "Help is on the way."

He jerked his chin as if help didn't matter. "Tell her..."

The fingers that circled my wrist were clammy.

My shirt was near useless in staunching his blood. "Hush. Help is coming." I hoped to God I wasn't lying.

His Adam's apple bobbed and his mouth worked its way around words. "Tell her I love her."

"You can tell her. Just stay with me," I begged.

The light filtering through the bleachers shifted, revealing his eyes—glazed with pain, pleading.

"I'll tell her. Who is she?"

"Hands in the air!"

I glanced over my shoulder. Maynard, the security guard who'd been at Suncrest since I attended, pointed a shaky gun at me.

I gave him the same amount of respect that Grace and her friends did. I ignored him.

"Hands up!" He cocked his gun.

"Officer Hodgins, it's Ellison Russell. This boy has been hurt. Call an ambulance."

The fool man didn't move. Maybe he wasn't used to school parents covered in blood. Or maybe it was the bra. Purchased in

Paris, it was made of silk and lace and seductive promises I had no intention of keeping. Ever. "Ambulance," I snapped.

He lowered his gun but didn't move.

"Call an ambulance. If you can't manage that, see if there's a doctor in the stands." There were probably twenty—surgeons and cardiologists and neurologists and oncologists. I bet none of them dealt with trauma. None of them knew how to deal with a gaping hole in a teenage boy's chest. Even so, they had to know more than I did. "Get. Help."

A man pushed past the useless guard. He was probably the father of a student. He had the look—a crisp button-down shirt, an I-run-things-get-out-of-my-way attitude, and madras pants in the school colors.

It was too late in the year for madras. *His wife should have made him change.* The thought bobbed across the surface of my brain. Just goes to show Mother's influence can't be drowned. Not even by a sea of blood.

His gaze scanned the scene, my scandalous brassiere, then—quickly—the scene again. He dropped to one knee next to Bobby and demanded, "What happened?"

"No idea. I found him. Are you a doctor?"

He answered with a quick jerk of his chin. "No. What are you doing down here?" The question sounded like an accusation.

"I dropped my lipstick."

His lips thinned. "Flashlight." His voice brooked no arguments.

Maynard, who'd ignored my every request, immediately handed over a striated silver tube. Apparently, the guard preferred taking orders from a man.

The man shined the light at the boy's chest, then he lifted my sodden shirt and gingerly poked at the boy's t-shirt. "You've been applying pressure?"

The boy moaned.

"Yes."

He looked up from the boy's chest and directed his gaze on

Maynard's unfortunate face. "Ambulance. Police. Now."

Maynard Hodgins finally moved. In fact, he spun on his heel and rushed through the open gate.

"Pressure?" I asked. The boy could die while the man directed Maynard.

I snatched my shirt back and applied it to the wound.

Sirens.

Someone smarter than the high school's cantankerous guard had called for help.

The boy's hand tightened on my wrist. I leaned forward, straining to hear his raspy whisper. "Tell her..."

"I will," I promised.

"What did he say?" the man demanded.

Bossing Maynard was one thing, bossing me another. I ignored him.

Activity engulfed us—paramedics and a uniformed police officer and two men with a gurney. Each one paused and stared at my lace bra and bloodied hands. I ignored the embarrassed heat prickling my skin. Let them look. The bleeding boy had needed my shirt far more than I had.

One of the men pried the boy's fingers loose from my wrist. Another replaced my bloodied shirt with fresh gauze. A hand gripped my elbow and lifted me out of the way.

"You're bleeding," a medic said.

How could he tell? The boy's blood covered my arms.

He pointed at a gash near my wrist. It must have happened when I reached through the slat in the stands. I hadn't noticed it.

"Have it looked at," said the man in the madras pants. "Get in the ambulance."

Who the hell did he think he was?

Really? Who was he?

He bent, scooped up a gold, square-shaped tube of Guerlain lipstick and held it in front of me. "If you want it back, get in the ambulance."

I held out my hand and waited for the gold tube to land in my palm. I dropped the blasted thing into my purse, stumbled through the gate and let one of the paramedics load me onto the ambulance, which is how I ended up holding Bobby Lowell's hand when he died.

TWO

I waited in the ER in a room created by ugly curtains. My wrist and hand, wrapped in clean white bandages, throbbed. I wanted home. I wanted a shower. Failing that, I wanted a scrub-brush and strong soap, because each time I closed my eyelids I saw my fingernails painted with Bobby's blood.

Finding another body was not what I had planned. Our return home from a summer of wandering through Europe was meant to be a return to solid, familiar ground. Grace would be surrounded by caring friends. She'd go back to school and a sustaining routine. I would paint. The raw pain caused by death would begin to fade. We both would heal.

Instead, one of Grace's oldest friends was dead. Murdered.

Tears gathered in the corners of my eyes and I blinked them away. Thinking about Bobby Lowell was a mistake; it made my throat swell and my jaw ache. I couldn't afford muzzy thinking, not when a police detective waited for me. One who probably had a list of questions longer than the strip of gauze circling round and round my wrist.

As a distraction, I rendered my little cubicle on an imaginary canvas. Oatmeal-colored vinyl curtains hung on grommets, mysterious machines sat quietly. The bed, which I'd abandoned in favor of an uncomfortable chair, was metal with a thin blue mattress and an abandoned tangle of scratchy sheets. The whole place stank of iodine and desperation. It would make a terrible painting.

I narrowed my eyes and let the colors run together—the

oatmeal of the curtains, the silver of the bedrails, the obnoxious blue of the mattress. It was still a terrible painting.

A nurse yanked the curtain along its pole. Its metallic screech set my teeth on edge. "The police are ready to see you now."

Some nurses are sadists who've figured out how to get paid. This one wasn't so bad. She'd injected my arm with lidocaine before the doctor sewed quick, neat stitches from the base of my wrist to the base of my thumb, and she'd found me the top to a set of scrubs so I didn't have to sit around wearing just my bra.

It was that second kindness that earned her my undying gratitude. Talking to the police in my bra was even less appealing than a holiday cruise. Mother insisted Grace and I couldn't spend Christmas in the house where Henry died. Her answer was a flight to San Diego and a cruise to Mexico. For all of us. Nothing says holiday spirit like being stuck on a boat for six days with a woman whose telling sighs probably weighed more than the anchor. Thank heavens for Daddy; he flatly refused to eat Christmas dinner on a boat.

The nurse led me to a room with real walls, paused outside the real door, then offered me a gentle pat on the shoulder. "Is there someone I can call to come pick you up?"

I shook my head. Libba was taking care of Grace. I'd talked to them both, assured a teary Grace I was fine and promised to be home soon. Calling any of my other friends would mean a lengthy explanation. I had only one explanation in me and it was reserved for the police. "No, thank you."

"Not your husband?"

"I'm a widow."

She sucked in a breath. "I'm sorry."

I wasn't. Even if he was still alive, it was unlikely Henry would have gone to the trouble of picking me up from the hospital. "Thank you for offering. When I'm done, I'll call a cab."

I smoothed the loose folds of my shirt. Why did I never talk to the police looking polished or put together? Then I entered the room.

Detective Anarchy Jones sat at the table inside.

My feet stopped moving forward, my intestines defied the laws of science and turned from solid to liquid in the time it took me to blink. My knees no longer seemed strong enough to support me. Only my mouth continued to function.

"What are you doing here?" I lifted my unbandaged hand to cover it before it said anything else.

Detective Jones stood. A smile that webbed the corners of his eyes and quirked his lips ghosted across his lean face. "The usual. Investigating a murder where you found the body."

"Oh." It barely qualified as a sound, much less a word. It was still infinitely better than *I'm sorry I didn't call you and let you know I was back.*

"Have a seat, Mrs. Russell."

Mrs. Russell. Oh dear. When had I gone back to being Mrs. Russell? I preferred being called Ellison and he knew it. I carefully lowered myself into a chair.

"Are you all right?" he asked.

I held up my arm. "Eight stitches."

He sat across from me. "That's not what I meant."

"I know." *Mrs. Russell* wasn't about to tell him that she and Grace were still muddling through Henry's death or that she wasn't ready for another man in her life.

"Are you? All right?"

Aside from my poor judgment in men—my liking him wasn't exactly a point in his favor—and my questionable taste in lipsticks, I was fine. Then again, maybe he was just asking if I was all right after finding poor Bobby.

He waited for me to say something.

I stared at the table and wished I was at home. He should have figured out by now that the emptiness of silence doesn't bother me. I won't speak just to fill it.

He gave up. Sort of. Anarchy Jones will lose a battle to win the war. Being the first to speak was a very small battle. "You knew Bobby Lowell?"

I nodded. "Since he was five. He and Grace were in kindergarten together."

"What happened tonight?"

I told him everything—my dropped lipstick, the unlocked gate, the person who knocked me down.

Anarchy leaned forward and rested his forearms on the table. "Man or woman?"

"A man, I think. I wouldn't swear to it. It happened so fast..."

He gave me *the look*. The disbelieving one that police save for an unreliable witness who can't tell who's knocked her on her keister. "Then what happened?"

"I went under the stands to find my lipstick. I found Bobby."

"Did you know it was him?"

My throat swelled and my jaw ached. "No. Not at first." I swallowed an unwelcome lump. "I just knew it was someone who'd been hurt."

"What kind of a kid was he?"

I have a Polaroid of Bobby and Grace at their third grade Halloween party. Bobby is a grinning, gap-toothed Superman. Grace is Dorothy from the Wizard of Oz. His arm is draped around her with the sunny confidence of a boy who excels at everything. That boy lay in a morgue. "He was a good kid."

"Really?" Detective Jones' left eyebrow rose. "That's not what I heard."

Bobby asked Grace to the seventh grade dance. He showed up on our front steps looking as if his striped tie might choke him to death. He brought her a corsage—a pink rose. The next morning I helped Grace press it between the pages of a book. She still has it, the first flower a boy ever gave her.

"He took Grace to a dance once." Henry snapped pictures before we sent them down the front walk where Bobby's mother waited to drive them. Poor CeCe. "Bobby's parents divorced a couple of years ago. It was...ugly. Bobby's been going through a rough patch."

"Maybe some part of that rough patch got him killed?"

"Or maybe he was just in the wrong place at the wrong time."

"You don't seriously believe that, do you?"

I didn't. When the stranger knocked me down I'd thought sex or drugs. I lowered my forehead into the palm of my uninjured hand.

"Ellison, tell me what you know."

Ellison. He'd used my first name. I lifted my gaze and searched his face—lean cheeks, expressive mouth, eyes that could make married women forget their vows—and I wasn't married. He'd picked up a tan over the summer. It made him even more attractive. I shook my head. "I don't know anything."

He snorted softly. "I have to know why Bobby was killed before I can figure out who did it. Please, help me."

"How? I haven't seen him in at least a year. Maybe longer."

"Did he say anything?"

"He asked me to tell her he loved her." My hard-won dry eyes suddenly swam in tears. Bobby *wasn't* a bad kid. With his dying breaths, he'd expressed his love for someone.

"Was he in love with Grace?" Anarchy asked.

"No." Bobby and Grace hardly saw each other.

"Then who?"

I shook my head. "I have no idea."

He stared at me for a moment. Waiting for me to say more? He leaned back in his chair. "You're telling the truth."

I sat up straight and crossed my arms over my chest, careful to keep the injured arm on top. "You can read me that easily?"

He chuckled. "Anyone can read you. You scratch the end of your nose when you lie."

The black expression I directed across the table seemed amusing to him. He grinned.

I lifted my non-itching nose in the air. "If you have nothing further?" I stood.

"Nothing this evening. But I will be in touch."

Exactly what I was afraid of.

* * *

The cabbie dropped me off in front of a house ablaze with lights. I glanced at my watch, saw the time—one in the morning—and sighed. I'd been holding onto a cowardly and apparently vain hope that Grace might be asleep, that I might stow my grief in a sock drawer and avoid dealing with hers until morning.

I trudged up the front steps and unlocked the door.

Max the Weimaraner met me with a sleepy sniff and quick rub of his head against my leg, his version of a doggy hug. Maybe he'd finally forgiven me for leaving him with our housekeeper Aggie all summer. I scratched behind his silken ears, then followed voices into the kitchen.

Libba and five teenage girls stood around the kitchen island, its marble top hidden by open bags of chips, a bowl of popcorn, an empty Eggo box, syrup-covered plates, Tab cans, a spill of strawberry Pop Rocks and one extra-large, extra full glass of wine. Annoyance flared within me like a Roman candle on the Fourth of July. I'd watched a boy die and Libba had okayed a slumber party?

"I hope you don't mind," she said. "Grace wanted to have a few friends over."

Nothing like putting me on the spot. "Of course not." I offered her a sugary smile. She deserved torture, "Seasons in the Sun" until her brain melted and leaked out her ears.

The flare of annoyance sputtered and died when I looked more closely at the girls' faces. Tears stained their cheeks and their eyes were red and puffy. They'd gathered to support each other and share their grief. Who was I to deny them that comfort? "Hi, girls."

They answered with a collective, "Hello, Mrs. Russell."

Debbie, Peggy, Kim—all girls I'd watched grow up—and someone I didn't know. She held out her hand. "I'm Donna Richardson, Mrs. Russell. It's nice to meet you."

I shook the girl's hand. It had all the weight of a skein of cotton candy. Her face was delicate too, with pale skin framed by a sheet of dark brown hair. She looked brittle. If someone poked her, she might break. “Welcome, Donna. It’s nice to meet you too.” I let go of her hand and my gaze swept over the group. “It’s late, don’t you think you should be in bed?”

I’m not sure what it says about Libba that *six* sets of eyes rolled.

“Mom, what happened? You have to tell us. Everyone’s saying Bobby is dead.”

Telling a teenager that one of her friends has died is brutal. There are no gentle words. At least not ones I could think of. Tears wet my eyes and I nodded. “I’m sorry.”

Grace looked wan beneath her tan, as did Peggy, Kim and Debbie. Donna was already so pale, it was impossible to tell if her skin blanched as well.

An eternity of silence ticked by before Grace took a ragged breath. She dragged the back of her hand across her eyes. “Everyone’s saying he overdosed.”

“No.” I shook my head.

“What happened?” asked Kim. Her voice shook, making six syllables out of what should have been three.

I didn’t know for sure. A knife? A gun? All I’d seen was a bottomless well of blood. “The police are looking into it.”

For one horrific instant, Grace swayed. The child had dealt with more murders over the summer than most people encounter in a lifetime. I’d just presented her with another one. Her hands grabbed the edge of the counter and the swaying stopped. Her friends drew closer to her, as if their proximity could give her strength.

“Was he...” Donna covered her mouth with her hand. Her dark blue eyes looked too large for her face. China doll eyes, perfect for her porcelain skin. “Was he alive when you found him?”

“Yes.”

Somehow, Donna’s eyes grew even bigger.

“Did he suffer?” asked Kim. Her eyes looked even larger than Donna’s. And wet. As if she was holding back a tidal wave of tears.

I was bone tired, in no shape for a storm of teenage emotion.

"No. Not at all." My nose itched like hell. I ignored it. "You girls should go to bed." My gaze lingered on Libba's extra-large, half-empty glass of wine. "Libba, maybe you should spend the night too."

No one moved.

"I mean it, girls. Go to bed. Go to sleep." I borrowed one of my mother's baleful expressions. "We can talk about this in the morning."

Slowly they pushed back from the counter.

"Go." I used my good arm to point toward the back stairs.

One by one they filed up the stairs until only Grace and Libba remained.

"There are extra blankets and pillows in the linen closet," I said to Grace. "I think the extra sleeping bags are in the closet in the blue guest room."

She didn't move.

"Your friends are waiting for you upstairs." I picked up a dirty plate and put it in the sink.

"Mom."

I turned and looked at her.

"Are you all right?" she asked.

"Are you?"

Her mouth twisted and she scratched the end of her nose. "I'm fine."

I opened my arms and Grace walked into them. We both needed a hug. The almost-woman in my embrace smelled of strawberry shampoo and Love's Baby Soft. Underneath those scents I detected hints of sunshine and sweat and something uniquely Grace. My whole world. "We'll talk in the morning," I promised.

"Okay." She pulled away from me. It's a monumentally unfunny cosmic joke that children grow up and leave home. Even less funny is the fact that good parents encourage them to do so. Damn it. My skin tingled from the loss of her touch and my chest constricted.

Grace's steps reached the top of the stairs, then I turned on Libba. Her hair, which usually hung in a perfect dark curtain around her shoulders, was mussed and her brown eyes looked unfocused.

"How is it I have four extra girls here?" I asked.

She swallowed a deep, sheepish sip of wine. "It started with one and then snowballed."

Teenaged girls do that. I picked up a syrup-covered plate and put it in the sink. "Kim and Peggy and Debbie I understand, but who is Donna?"

"Do you remember India Easton?"

I put another plate in the sink. Cleaning up one-handed wasn't easy. "No. Care to help?"

Libba opened the cabinet beneath the sink, pulled out the trashcan, and swept an avalanche of Pop Rocks into it. "You should remember her. She was three years ahead of us at Suncrest. She went to Wellesley."

I stared at her blankly.

Libba put the trashcan down, sloshed some more wine into her glass, and leveled her blurry gaze on me. "She was a cheerleader. She dated Harrison Granger."

I shook my head. "I don't remember her."

Libba waved away my faulty memory with an elegant flip of her wrist. "At any rate, she went to Wellesley."

"You already said that." I considered the two fingers of wine left in the bottle. The emergency room doctor had forbidden drinking, but it was oh so tempting.

"She met a boy at Harvard and they got married and moved to Stamford, Connecticut."

None of which explained why Donna Richardson was in my house. The wine was looking better and better.

Libba reached for the bottle and emptied the last of it into her glass.

My eyes narrowed. Damn it. She deserved "Seasons in the Sun" ad nauseum.

"He made an absolute pile of money doing..." She waved her hand. "Something. Anyway, he died. A couple of years ago, I think. India remarried and came back to Kansas City."

Aha! Donna must be India's daughter. That still didn't explain why she was sleeping in my house with girls who'd been inseparable since they were six.

Libba brought the glass with the last of the wine to her lips. "I don't speak teenage girl, but I think Kim took Donna under her wing this summer and insisted that she come tonight."

I nodded, finally understanding. The apple didn't fall far from the tree. Kim's mother organized things—parties, luncheons, charity committees, and people—with an efficiency that I only dreamed of. Well, Mother dreamed of it for me.

"I am sorry about the slumber party," said Libba.

She didn't look sorry. She looked drunk.

"It's not a problem. I just wanted to know who she was." I opened the back door and tossed the popcorn onto the patio for the birds and squirrels, then I turned on the hot water in the sink and watched the syrup melt off the plates. "Would you close those chip bags? Aggie can finish cleaning the rest of this up in the morning." My bed sang a siren's song. Its voice floated through the upstairs hall and down the stairs to the kitchen—*come to me, come to me, come to me.* I was ready to answer its call. Even without wine, I could barely keep my eyes open. "I assume you're spending the night?"

"If you don't mind."

"Of course not. Is the blue room okay for you?"

"Fine, but can we catch the end of the *Tonight Show*?" She stumbled toward the den.

I swallowed a sigh and trailed after her. The *Tonight Show* had long since ended, but someone had to tuck a blanket around Libba when she passed out on the couch.

She turned on the television, flipped the dial to NBC, and collapsed onto the sofa. Images flickered across the screen. Mikey spooned Life cereal then Tommy ate Libby's fruit cocktail. From her corner of the couch, Libba squinted at the television. “Where’s Johnny?”

I glanced at my watch. We’d missed Johnny by a wide margin. “He’s gone to bed.” Exactly where we should be.

The woman on the screen raised her arms to prove that Arrid kept her extra dry, then George Peppard’s face appeared.

Libba leaned forward, scrunched her nose and slitted her eyes until—presumably—she could make out a face on the television. “I like *Banacek* too.”

Great. I claimed the other corner of the couch and my eyelids drifted shut.

They might have stayed shut all night were it not for the scream.

THREE

The scream ripped through my nerve endings and I leapt seven, maybe eight, feet straight into the air. Well, my heart did.

Libba jerked awake. “What the hell?”

Exactly. I left her on the couch, raced up the stairs, ran down the hall toward Grace’s room and threw open the door. Inside, girls with long legs, fading tans and short cotton nightgowns surrounded Donna. She huddled amidst a sea of sleeping bags, pillows and extra blankets. She’d wrapped her arms around her knees, lowered her head, and rocked back and forth.

Grace knelt next to her and stroked her hair.

Peggy sat next to her on the floor and crooned, “It was just a bad dream.”

Donna didn’t respond.

Kim sat across from her with her legs crossed, her arms crossed and her brow slightly wrinkled. “It’s only a dream. It’s not real.”

Next to her, Debbie hid a yawn behind the back of her hand.

Peggy closed her hand around Donna’s arm and shook gently.

The girl flinched and jerked her arm away. Then she raised her head an inch or two from her knees. Her brows were raised, her eyes as big and round as the bowls of my grandmother’s sterling soup spoons, and her lips looked taut and pale.

“It can’t hurt you.” Peggy’s soft tone acquired a bit of an edge.

“Peggy’s right, Donna. It was just a dream.” Who was I kidding? A boy had been murdered. It was a miracle they weren’t all having nightmares.

Donna lowered her head and resumed her rocking.

Debbie snorted softly. “Think about something nice so we can go back to sleep.”

I stepped into the room, knelt and draped my arm around Donna’s slender shoulders. Her muscles tensed beneath my touch, but she didn’t shake me off. She sniffled and made a wet sound deep in her throat.

“I think you could do with some hot chocolate or warm milk.”

Donna stopped rocking and looked at me, taking my measure. A few seconds ticked by before she nodded.

I helped her to her feet, then directed my gaze to the bed where Kim and Debbie sat, their backs against the bed, their arms still crossed. “This has been an upsetting night for all of you and you’re all going to process Bobby’s death differently.”

Neither girl spoke. They would when the door closed. I shifted my gaze to Grace and she offered me a near imperceptible nod. No one would speak ill of Donna for having a nightmare.

I led Donna from the room.

Libba and Max loitered in the hallway. She leaned against a wall with her eyes half-closed. His amber eyes looked somehow sleepy and alert at the same time.

“Go to bed,” I said to both of them. Libba looked fuzzy from too much Blue Nun, in no shape to make hot chocolate, much less comfort a frightened teenager. As for Max, if he went downstairs, he’d want to go out. If he went out, he’d eat all the popcorn I’d thrown for the squirrels. I’d have five teenagers, a drunken friend and a dog with an upset stomach to deal with.

Libba nodded and disappeared into the guest room. Max nodded and disappeared into mine.

“Let’s get you some hot chocolate.” I gave Donna’s shoulder a gentle squeeze and together we descended the stairs.

I flipped on the lights in the kitchen. “You do want hot chocolate, don’t you? I could warm milk if you’d prefer that.”

“Hot chocolate, please.”

Dealing with death was enough to rattle anyone, but Donna seemed about to shatter.

"Good choice. I can't stand warm milk, but some people seem to like it."

The girl shuddered. Smart kid.

"Sit down." I nodded toward a stool not pushed under the lip of the counter, pulled a small pan off the pot rack and poured in some milk. "You're in luck. Hot chocolate is one of the few things I'm good at making. My secret is a dash of vanilla. Do you cook?"

She didn't answer. Instead, she stared at the painting hanging on the wall. One of mine, the canvas depicted a tossed salad and was perfect for a kitchen.

The milk bubbled at the edge of the pan. "How chocolaty do you want it?"

Again, she didn't answer. Instead, she rose from her seat and peered closely at the canvas, almost as if she was studying the brushstrokes. Since they were *my* brushstrokes, I couldn't hold her silence against her.

I spooned Swiss Miss into a mug, poured the milk over it, added my signature dash, then stirred. "Marshmallows?"

She looked away from the painting. "I'm sorry?"

"Do you want marshmallows?" I held up the mug. "In your hot chocolate?"

"No, thank you."

I put the cocoa in her hands. "You know, sometimes talking about a bad dream makes it better."

Donna shrank. Her shoulders hunched. Her chin lowered to her chest. If she hadn't been holding a mug, she probably would have crossed her arms over her body again.

"I can call your parents to come get you if you want."

The mug hit the floor in an explosion of hot chocolate and broken pottery.

"Oh my God, I'm so sorry." Donna fell to her knees. She picked up a shard of broken mug with one hand and dashed at a tear with the other.

"Don't touch that, you'll cut yourself. I'll get a broom."

She continued to pick up bits of broken pottery. The white

flounce of her nightgown absorbed enough cocoa to turn a soft brown. Her shoulders looked so hunched, so taut, it was a wonder her tendons didn't snap.

"Donna, stop."

A tear traced down her cheek and plopped into the mess on the floor.

I bent, closed my hand around her elbow, and forced her to her feet. "Sit."

"But..." Her gaze remained locked on the mess.

"No buts. Sit."

She sank onto a kitchen stool.

I grabbed the trashcan from the cabinet beneath the sink and held it out to her. "Throw those away."

She dropped the pieces of mug into it. Then she clasped her hands in her lap.

I unspooled a length of paper towel and dropped it to the floor. Like Donna's nightgown, it quickly turned brown.

"We'll get you a clean nightgown before you go back to bed. Shall we try again?"

"I'm sorry."

"It's just a mug. Do you want more cocoa?" I poured milk into the saucepan and put it on the heat.

"Thank you." Her cheeks were as pale as the unstained white linen of her nightgown. Poor kid. The silence between us stretched, awkward and uncomfortable as new golf shoes.

I cleared my throat and searched for something to say. "When did you and your family move to Kansas City?"

"June." Her voice was barely audible. The taut line of her shoulders loosened.

"Just in time for the heat." No wonder teenagers thought adults were stupid and boring. We said stupid, boring things.

She lifted her head, turned it toward the brick wall. "That painting is amazing. My father had a friend in Connecticut who collected that artist. At least I think it's the same one. The brushwork is the same."

"You like art?"

"I do." She offered me a tremulous smile. "I want to be an artist."

"The painting's mine."

She blinked. A classic, teenage "duh" blink. It was obvious I owned it.

"I mean, I painted it."

Her brows rose high enough to be insulting.

"I'm surprised the girls didn't tell you I painted."

"They did but..."

She'd thought I painted amorphous rainbow-colored horrors, the kind that proliferated at craft shows. Maybe she'd imagined diaphanous women in oversized hats walking through swirls of pastel. That or big-eyed children who reflected a world-weariness usually reserved for adults.

"Thank you for being so nice. I'm sorry about the mug."

"Don't give it another thought."

Her gaze returned to the painting. "Do you teach?" Her voice was small.

"I never have."

"But you could?"

I could. I could also spend every afternoon playing bridge with Mother. Just because I could do something didn't mean I wanted to.

"Would you teach me? Please?" With her lashes still spiky from her tears, her blue eyes looked enormous in her face, rather like one of the big-eyed children.

I swallowed. "Teach you?

"To paint. I can draw but I've never had painting lessons." Her enormous eyes, which only minutes before had been haunted by dreams of violent death, implored. "Please?"

I couldn't tell her no. Not after the night we'd all had. "Let me see your portfolio."

"I'll bring it by tomorrow...I mean, later today." She bit her lips, glanced again at the painting, then picked up a strand of her hair and began to twist it. "My parents don't really approve of art—as a career, I mean. It might be better if we didn't tell them."

An out. "Donna, I can't go behind your parents' backs."

"Maybe we could just tell my mom."

"Let me think about it."

Her shoulders fell.

"Bring your portfolio and we'll see. Are you done with that?" I nodded my chin at her empty mug.

She nodded, and I took it from her hands then put it in the sink. I added the dirty pan, mouthed a silent apology to Aggie, then said, "Shall we go to bed?"

"You'll look at my sketches?"

"I will."

Banging on the front door is never a good thing. Banging on the front door at—I turned my head and glared at the clock—seven-thirty on a Saturday morning is a terrible thing.

I got up, grabbed one of the silk peignoirs I bought in Paris, jammed arms into the sleeves and hurried down the front steps with Max at my heels.

I yanked the door open before whoever was on the other side woke the whole house.

The man from under the bleachers, the bossy one who'd held my lipstick hostage, stood on the front stoop holding my newspaper.

He stared at me, perhaps placing where he knew me. His gaze shifted to my bandaged left wrist. "You're the woman from under the stands."

"I am."

"I'm sorry to disturb you so early on a Saturday morning. Your paper." He handed it to me, then flashed a charming smile.

Henry had a charming smile. I don't trust charming smiles.

I glanced at my wrist, at the spot where my watch would be if I wore one so early on a Saturday.

His gaze rested on the gauze. "It looks as if you needed stitches. I told you that you needed a doctor."

Seven-thirty, a charming smile and an I-told-you-so. Whoever he was, I didn't like him.

"I heard the boy..."

"Yes." My tone ended further discussion.

Except, it didn't. The man shook his head. "What a tragedy. You knew him?"

I narrowed my eyes.

"I'm sorry." He thrust his hand at me. "Jonathan Hess. I'm Donna's father."

I offered him a dead-fish handshake—the kind you give a man who's awakened you after too few hours' sleep.

"What do you think happened?"

It's hard to look down your nose when looking up at someone. Mother can do it. Effortlessly. I tried. Probably failed. "No idea."

"He didn't say anything?"

"He died." My voice was flat as the pancakes I'd promised the girls for breakfast. Real ones, not some cardboard facsimile that tasted like the box they'd come in.

He shook his head again. "Pity." He peered past me into the foyer. "I'd like to take Donna home."

"She's asleep."

Max yawned as if suggesting that was where he'd like to be.

Jonathan Hess reprised his charming smile. "Teenagers would sleep 'til noon if they could. I'd like to take her home."

I tossed the paper into the front hall then pulled the silk of my robe more tightly around my body. The man in front of me looked like any other man I knew would look on a Saturday morning—except for the madras pants. Didn't he realize it was September? Pure contrariness straightened my shoulders. "The girls were up late. They're all still asleep."

He raised his chin. "Then wake her. Please. I'd like to take her home now."

That and twenty-five cents would get him a cup of coffee.

"Mr. Hess, there are five girls asleep upstairs. I prefer not to disturb them. I'll be happy to bring her home when they wake up."

The charming smile faltered then rebounded. "My wife didn't okay this slumber party with me. We have plans for this morning and I'd like to take her home now."

He was a *stepfather* of recent vintage and he had the right to okay sleepovers? That took controlling to a whole new level. I dug my heels in deeper. "Does Donna have a practice or something? Because if she doesn't, we should let them sleep. The girls had a rough night. Bobby's death upset them terribly and sleep is the best thing for them. I'll bring her home in a few hours. In the meantime, she's safe and secure."

He stepped toward me. A step that brought him too close. I had either to retreat or share a space too small for the both of us.

Max growled. He even showed his teeth. Nice, long white ones that gleamed pearly bright and deadly in the morning light.

I used to think Max was a good judge of character. I know better now. Max could easily snuggle up with a serial killer and bite a saint. Jonathan Hess probably wasn't either. He was just a man used to getting his way.

I dropped my hand to the top of Max's silken head then lowered my fingers to his collar. If he decided to bite Jonathan Hess, I could stop him. Maybe.

Someone tapped my shoulder and I turned. Donna stood in front of me with her head bowed and her gaze focused on the floor. "I'm ready to go," she mumbled. "Thank you for having me, Mrs. Russell."

I swallowed a sigh. Just because her stepfather was one of the bossiest men I'd ever met didn't mean I could keep her at my house indefinitely to spite him.

Jonathan Hess's hand circled her thin arm like a shackle.

It was just silly. Why couldn't she stay and have breakfast with her friends?

Max growled again. I tightened my fingers around his collar. "Thank you for coming, Donna. You're welcome any time."

Now that he had what—who—he came for, Jonathan Hess' charming smile appeared again. I wasn't charmed. I'd lived with a man who had to be in control all the time and I didn't envy India—or Donna—one bit. "Thank you for having her, Mrs. Russell."

He led Donna to the black Cadillac parked in my driveway.

I stood in the doorway and waved goodbye.

Donna seemed nice enough, but her stepfather was a prized ass.

I decided right then, without even seeing her portfolio, Donna Richardson was getting her painting lessons.

Donna getting up woke the other four girls. They oozed bonelessly into the kitchen, their hair tangled, their cheeks still marked with sleep. Kim asked for orange juice. Peggy wanted grape juice. Debbie and Grace wanted coffee. I did too.

When we were all provided with beverages, I got out a mixing bowl, a box of Bisquick, some eggs, milk and a carton of blueberries. "Pancakes?"

They all nodded. Peggy and Kim added, "Yes, please, Mrs. Russell."

Pancakes are so easy even I can make them. The girls wolfed them down as if it had been days not hours since their junk food binge. Then they disappeared up the stairs, leaving me with a messy kitchen, a bandaged hand and the unfortunate realization that it was Saturday and Aggie wasn't coming.

I fetched the paper from the foyer, poured myself another cup of coffee and settled onto one of the stools that surrounded the kitchen island.

Youth Murdered at Elite School

Law enforcement officials are seeking information regarding the shooting of a juvenile male that occurred in Kansas City, Missouri on Friday.

Shortly before nine o'clock, officers responded to an

emergency at Suncrest Country Day School. When they arrived at the scene, police discovered a gunshot victim.

The victim, Robert Carsington Lowell, is the scion of a Kansas City family known for its support of the arts. He was transported to St. Benedict's Hospital where he was pronounced dead on arrival. Sources close to the incident report the body was found by a parent attending a football game between Suncrest Country Day School and its cross-state rival Burroughs School.

The victim's great-grandfather, Carsington Phipps Lowell, was an influential architect and designed many of the city's public buildings.

An investigation is underway and anyone with information is urged to contact the police.

I stared at the paper. That was it? First off, I could write better headlines with my eyes closed. Second, the article didn't actually say anything. Well, aside from the fact that Bobby was dead and that he'd been shot. They must have received the information right before they went to press. When they had more, Bobby would be front page news.

My vision blurred and I swiped at my eyes with the back of my hand.

An elephant had somehow gained access to the house and was careening down the back stairs—that or Grace was wearing Dr. Scholl's sandals on the hardwoods.

She burst back into the kitchen with a deafening clatter and a mug in her hand. "Is there any more coffee?"

I jerked my chin toward Mr. Coffee, who was keeping half a pot warm.

"Mom, you're crying."

"I am not." A fat tear plopped onto the newsprint. "I was just reading about Bobby. He was shot." Bobby's dying face filled my gaze. "Had he been dating anyone?"

"Not that I know of." Grace slipped out of her sandals, and

walked barefoot and quiet to the coffee pot as if a loud noise might set me sobbing. She poured. "Why?"

"He asked me to tell her he loved her, but I don't know who to tell."

She walked toward me, bringing the coffee pot with her, and filled up my mug. "I'll find out and let you know."

Kim, Debbie and Peggy stampeded down the steps—all in Dr. Scholl's sandals, all unaware that between the slapping of their heels and the knock of wood on wood, they sounded like a herd of pachyderms.

"Hey," Grace said. "Was Bobby dating anyone?"

The girls looked at each other. It wasn't a we're-teenagers-and-adults-(even cool ones like Grace's mom)-just-don't-understand-and-we-must-keep-this-secret-forever look. It was more of a what-the-heck-is-she-talking-about look. Two heads shook.

Kim's did not.

"Do you know anything?" I asked her.

Her "no" came a second too late and too loud to be convincing.

"You're sure?"

She looked me straight in the eye. "Positive."

Maybe she was telling the truth. Maybe she wasn't.

"I should go. Thank you for having me, Mrs. Russell." Then Kim and whatever she knew walked out of my kitchen, leaving me no closer to finding Bobby's mystery girlfriend.

FOUR

I hobbled up the long, bricked walkway that led to CeCe Lowell's door. The Parisian salesgirl had sniffed and told me that pain was a small price for beauty. My feet disagreed. That the navy of my pumps exactly matched the navy of my dress was of little import to toes crammed into pointy shoes. They'd stopped whispering their discontent. They were yelling.

I ignored them and rang the bell.

CeCe answered it herself.

The poor woman looked as if she hadn't slept. She also looked disappointed, almost as if she was expecting someone else. It was a fleeting impression. One I dismissed when she grabbed my good wrist and pulled me into a hug.

She released me. "Thank you for coming."

"I tried to call." Five times over the course of an hour I'd received a busy signal. Then the need to find the name of the girl Bobby had loved and to offer CeCe my condolences had compelled me to don my too-tight shoes and drive to her home.

"I left it off the hook." She rubbed her red-rimmed eyes. "She kept answering it."

Who? One of CeCe's sisters? "If now is a bad time, I can come back later."

"No!" She snatched at my wrist again. "I mean no, of course not. I'm glad you're here. Come in. May I offer you coffee?" She led me toward the living room.

Something was off. Wrong. Grief thicker than fog wrapped around her yet she seemed manic, desperate. I understood why when I crossed the threshold into CeCe's living room.

Kizzi and Alice Standish shared a flowered couch.

Kizzi lived behind a curtain sewn from dry gin martinis. Her daughter Alice was nuttier than the little bowls of mixed almonds and cashews the club puts out for bridge snacks. Word on the golf course was that Howard Standish was considering having them both committed—to different facilities, of course.

Alice launched herself off the couch and into my chest. Her arms circled my neck and she buried her face against my shoulder.

"You found him," she wailed. "Did he say anything about me?" She released her lock on my neck and took a miniscule step backward. "Did he say anything about me before he"—she brought her hand to her throat and dragged in an audible breath—"before he passed on?"

Bobby loved Alice? I closed my eyes, tried to picture it, and couldn't. Boys like Bobby fell in love with homecoming queens with golden auras. They fell for class brains who magically transformed into Charlie Girls as soon as they removed their glasses and loosened their ponytails. They even, on occasion, fell for funky, artsy girls who carried guitar cases wherever they went so they could sing about peace. Boys like Bobby Lowell didn't fall for unstable waifs with heavily kohled manic eyes nearly hidden by a dark fringe of hair. Did they? Maybe I had it all wrong. Maybe Bobby preferred a girl with knobby knees and gangly limbs like the one who'd half-choked me with her embrace.

"Alice, give Mrs. Russell room to breathe," said Kizzi. She lifted a glass of clear liquid to her lips. Gin?

Alice backed away, a tiny step. "Bobby loved me. That's why I had to come over and keep Mrs. Lowell company. I knew he'd want me to be here."

"Have you been here long?" I asked. Poor, poor CeCe. As if Bobby's death wasn't traumatic enough, she'd also endured a morning of sheer crazy? No wonder she looked as if she was four-fifths of the way to a nervous breakdown. Even if Bobby had adored Alice, that didn't mean his mother did.

"I came over a few hours ago." Alice glanced over her shoulder at Kizzi, who'd made a decided dent in the level of liquid in her glass. "Mother came to get me but I convinced her we needed to stay."

"That's very thoughtful of you," I deadpanned.

Alice simpered. Apparently, she was immune to sarcasm.

Where the hell was Howard Standish? How had he let his family invade CeCe's grief? "CeCe, may I please use your phone, just for a minute?"

"Do you want to use the one in the kitchen? It's more private there."

"Lovely. Thank you."

My crumpled toes and I limped into CeCe's harvest gold kitchen, picked up the phone and dialed.

Flora answered in three rings. "Walford residence."

"Flora, it's Ellison. May I please speak with Mother?"

A few seconds later Mother was on the line. "Is it true?"

I leaned against the counter and breathed deep. "I found him."

"Ellison, you simply must stop enmeshing yourself in these scandals. You ought to be—"

"Mother!" I didn't need her advice, didn't want it. But that never stopped her. She probably had a monologue of helpful tips for avoiding dead bodies ready. "I'm at CeCe Lowell's and Kizzi and Alice Standish are here. Is there any way you can track down Howard? He needs to come get them. I don't think CeCe can take much more."

I listened to a moment's worth of silence. Mother was probably weighing the satisfaction of telling me how to run my life with the joy of having a purpose. Thankfully, joy won. "He'll be there in thirty minutes if I have to drive him myself."

He would be too. Once Frances Walford decided upon a thing, it was as good as done. "Thank you, Mother." I hung up the phone.

I returned to the living room, my toes cringing with pain at every step. Alice had returned to her mother's side where she daubed beneath her eyes with a crumpled tissue. Kizzi still perched on the edge of the couch with her drink locked into her hand. CeCe looked as if she might start drinking straight vodka. I didn't blame her.

I claimed a flame-stitched wingback chair. "Alice, are you a sophomore or junior this year?"

She daubed again. Sniffled. "Sophomore. Same as Bobby was."

"Are you enjoying school?"

"Enjoying school? My whole world has crumbled and you want to know if I'm enjoying school?" The tiny bit of her eyes visible beneath her heavy bangs narrowed. "How can you ask me something like that?"

Kizzi roused herself enough to try to pat her daughter's knee. She missed. For one ephemeral instant she leaned forward in space and hung there—a lob shot in tennis, a perfect chip in golf. In the next heartbeat, she fell, wedging herself between the brass coffee table and the couch with her glass still firmly gripped in her hand. The contents sloshed, but not a single drop spilled.

I gasped. CeCe did too. We both rose from our chairs.

Not Alice. She crouched. "Oh, Mother. How could you?"

I wondered the same thing and more. How could Kizzi let Alice intrude on CeCe's grief? How could Kizzi come here and get sauced? How could she not see that her daughter was disturbed?

With an ease that spoke of heartbreaking regularity, Alice shoved her forearms beneath Kizzi's armpits and stood, lifting her mother with her. When they were both standing, Alice pushed her mother back onto the couch then offered CeCe and me an apologetic smile. "Mother has a problem with balance."

Mother had a problem with gin. "Perhaps you should take her home?" I suggested.

Kizzi patted her hair. "I just slipped."

Alice nodded. "She's fine. Besides, we couldn't leave."

CeCe made a sound that might have been a sob—probably was a sob—then sank back onto her chair.

I glanced at my watch. Mother still had fifteen minutes.

I could have asked them to leave. Should have. But Kizzi

Standish's mother-in-law, Alice Anne Standish, scared the hell out of me. Not just me. She scared everybody. Maybe even Mother. Alice Anne possessed all the delicacy of a Sherman tank. She flattened people in her campaign to remake the world the way God should have made it. Her way.

I shifted in my chair and cast about for something—anything—to talk about.

Alice beat me to it. She leaned forward, rested her elbows on her knees and said, "Bobby and I were in love."

Not that.

"It's true." She nodded as if the bobbing of her chin could convince me she was telling the truth. I didn't need convincing. She was telling the truth—sort of. She *believed* Bobby had loved her. She definitely had loved him—if delusion counted as love.

CeCe covered her mouth with her hand. From where I sat, it appeared she might be biting the palm. To keep from screaming? Kizzi held up her empty glass and stared at it in wonder. Where had the liquid gone? I squirmed in my chair.

How had CeCe allowed a sixteen-year-old girl to hijack her living room sofa and her grief?

"I had everything planned." Alice sat up straight. Her chin resumed its nodding. "We were going to finish high school, go to college, then get married. That girl meant nothing to him."

I knew it! Alice *couldn't* be the girl Bobby had loved. She was simply too odd. "What girl?" I asked.

Alice shrugged. "No one important."

"If that's true, why mention her?" I asked.

She scowled at me. The expression in her eyes was...feral, frightening, predatory.

I shivered, suddenly chilled.

"Bobby knows—knew," she corrected, "I wouldn't stand for him and another girl."

The sound of my heart thudding in my chest echoed in my ears. I gripped the arm of the chair. Had Alice Standish killed Bobby Lowell?

The doorbell rang and CeCe sprang from her chair. "I'll get that." She rushed from the room leaving me with the girl who might have killed the boy who rejected her.

A moment later, a man's voice drifted down the hall. I crossed my fingers in my lap. Then I heard a second voice—Mother's. I owed her. No doubt she'd collect.

Howard Standish strode into CeCe's living room. "Kizzi, Alice, it's time to go home."

His wife and daughter stared at him.

I did too. There was a trace of lipstick on the collar of his white shirt. Red lipstick. A shade similar to *Rouge Chaud*. Where had Mother found him? And with whom?

"I don't want to go," said Alice. "Mrs. Lowell *needs* me. Bobby would want me to be with his mother."

"Bobby would understand, Alice." CeCe stood in the doorway. Her voice was soft but determined, almost as if Mother's arrival with Howard Standish had given her strength. "Besides, I'd like to be alone for a while."

"Fine," Alice huffed. "But I'll be back."

I stared at Howard. Mother cleared her throat and muttered his name.

Howard found a backbone. Finally. "No, Alice. You and Mrs. Lowell both need space to grieve. You're not to come back here."

Alice raised her pointy chin. "And if I do?"

He leveled his gaze on her. "Then you won't go to the funeral."

She muttered something about wanting to see him try and stop her, but she stood. She even pulled her mother to a standing position.

Howard Standish ushered his family away.

CeCe turned to Mother. "Thank you, Frances. I couldn't get them to leave and—" Her voice hitched. "Thank you."

Mother gave CeCe one of her tight, controlled, almost hugs. "Don't mention it. The next time Alice shows up, don't let her in."

"Bobby asked her out once. One time." CeCe held up her index finger and jabbed it into the air. "I think he did it to be kind. He came home and said that compared to Alice's family, Rob and I looked like Ward and June Cleaver." She caught her lower lip between her teeth and looked up at the ceiling.

While CeCe had better pearls than June, she hadn't possessed a husband who came home every night. If the talk around the bridge table was true, sometimes he failed to come home for weeks at a time.

"That poor girl needs professional help." Mother shook her head. "Lorna told me they've had her to several doctors but as soon as they hear bipolar they walk out of the office."

"She's not dangerous, is she?" asked CeCe.

Someone cleared her throat and as one, Mother, CeCe and I looked toward the entrance to the living room.

Alice stood there, crackling with crazy, dark, bone-deep anger. She raised her nose in the air, marched past us, bent and picked a small black handbag off the rug by the couch. "Mother forgot her purse."

She'd heard everything we said. How else to explain the drawn brows, the narrowed eyes, the tightening around her lips? She looked positively frightening.

Had Alice killed Bobby? Whoever had knocked me down by the football stands was tall. I stared at the teenage girl who was trying to murder me with just a look. Alice was tall enough to knock me flat, but...

Without another word, Alice turned and stalked out.

Mother—brave, brave Mother—followed her.

CeCe and I stood frozen and quiet, caught in a surreal tableau where children were murdered and teenage girls looked guilty.

Mother returned, tsked and shook her head. Hard to tell if she was exasperated or sympathetic. "They're gone. Howard and Kizzi shouldn't let that girl out of the house." Exasperated.

"Thank you, Frances, for bringing Howard, for coming to my rescue. And Ellison, thank you for calling the cavalry." CeCe took a deep breath. "Every time I asked them to leave, Alice insisted she *had* to be here."

Mother reached out and took one of CeCe's hands in her own.

"I can't believe this is happening," murmured our hostess.

Mother made a vague clucking sound in the back of her throat.

I stepped forward and rubbed a small circle on CeCe's back. I hated to say anything, but I felt honor-bound to fulfill Bobby's last wish. CeCe would want that too. "Bobby's last words were 'Tell her I love her.' I don't think he meant Alice."

CeCe choked, the sound halfway between a laugh and a sob. "He didn't mean Alice."

"Who?" My voice sounded too eager, as if I was in a hurry to discharge Bobby's request and move on with my life. I was. I was also terribly shallow. Poor CeCe would grieve for a lifetime. I rubbed another circle on her back, lowered my voice and said, "Do you know who it was?"

"He'd met a girl and he was head over heels in love with her."

"What's her name?" I leaned forward.

"No idea." Again, CeCe's voice caught.

Why was nothing ever easy?

She wiped her eyes and sniffled. "He said she was perfect. He seemed...happy. Everything about him changed. It was like the old Bobby had returned. He met her at the beginning of summer, right about the time..." Her face flushed.

Right about the time my husband got himself murdered.

Mother tsked. I don't think she can help it. She does it every time anyone comes close to mentioning Henry.

CeCe covered her eyes with the tips of her fingers. "Thank you for not saying anything about love while Alice was here. The girl needs help."

Both Mother and I snorted. The girl needed a mental institution.

"Did he...did Bobby..." CeCe didn't look at me. Maybe she couldn't. Maybe the blank wall really was fascinating. The muscles in her face looked frozen, taut, almost painful.

"He didn't suffer at all. It was like he was falling gently asleep." My nose itched like hell.

Mother gave me a short nod—she at least knew I was lying—then she draped her arm around CeCe's shoulders and led her to the couch. "Ellison, would you please get CeCe a cup of coffee? Or would you prefer tea?"

"Coffee's fine."

In the kitchen, I found and filled three mugs—Tony the Tiger, Ronald McDonald and one that detailed a Virgo's personality. CeCe didn't look up to handling a china cup and saucer. I found a tray, put a sugar bowl and a small creamer on it and carried it all to the living room.

Mother's eyes narrowed when she saw the mismatched assortment on the tray.

Virgos—observant, precise and inflexible. The mug had Mother pegged.

We sat for a moment, letting the warmth from the mugs seep into our hands. Then Mother said, "CeCe, Alice was right about one thing. I don't think you should be alone."

"One sister is driving in from St. Louis. She should be here anytime now. The other one is flying in from Charleston. And..." she swallowed, "I tracked Rob down in Thailand. He's flying home."

"Thailand?" Mother asked. "What's he doing in Thailand?"

She was too far away for me to kick. That and my toes already hurt. Mother thought Thailand was a vacation destination? It must be nice to have a husband who isn't into kinky sex. Time for a change of subject. "CeCe, I promised Bobby I'd tell the girl how he felt. Do you have any idea how I might find her?"

"None." CeCe dropped her forehead to her hand. "I can't seem to think straight."

Mother scowled at me as if *I'd* said something out of line. Hell. She was the one asking questions about Thailand.

The doorbell rang.

"Ellison, why don't you get that?" Mother asked.

I stood, ignoring the pinching sensation near my toes. Cutting my toes off with pinking shears would be less painful than the shoes. But kicking the damned things off wasn't an option. I'd never get them back on. I opened the door. BeBe Sullivan stood on the other side.

"Thank God." She pushed past me. "Every time I pulled off the highway, I tried to call. The phone has been busy for hours. I'm glad she's not alone. She is all right, isn't she? Where is she?"

"Living room," I murmured. BeBe wouldn't have heard me if I yelled. She was already bustling down the hallway.

"CeCe," she called. "I'm here."

I followed her at a more sedate, painful, gimping pace. Somehow I'd forgotten that CeCe's sister was a force of nature, probably a Virgo like Mother.

By the time I reached the living room, Mother was taking her leave. "CeCe, call me if I can do anything. Promise?"

CeCe nodded.

"We'll leave the two of you alone." Mother scooped up her handbag and mine then glided toward me. "We can see ourselves out."

"Thank you, Ellison," CeCe said.

"You're welcome. Call if you need anything."

She offered me a smile. It didn't come close to reaching her eyes. "I will."

"BeBe, lovely to see you. Come along, Ellison."

I followed in Mother's wake.

Outside, the sun touched on leaves just beginning to turn.

"What their parents were thinking I'll never know. Those names." Mother shook her head.

Three sisters—Belinda, Cecily and Delia—BeBe, CeCe and DeDe. I shrugged; there was no accounting for what parents did to their children. In the general scheme of things, matching nicknames seemed preferable to wedging yourself between a couch and a coffee table.

Mother focused her Virgo gaze on me. "What's wrong with your feet?"

"Nothing. My shoes hurt."

"Don't wear them tomorrow."

"Tomorrow?"

"Tomorrow when you have brunch with your father and me. I thought afterward we might play a round of golf."

I owed Mother a favor. We both knew it. I just hadn't thought she'd call in her chit so quickly. She had something up her sleeve. Probably Hunter Tafft. "Just the three of us, right?"

Mother's response was a pleased smile, as if she held a hand full of trump cards.

I glanced at my bandaged wrist and somehow managed *not* to smile. I had a trump card too—and it was the ace.

FIVE

I arrived early for brunch—not because if I beat the crowd, I beat the scrutiny, not from an eagerness to see my friends and neighbors eat their weight in heavy food, and certainly not from eagerness to see Hunter Tafft, the man Mother had selected as my next husband. In fact, the mere thought of seeing him made my stomach go all fluttery.

I arrived early for strategic purposes. First, picking my chair at the table was essential. If I was spending the morning brunching with Hunter, I shouldn't have to endure having my back to the room as well. I wanted the seat with my back to the lovely view of the golf course, the one next to the French doors that led to the terrace, the seat with the built-in escape route. Second, Jane Addison always brunched early. She had to—she had to finish in time to sit on open houses. Arriving thirty minutes early was worth it if I talked to Jane.

If you want to know the latest, befriend a real estate agent. A good one knows almost everything. After all, marriages, the last kid leaving for college, divorces, and deaths all sell houses. A really good agent also knows little things—who was spotted leaving a house not his own at three in the afternoon on a work day, whose trip to a "spa" was really a trip to rehab, and what Judi Barton paid for her most recent facelift. Too much. The poor woman's skin is pulled so tight she looks like a vampire. A real estate agent as good as Jane might even know who Bobby Lowell had loved.

Elaine, the club hostess, led me to Mother and Daddy's usual table. We passed a long, linen-skirted buffet loaded with enough food to end world hunger. Dilled crepes filled with sour cream and nearly transparent slices of smoked salmon sat next to a potato *galette* topped with bacon-wrapped kidneys. Country ham, cut paper-thin and served on beaten biscuits, vied with ham croquettes. Corn muffins dotted with sausage, a bottomless chafing dish of scrambled eggs, and broiled tomatoes with Chef Pierre's special watermelon chowchow on the side beckoned. Brandy snifters filled with cantaloupe, honeydew and strawberries garnished with a sprig of mint and a dollop of whipped cream tried to compete with the pastry chef's peach upside-down cake.

At a separate station, one of the sous chefs cooked made-to-order omelets. Next to him, nearly hidden behind a mountain of strawberries, another sous chef ladled batter into a waffle iron.

No one left brunch hungry.

Or thirsty. The bartender's Bloody Marys were just spicy enough. I asked Elaine to have a waiter bring me one then scanned the already crowded dining room for Jane.

The tinkle of ice in glasses provided the background music for the hum of polite conversation. A few members might have been discussing their minister's sermon. Most weren't. They were probably talking about golf or football or Bobby's death.

Mother and Daddy's preferred table is the one farthest from the buffet. Anyone wishing to interrupt their meal must make an effort—no pretending to breeze by, then happen to stop for a brief chat. Nope, anyone who weaves their way through the tables to the Walfords' domain has a purpose.

Young Jack McCreary had a purpose.

"Mrs. Russell," he said, "good morning. It's nice to see you."

The waiter arrived with my drink and I sipped. Heaven. "Good morning, Jack."

He shifted his weight, jammed his hands in the pockets of his khakis, then pulled them out and adjusted his tie. "I...you...that is to say..." He lifted his horn-rimmed glasses off the patrician bridge of his patrician nose, peered through the lenses from a distance of a few inches then put them back where they belonged. Next he pulled at the bangs that covered his forehead.

I arched an eyebrow. No way was I making things easy for the kid who'd tormented Grace when she got her first bra. At the time, Henry claimed it was because Jack *liked* Grace. It was a *guy* thing. Easy for Henry to say when he wasn't ever around to dry Grace's embarrassed tears. Humiliate my daughter, make her cry, and I'll hold it against you for all eternity. It's an *Ellison* thing.

Jack rubbed the bottom of his squared chin with the back of his hand, cleared his throat and said, "You found Bobby."

My fingers tightened around my glass. "I did."

He shifted his weight again, glanced at the rug then at the ceiling. "Did he say anything?"

I tilted my head slightly to the side. "What would he have said?"

"I don't know." One hand disappeared into a pocket, the other pulled at his tie as if it was choking him. "Did he say anything about me?"

Why did he want to know? Had Jack been the one who knocked me down by the gate? I compared the boy standing in front of me to my memory of the person who'd knocked me down. Was Jack too tall? Too thin? Too young?

"It's just..." He gave up on his collar and stared at his feet.

Perhaps I should have more sympathy. He'd lost his best friend and was obviously hurting. Perhaps, just for today, I could let go of my dislike. I shook my head. "He mentioned a girl."

A hand landed on Jack's shoulder. The boy jumped.

"Ellison, lovely to see you. I hope Jack isn't bothering you."

Jack winced. Embarrassment? Or was John McCreary squeezing his son's shoulder hard enough to hurt?

"Jack is never a bother." I glanced around the quickly filling dining room. "Is Amy with you?"

"Just us boys today." John chuckled as if he'd said something funny. "Brunch and a round of golf."

"Please give her my regards." When Mother said something like that, it was a dismissal. People murmured quick goodbyes and disappeared. When I said it, nothing happened. Neither John nor

Jack moved. Instead, they stared at me through their tortoiseshell frames as if they expected me to say something more. I cleared my throat. “I imagine she’s enjoying her day with the girls.”

Jack snorted. Apparently, the idea of spending the day with his sisters wasn’t particularly attractive.

“I imagine she is,” said John. “You’ve had a rough weekend.” He jerked his chin toward my still-bandaged wrist, my *sorry-no-golf-for-me-today* injury, my ace of trump in Mother’s little game.

I nodded.

“Tragic loss.” John didn’t even pretend to look saddened. “Tragic.”

Jack looked sick. Five-too-many-ham-croquettes-followed-by-a-huge-slice-of-peach-upside-down-cake sick. Miserable sick. Your-best-friend-died sick. He opened his mouth as if he meant to say something, glanced at his father, then snapped it shut.

I stirred my Bloody Mary with a celery stalk. “Bobby was a great kid.”

The muscles around John’s mouth tightened and for a fraction of a second the left corner of his lip curled. “Like I said, tragic loss.”

What the hell was going on?

“John, how lovely to see you.” Mother swept up to the table. “And Jack, it’s nice to see you too.”

Daddy stuck out his hand and John was forced to give up his hold on his son’s shoulder to shake it.

“Where’s Amy?” Mother glanced around the now-crowded dining room.

“She’s at home with the girls.”

Mother smiled as if he’d just described an enormous treat. “How lovely for her.”

She nodded to Daddy and he pulled out a chair for her. When she was settled, he leaned over and kissed my upturned cheek.

Mother opened her napkin and smoothed it onto her lap. “Do give Amy my regards.”

With a lantern-jawed grimace, John McCreary muttered a goodbye and left. He even dragged Jack with him.

"What did *they* want?" Mother asked.

I shook my head. "No idea."

"John McCreary's grandmother and my mother were dear friends. I believe they were in the same bridge group for something like thirty years." Mother patted my hand to emphasize what she wasn't saying. *Don't you dare implicate him in something sordid.* She might not care for him but our families shared a history.

Mother had me all wrong. I didn't want to implicate anyone. Finding the girl Bobby loved and telling her what he'd said was my plan. Then I'd return to a normal, uneventful life. A life where I painted and played bridge and tennis and golf. A life where Grace went to school and hung out with her friends and argued with me over the length of her skirts. Bring on the hum-drum, the ordinary, the loads of laundry, the sink full of dishes, the reruns of *McMillan & Wife*, and Mother's and my endless tug-of-war over said life. "Thank you again for coming over to CeCe's yesterday."

"That poor family..." Mother looked down, shook her head, and tsked.

"Where did you find Howard?" I asked.

"At home. I called to tell him I was coming and the dratted man still kept me waiting on the stoop for a full five minutes. I had to ring the bell at least three or four times. Why do you ask?"

I hid a smile. He'd kept her waiting and she'd only rung three or four times? Not likely. I'd bet a year's worth of Sunday brunches she'd rung the bell at least nine or ten times. "No reason." If Mother hadn't noticed the makeup on his collar, I wasn't going to point it out. The Standish family had enough problems without rumors of Howard's infidelity floating around.

"That girl, Alice, is a mess." She glanced at my father. "Harrington, dear, flag down a waiter. I want a Bloody Mary, spicy with a double shot of vodka." She returned her attention to me. "It's not entirely the girl's fault." She lowered her voice. "With a mother who drinks like that, there aren't too many possible outcomes."

I refrained from commenting. So did Daddy. We were both too fond of breathing to say anything about double shots of vodka.

Mother's eyes narrowed as if she'd read my thoughts. "Isn't it a bit late in the season for that dress?"

The dress, a Diane Von Furstenberg wrap, was brand new. "I don't think so."

"Really?" She raised a brow. "The color seems awfully summery to me."

The color fell somewhere between coral and bittersweet. It was perfect for autumn. "I like it."

"You look lovely, sugar." Daddy grinned at me. His eyes twinkled as if he found Mother's snitty mood amusing.

Mother sniffed and looked at her watch. She might have even tapped her foot beneath the cover of the tablecloth.

My insides—vital organs like my heart and stomach and large intestines—began to liquefy. Any moment now, Hunter Tafft would walk through the door, and I wasn't ready to see him.

At least it was just brunch. Anyone could endure brunch. My bandaged wrist meant I could escape the much longer round of golf. I cleared my throat. "Mother, about golf this afternoon." I held up my arm. "I think I'm going to have to beg off."

"Are you sure, dear?" she asked. "It's a lovely day."

"I don't think I could grip a club."

"Well..." She patted her lips with the edge of her linen napkin. "I imagine you know best."

That was it? I held up a bandaged wrist and I was off the hook? It was as if she'd offered me a gimme for a twenty foot putt, an occurrence only slightly less likely than hell freezing over. Something was up. It had to be. In my whole life, I'd never been able to subvert Mother's plans so easily. Maybe Hunter wasn't coming. "I appreciate your understanding."

"We'll reschedule for when you're feeling better."

I stared at my wrist. Too easy. Something was rotten in the state of Missouri.

The scent of Aramis overwhelmed the aroma of my coffee. I looked up.

"How are the two prettiest ladies in town?" A man wearing the ugliest plaid sports coat I've ever seen—burnt sienna, burnt umber, cadmium deep yellow—stood in front of us.

Mother smiled. Daddy stood and thrust out his hand. Quin Marstin shook it. I looked from Mother to Quin to the empty seat at the table. Oh dear Lord.

"We're so glad you joined us." Mother's smile didn't mean a thing. The expression certainly didn't touch the rest of her face. Was Quin a last-minute addition because Hunter hadn't wanted to come? "Please sit."

Quin sat.

Next to me.

When we were in high school, Garret Hargrove Marstin V, more commonly known as Quin, was the class president, the starting quarterback for a football team that won the state championship and the boy named most likely to succeed. As far as I knew, our senior year was the apex of his life. He'd been young, popular, and almost every girl at school had wanted to date him. The world had changed. Quin hadn't noticed.

He leaned back in his chair and grinned at me. "Ellison, looking good, babe."

Babe?

Next to me, Daddy tensed. Across from me, Mother washed away a sour-pickle expression with a deep sip of Bloody Mary. I shifted in my chair, inching as far as possible from Mother's idea of a set-up. Had she lost her mind? "Thank you," I murmured.

The man positively reeked of cologne. What's more, I'd bet, hidden beneath his white shirt, boring tie and that appalling blazer, there was a gold chain with a medallion nestled among his chest hairs. Bleh.

"How's single life treating you?" Given that I was single because my husband had been murdered, I wasn't quite sure how to answer. True, Henry had been a cheating low-life and I didn't exactly mourn his passing, but...He scooted his chair closer to mine. "Chick like you, you don't have to stay single long."

Across the table, Mother choked on her drink.

Quin leaned toward me and his Aramis assaulted my nose again.

Maybe his sense of smell was gone. Maybe when he looked in the mirror, he didn't see the thinning hair. Then again, how could he, hidden beneath a toupee the way it was? Maybe he didn't notice the thickening waist that threatened to become a paunch. The man remained a legend in his own mind.

I inched farther. So far, I risked falling off my chair. Maybe Daddy would catch me. Although...he looked frozen in horror. No help there.

"What are you doing now, Quin? For a living, I mean," I asked.

Clipping coupons off the bonds his grandfather and father had amassed. We all knew it. Then again, cutting along a straight, dotted line is *something* of a skill.

He sat up straight, grinned, then leaned against the back of his chair. "I'm thinking of investing in a chain of incense stores. Not too late to get in on the action. You interested, Harry?"

This time Daddy choked on his drink. I patted his back and looked for a waiter. With everyone choking, we were going to need more ice water. No waiter—but I did see Jane Addison walking toward the ladies' lounge.

I gave Daddy one last pat then pushed my chair away from the table. "If you'll excuse me, I need to powder my nose."

I followed Jane into the ladies' lounge, a room filled with nautical prints, lobster traps and—a tiny nod to the Midwest where we actually lived—a vase of sunflowers.

"Ellison," Jane exclaimed. "I didn't expect to see you today."

I held up my wrist. "I wasn't badly hurt."

"Still...you found Bobby. I can't even imagine how awful that was." Jane glanced at the mirror then patted a wisp of auburn hair back into place. "Although...I suppose you're used to it."

From anyone else, such a remark would count as utter bitchiness. Not Jane. She might gossip—endlessly—but she meant no harm.

She shook her head and the wisp fell. She frowned at herself in the mirror. "Poor CeCe. To lose a child...Do you have any hairspray in your handbag?"

"No."

She wet the tips of her fingers under the faucet then patted the rebellious strand into place.

"Was Bobby seeing anyone?" I asked.

"Bobby?" Jane daubed lipstick on her lips then pressed them together. "Not that I know of. Why?"

I doubted Bobby Lowell would have wanted his last words shared with the biggest gossip in town. "No reason."

She shrugged, apparently willing to accept my lie. "How are you and Grace doing all alone in that big house? I have a property coming on the market next month that would be perfect for you."

Such were the perils of talking to a real estate agent. "We're not moving."

She raised a brow as if she couldn't believe I'd want to stay in the house where my husband was murdered. "Well, if you change your mind, you know who to call."

"I do."

Jane glanced at her watch and gasped. "Is that the time? I've got to run. It's lovely to see you, Ellison. Call me and we'll have lunch." She breezed out the door.

Mother breezed in.

I pulled a compact out of my purse and did what I'd promised. I powdered my nose and glared at Mother in the mirror. She was delusional if she thought I'd ever find Quin Marstin remotely attractive.

"Do you want to tell me what you were thinking?"

"That's the type of single man who's available."

I shuddered.

Mother took out her own compact. "I blame Ford. If he hadn't divorced Tinsley and married that *woman*, Quin might not be so..."

"Slimy," I supplied.

She shrugged. "You could do worse."

"How?"

"Well, maybe not." The words Mother didn't say—*you could have Hunter Tafft*—echoed through the lounge.

If I ran now, I might make it. If I raced down the front hallway, blew through the entrance, jumped into my convertible and drove away, Mother would never catch me. Or...I could act like an adult. "I don't want a man in my life and you need to stop meddling."

She snorted and her cheeks flushed beneath her tan.

"You asked Hunter to brunch, didn't you?" My stomach twisted. "You asked him and he declined. He doesn't want you meddling either." Had he declined because of Mother's machinations or did Hunter not want to see me?

What little appetite I had, the tiny bit not obliterated by the scent of Aramis, died. "I believe I'll head home now."

Mother's mouth opened then shut. Then it repeated the exercise. Twice. "You wouldn't dare."

I would. "Give Daddy my regards."

One of Mother's hands settled on her hips, the other wagged in my face. "What am I supposed to tell Quin?"

"Ask him about incense. He won't even notice I'm gone." Before Mother found a compelling argument to keep me, I escaped.

SIX

I walked into the kitchen with Max at my heels, an empty stomach and a chest swollen with I-am-woman-hear-me-roar pride. Standing up to Mother still held an empowering novelty.

Grace sat at the kitchen counter with the phone plastered to her ear. The cord was stretched to capacity, an avocado green line instead of a coil. She stared at me for a moment then spoke into the phone. "Gotta go." She stood, made the trek back to the cradle and dropped the receiver onto the hook. "You're home early."

"Your grandmother ambushed me."

"Mr. Tafft?"

If only. "Quin Marstin."

"Ew." She wrinkled her nose. "Do you think his hair is real?"

Not in a million years. I shook my head to erase the image of what Quin Marstin might look like without the blonde rug on his head. "Who were you talking to?"

The phone rang.

Grace picked it up and listened for a moment. "I can't talk right now."

Whoever was on the line kept talking—and talking.

Finally, they stopped for breath and Grace got a word in edgewise. "I don't know. I'll ask her. Gotta go. Bye." She put the receiver on the hook.

"Who was that?"

"Kim."

"What did she want?"

Grace left her post by the phone, crossed to the fridge and

grabbed a Tab and a bowl of sliced limes. "You want one?"

"Sure."

She grabbed a second Tab, put the cans on the counter and reached into the cabinet for glasses. "Ice?"

Grace was stalling. "What did Kim want?"

My daughter put down her Tab. Her hands gripped the edge of the counter. "The whole world thinks Bobby got killed because of drugs. Kim wanted to know if you noticed anything."

Kim wanted juicy gossip.

"Do you think it was drugs?" I asked.

Grace shrugged. "I don't know. There aren't too many reasons to be under those stands."

"Could he have been meeting a girl?"

Grace caught the corner of her lower lip between her teeth. She loosed her grip on the counter and twisted a strand of hair around her index finger. "Why wouldn't they just meet at his car?"

Excellent question. The area beneath the stands—with its noise, cigarette butts and view of feet—was hardly a spot for a romantic rendezvous. "What kind of drugs?"

"Pot." She said the word quickly, decisively. Was she positive or was she covering for her old friend? Please God, please not heroin or LSD. The tip of her finger turned purple but she coiled the hair even tighter. "Some people are saying Bobby was dealing."

Gulp. "Was he?"

Her gaze fell to the countertop and stayed there. "I don't think so. I don't know. Maybe."

I circled the kitchen island and draped my arm across her shoulders. I even stroked her hair. She let me—for a moment—then the teenager emerged. The young woman who didn't need her mother and was offended I might think she did. *She* shrugged me off, turned her back on me, returned the limes to the fridge.

The place where she had stood bristled with annoyance; it felt cool, it felt empty. I swallowed the urge to tell her everything would be all right. For Bobby and his family, nothing was all right. Besides, Grace would think I was being patronizing. When in doubt, change the subject. "I think Kim knows something about Bobby. Was she going out with him?"

With her back still to me, she shook her head. "Nope. She and Sam are still together."

"You sound surprised."

She turned. "I am. Before we left for Europe, I wouldn't have given them two weeks."

Sam was exactly the kind of boy Mother wanted for her daughters. Smart, handsome and from a fine, old family. She wanted it so much that, just to please her, I convinced myself I was in love with Henry. "Does Kim really like him or is she dating him to please Ginny?"

"Yeah, right. No one would stay with someone just to please their mother."

If she only knew.

Maybe Aggie would be able to help find the mysterious girl. My muumuu-wearing housekeeper had once worked as an investigator. I made a mental note to ask her.

The phone rang. Again.

Grace was there, with her hand on the receiver before it completed its first *brrnngg*. She waited until it had completed three before she answered. "Hello, Russell residence."

She listened then a smile flitted across her face. She held out the receiver and mouthed "*You're in trouble.*"

Mother was calling already? I'd counted on at least a few days of the silent treatment. I took the phone. "Hello."

"I'm at the club." Libba's voice was slightly breathless.

"Oh?"

"You're not."

"Obviously. You called me at home."

"Did you really walk out on Quin Marstin?"

I paused. It wasn't *just* Quin. It was Mother and ham croquettes and Jack McCreary and not enough Tabasco in my Bloody Mary.

Libba took my silence for a yes. "Oh. My. God. You did. Was it the toupee? Or did he try to sell you on those damned incense shops?"

"Libba," I snapped. "Don't embarrass him. Tell everyone I'm ill...still shaky after finding Bobby."

Libba snorted. Her eyes probably rolled.

"Please?" I begged.

"Fine," she conceded. "You owe me."

I was racking up debts faster than a golfer breaks tees. "I owe you."

The doorbell chimed. Grace disappeared into the front hall.

"Libba, someone's at the door. I'll talk to you later."

"Fine," she huffed. "But don't forget, you owe me."

As if she'd let me. I hung up the phone. Should I take the receiver off the hook and leave it off? Anyone calling would get a busy signal and I'd get some peace. Grace would never stand for that. The telephone was her lifeline.

I let go of the receiver and stepped away from the phone.

Grace led Donna into the kitchen. The girl clutched a black leather portfolio to her chest. When she saw me, she pasted a tremulous smile on her lips. "I brought you a couple of my sketchbooks and a few watercolors."

I'd forgotten all about my promise to look at Donna's work. "Would you leave them here? Just for a day or two? I want to take my time with them."

She nodded then put the bundle on the counter. "I just appreciate you looking at them." Her gaze slid to the kitchen window, to the back door, to the exposed brick wall. "I...um...that is...um, I'm sorry if my stepfather was rude."

Her stepfather wasn't rude. He was beyond rude, he was a bona fide jackass. "He was just worried about you."

Her eyes narrowed, her nose wrinkled, her upper lip raised. Scorn. The expression flitted across her face so fast that if I hadn't been looking right at her, I would have missed it. It was replaced by the bland expression everyone I knew wore when they were discussing someone they didn't particularly like.

The phone rang. Again. Phones are like that. They mock you with silence when you want them to ring. They ring off the hook when all you want is a moment's peace. I should have left the receiver off the cradle.

"We could let it ring," I said.

"Yeah, right," said Grace. Apparently an unanswered phone ran contrary to some unwritten teenage law. She picked up the receiver. "Russell residence."

She listened for a moment then, without a word, held out the phone to me.

What now? I took it from her. "Hello."

"Ellison, it's Anarchy Jones. Would you come up to Suncrest? There's something I'd like you to see."

My heart, which had been beating like hearts should—a nice steady lub-dub—plummeted faster than Gerald Ford's popularity. "Is everything all right?" I asked.

"Fine."

One word that told me nothing. "I'm on my way." That was the way words were supposed to work. They were supposed to communicate some useful bit of information. I hung up the phone. "Girls, I have to go."

"Why?" Grace asked. "What's going on?"

I shook my head. "I have no idea."

If someone had asked me the place I'd least like to go in the whole world, the football field at Suncrest would have topped the list. Bobby's death was too recent, too raw.

I pulled into the parking lot but couldn't quite get out of my car. Instead, I let the autumn sunshine warm my shoulders. I peered into the rearview mirror and repaired the damage the wind had done to my hair. I dug in my purse for a lipstick and came up with the one I'd lost in the stands. I dropped the cursed thing back into my bag. My lips went untouched.

My hands were long since scrubbed free of Bobby's blood but I could still see rusty red—under my nails, near my cuticles, in the grooves of my skin. My fingers closed around the steering wheel and tightened until my knuckles turned white.

"Are you getting out?"

I looked up into Anarchy Jones' handsome face. The dark lenses of a pair of aviator sunglasses hid his eyes. His lips curled into a half-smile, as if my inability to get out of the car somehow amused him.

"Of course." I reached over to the passenger's seat and grabbed my handbag.

He opened my door and extended a hand to help me out of the car.

It would have been churlish not to take it.

His fingers, cool, callused and strong, closed around my hand and once again the regular lub-dub of my heart gave way to wild beating. I had to tug to pull my hand free. "What was it you wanted me to see?"

"Why did you park all the way up here?" he asked.

"Walking is good exercise."

He gazed at my feet—more specifically my shoes. Purchased in Italy, they were decidedly *not* walking shoes. At least this pair didn't pinch my toes.

I gazed at the hive of activity near the field—men and cars and yellow tape. "I don't want my car anywhere near that mess." I traced part of the length of the narrow black racing stripe on the car's satiny finish.

"Isn't this the car you—"

"Yes," I snapped. No need to relive the past. No need to remind me I'd run over my dead husband. Besides, nothing that happened was the car's fault.

The skin around his eyes crinkled. "Any luck finding the girl who Bobby loved?"

"How do you know I'm looking?"

He smiled. "You're you. I figure a kid asks you to do something with his dying breath, you're gonna do it."

"I haven't found her. Whoever Bobby was seeing, he was keeping secret."

"Maybe it was a message for his mother."

I shook my head. "CeCe says it's not."

"You talked to her?"

"Yesterday."

"I tried talking with Mrs. Lowell but she'd taken so many Valium I couldn't make sense of what she said."

A strand of hair blew in front of my eyes. I smoothed it back into place. "Maybe the police make her nervous."

"Maybe she has something to hide."

I snorted.

"You disagree?" Anarchy asked.

"CeCe's husband took off with a girl half his age. Except for Bobby, she was alone."

One of Anarchy's brows rose above the wire rim of his sunglasses. He didn't understand. How could he?

"Aside from being able to keep a house, cook a flawless meal and entertain, CeCe has no skills."

Anarchy's other brow rose. "I bet she plays tennis or golf or bridge."

He still didn't get it. I tucked another strand of hair behind my ear. "She plays all those things, but you can't make a life out of them. Bobby was her son and she loved him, but he also gave her a purpose."

"What was she going to do when he went to college?"

Who knew? "Date or do more volunteer work or get a job in a boutique."

"She can do that now."

It was my turn to raise an eyebrow. "You think any woman in her forties wants to actually do those things?" Obviously he had no idea what most available middle-aged men were like. An unfortunate vision of Quin Marstin slunk across my brain. "As for volunteer work, you've obviously never sat on a women's committee. None of us want to do it. We feel as if we have to."

"What about a job?"

"CeCe has no work experience. Like I said, if she was to get a job it would be selling ladies dresses or fine china or cooking gadgets." I shuddered.

"So, CeCe Lowell had nothing to do with her son's death?"

"Absolutely not." I added an emphatic shake of my head.

"Any idea who did?"

"None." I glanced toward the hive of activity. "What was it you wanted me to see?"

"It's down by the field."

We walked across the parking lot and the back of the stands came into view.

The base of the fence was mounded with flowers. Above them, fluttering in the light breeze, was a length of red ribbon threaded through the chain links. In letters three feet tall, the ribbon spelled "SLUT."

My feet in their Italian pumps froze to the pavement.

My heart, already jittery from proximity to Anarchy Jones, thudded so loudly the sound echoed in my ears.

My hand, the one not wrapped in bandages, flew to my mouth and attempted—unsuccessfully—to smother a profanity.

"Who did this?" I asked.

"I was hoping you could tell me."

Alice Standish. Was she crazy enough to do something like this? From what I'd seen at CeCe's, the answer was definitive.

If I implicated her granddaughter with solid evidence, Alice Anne Standish would restring her tennis racket with my tendons. I shook my head. "I don't know."

"Any theories?"

I'd been more focused on finding the girl Bobby loved than the person who stole his life. "Not one."

"No one is talking," Anarchy said. "The kids cross their arms and slouch and roll their eyes and wait for their fathers' lawyers to show up. Their parents aren't talking either. I need your help, Ellison."

Damn.

He took off his glasses, rubbed the bridge of his nose, and gazed into my eyes. "I don't want more people to die."

Neither did I, but..."There's a reason people won't tell you things."

"They don't want to get involved."

I shook my head, looked away from Anarchy's warm brown gaze. "They don't want to rat out their doubles partner. It might make it hard to find another one."

"Will you help?"

I caught my lower lip between my teeth. There was no reason not to tell him what I'd heard. "The kids are saying Bobby was dealing drugs. Pot."

"What about the word in the fence?" He jerked his chin toward the ugly word. "Who did that?"

"Let me talk to her."

"You know who did this?"

"I can guess. If I'm right, I'll tell you." I wouldn't wish a police investigation on my worst enemy—well, maybe on Prudence Davies, but she's a special case. I wasn't dragging a sixteen-year-old girl into one if I could help it.

Besides, Alice's grandmother was a force of nature. If I set the police on Alice and I was wrong...the woman would make my life a misery.

SEVEN

Who was the slut? The girl Bobby had loved or someone else entirely?

I drove with the top down. The whoosh of the wind and the rumble of my empty stomach were the only sounds until I pulled to a stop sign. I turned on the radio and Elton John sang "The Bitch is Back."

Had Alice strung the ribbon through the fence? It seemed possible—even probable.

I pulled into the driveway, parked the car, and hurried up the front steps. No breakfast, no brunch, no lunch. I was starving and before I seriously considered who Bobby loved, if Alice had spelled "SLUT" with red ribbon, or who'd murdered a teenage boy, I needed a sandwich.

I opened the door. "Grace, I'm home."

No answer. Except for Max. He moseyed down the stairs, yawned then rubbed his face against my leg.

I scratched behind his silken ears and headed for the kitchen. Maybe he heard my stomach rumble, maybe doggie ESP told him I'd be opening the refrigerator, but rather than return to his nap, Max followed me. "Where's Grace?" I asked him.

I knew he was paying attention—especially when I took a cold roast chicken out of the fridge—but Max is the strong silent type. He didn't answer.

I put a bowl of grapes next to the chicken then grabbed sprouts, a tomato, an avocado and a loaf of whole grain bread. I didn't just *want* a sandwich, I *needed* it. That and a Tab. I popped the top off a can and drank deeply.

"You're home." Grace stood in the doorway.

I sprinkled sprouts on a slice of bread. "I am." The bread knife cut cleanly through the tomato.

"Isn't it kind of late for lunch?"

I glanced at the clock. Three. No wonder I was starving. "I haven't eaten yet today."

She scrunched up her face, an expression that could have meant *gosh, that's awful, Mom* or *boy, are you an idiot to wait so late in the day.* I was too hungry to care if Grace disapproved of my dining choices. I laid the tomato slices on top of the sprouts.

"What did Detective Jones want?"

I gently squeezed the avocado. "He asked me a few more questions."

She stared at me as if she could somehow discern I wasn't telling the whole truth.

I stared back. As far as I was concerned, my daughter need never know about the ugly word woven into the fence. She'd probably hear about it—the grapevine was too effective. But it wouldn't be from me.

After a moment, she shrugged. "Do you mind if I go out for dinner tonight?"

I sliced through the skin of the avocado. "Is your homework done?"

She nodded. "Yeah."

I cupped the half with the pit in my hand, whacked the knife at it, twisted, and pulled the pit free. "Who are you going with?"

Grace caught the end of her ponytail and twirled strands of honey-colored hair around her fingers. "Friends."

I added a few slices of avocado to my sandwich then pulled the plate of chicken closer. Next to me, Max sat up straighter. His pupils dilated until his eyes were nothing but liquid need melting into eternal devotion if only I'd give him a bite. I tossed him a bit of chicken. "Which friends?"

Grace mumbled a name.

"Who?"

"Jack McCreary."

A slice of chicken fell from my fingers onto the floor and Max inhaled it. "No."

"What do you mean 'no?'"

I put the knife down on the counter. "I mean no."

Her arms crossed over her chest. "Why not?"

I held up my hand so I could use my fingers to enumerate. "You came home in tears how many times because he teased you?"

She shrugged. "That was years ago."

"I don't like him." I ticked off another finger.

She crossed her arms. "I do."

"He may have had something to do with Bobby's death." He certainly had been behaving strangely enough at the club. It wasn't hard to extrapolate guilt.

Grace shook her head, dismissing my concerns. "That's just silly. Jack and Bobby were best friends."

I gave up on counting fingers and held my hands out to her. "Grace, there's been a murder. You yourself said it might have something to do with drugs. Suppose Jack was involved?"

"Why would you think that?"

"I saw him at brunch today and he was acting oddly."

She rolled her eyes. "Maybe that's because his best friend died on Friday."

"Fair enough, but today is Sunday and he wants to go on a date."

"It's not a date! It's two friends hanging out."

And one of those friends just might be a murderer. "I don't want you to go."

"Please. I'm sixteen." She was making my argument for me.

"Exactly."

"I'll be in college soon." Grace was not helping her case.

"What has that got to do with Jack McCreary?"

"I'm growing up."

My fingers gripped the edge of the counter. "Please tell me that has nothing to do with Jack."

She rolled her eyes. This time with more drama. "Don't be ridiculous."

Thank God for small favors. Grace's days of playing with dolls and thinking her mother knew everything might be behind her, but I wasn't ready for her to grow up too much.

"Are you forbidding me from going?" Something in her eyes dared me to do it.

"If I am?" I tasted other words on the back of my teeth. My lips even parted. I sealed them shut. *As long as you live in my house, you live by my rules*. That expression hadn't turned out too well for Mother. My sister rebelled by marrying a rubber manufacturer from Ohio—and no, not the tire kind. I made a more traditional choice, a banker. Mother was pleased until he got himself murdered.

"I might go anyway, Mother," she said, lifting her nose.

Mother? I wasn't Mother. I was Mom or Mommy or MaMa or even Mumsy. Mother was *my* mother. And we weren't anything alike. Were we? I hadn't uttered the *rules* sentence. Mother would have.

"I don't want you hurt."

She crossed her arms. "You don't trust me."

"You, I trust. I have my doubts about Jack McCreary."

She shook her head hard enough to make her ponytail whip back and forth. "You don't trust me to take care of myself."

Maybe I didn't. Then again, what mother trusts her only child with a potential killer? "I don't want you to go."

She stared long enough for me to remember all the psychology books I'd ever read. Grace was trying to develop an identity independent from me. The harder I fought, the harder she would.

"I'd prefer you not go."

She tossed her ponytail. "Well, I am." She turned her back, marched down the hall, stomped up the stairs and slammed the door to her room.

A second later the house thumped to the sounds of her stereo turned a million decibels high.

Short of locking her up, how was I going to keep her home? Since when was Grace dramatic? Since when did she rebel?

I stared at my sandwich. I wasn't hungry anymore.

The phone rang and I waited for Grace to answer it. Three rings, a short silence, then her voice tumbled down the stairs. "It's for you."

I picked up the receiver. "Hello."

"Thank God I caught you at home." Libba's voice was slightly husky, as if she'd been running (highly unlikely), or playing tennis (slightly more likely), or having sex (highly probable). "You know that favor you owe me?"

"Yes." Was it a word or a sigh? Hard to tell, even after the lone syllable escaped my lips.

"Well..." Her lone syllable promised the delights of Shangri-La, the endless adventure of jungle exploration and the excitement of a plunge on a rollercoaster. Shangri-La doesn't exist. Jungles overflow with snake and bugs. I hate rollercoasters.

"What, Libba?"

"You know Charlie, the man I've been seeing?"

"No, I don't. I was out of town all summer."

"Well, tonight's your lucky night." She paused. "He has a friend."

I dropped my forehead to my hands. It was gentler than beating it against a wall. "Just so we're clear, you want me to go on a blind date?"

She treated me to a moment's silence while she searched for an answer that wouldn't make me hang up the phone.

"Need I remind you I don't date?" I asked.

"Need I remind you that you owe me?"

"Why are we friends?"

Libba snorted. The sound carried, pin-drop clear, through the telephone wires. "We're friends because we've known each other all our lives and because you need me. Without yours truly, you'd lock yourself in your studio and spend all your time painting."

"That sounds like heaven."

"You say that now. Just wait 'til Grace goes to college—you'll be lonely."

Why must everyone remind me that Grace would be leaving for college? I still had two years with her. "Libba—"

"It'll be fun," she wheedled. "We'll go to the Magic Pan for crêpes. Charles knows this little club downtown and he wants to take us."

"I can't."

"Why not?"

"Grace wants to go out with Jack McCreary."

"And?"

"Jack McCreary was Bobby's best friend."

"And?"

"What if Bobby was murdered over drugs?"

"Grace is almost grown. You're going to have to loosen those apron strings."

I didn't want to. Those apron strings kept Grace close and safe and protected. She'd already lived through her father's murder. Proximity to a boy who might be doing—or dealing—drugs wasn't what I had in mind for her.

"I bet you fought."

How did a woman who'd never had children, who gave the impression she'd never wanted them, know so much?

"I'd call it a spirited debate."

"Did it end with a slammed door?"

Silence was my answer.

"And loud music? Is there loud music?"

I couldn't hear lyrics or melody, just a steady thumping beat, loud enough to shake the house. I didn't bother to answer.

"You have to let her make her own mistakes. You can't protect her from everything."

"I should be able to protect her from murderers."

"Do you really think Jack McCreary killed Bobby?"

I didn't think so—but I'd been wrong before. *Really* wrong. "No." Another lone syllable lost in the space between a word and a sigh.

"Let her go."

Easy for Libba to say. Near impossible for me to do. Unless...

"Let her go," Libba repeated. "She'll be fine. Besides, you'll be having such a fabulous time with Charlie and me and his friend, Upson, you won't have time to worry."

Upson? "Just dinner, right? Then my debt is paid."

"Dinner and one club."

I shook my head. "I don't want to be out late."

"Upson is in town on business. He's got a meeting in the morning so I doubt he wants to stay out late either. We'll have you home by eleven."

"Do you have a bridge in Brooklyn you'd like to sell me?"

"I promise. We'll have you home early."

"Eleven."

"Done. We'll pick you up at six. Wear something fabulous." She hung up before I could think of any other objections.

I rested the receiver in the cradle. Slowly, I lifted it. More slowly still, I inserted my finger in the three hole and rotated the dial. I'd promised to call. I hadn't. Not 'til now. Not 'til I wanted something. I dialed six. He had every right to hang up on me. It took only a second to dial the one. I rushed through the rest of the numbers, afraid I'd lose my nerve.

He answered the phone on the third ring. His voice, deep, cultured and ever-so-slightly pompous, made every word he uttered sound important. "Hello."

I swallowed, tried for a deep breath. "Hunter, it's Ellison." The words came out in a rush. I waited for him to say something...and waited.

Finally, he spoke. "Hello."

I swallowed again. In the history of bad ideas, calling Hunter Tafft won the prize. Worse than the decision to burglarize the Democratic National Committee headquarters at the Watergate.

Worse than making tapes of conversations pertaining to the break-in. Worse than keeping those tapes. I should have called him weeks ago when Grace and I first got back from Europe. But what was I supposed to say? *I'm grateful for your help, I think you're insanely attractive and my fingers itch to know if your silver hair is as soft as it looks. Oh, and, even though I want to touch your hair, I don't want to get involved. Not now. Maybe never.* Having your husband betray you with half the women you know creates trust issues. Big ones. I'd work on them. Someday. "How are you?" I croaked.

"Fine, thank you."

I really ought to have thought this phone call through before I made it. "Um, I don't know if you heard, but I found a body on Friday night."

"I heard."

I nodded then remembered he couldn't see me. My fingers tightened around the receiver. "It was Bobby Lowell. He was murdered."

Hunter offered me nothing but silence.

"There's some speculation that Bobby might have been involved in drugs."

I thought I heard a grunt. At least Hunter was still listening. Maybe.

"His best friend was Jack McCreary. They did everything together."

Another grunt.

"Grace has informed me she's going out with Jack McCreary tonight."

Silence.

"I'm worried and I need your help." I didn't give him a chance not to answer. "Please, Hunter."

To his credit, he didn't make me wait for an answer. "What do you need?"

"I was wondering if you had someone who could..." My grip tightened on the phone. "Keep an eye on her."

"You mean follow her."

"Yes," I admitted.

"You're sure about that?"

I stared at my bandaged wrist, remembered the warmth of Bobby's blood welling between my fingers, and nodded. "I'm sure."

"Why don't you do it?"

"She'd notice her mother following her around." I didn't add that I had a date. It wasn't information that would help my cause.

"What about Aggie?"

"I don't want to put her in that position." Aggie adored Grace. She wouldn't feel comfortable invading her privacy. Plus, Aggie was given to wearing toxic muumuus, loud—both in color and jingles—jewelry, and bright makeup. She was about as subtle as a crimson dress at a debutante ball. Not exactly ideal for following a teenage girl—or anyone else—around without being detected.

"I'll see what I can do." From Hunter, that meant it was as good as done.

"Thank you."

"It'll cost you."

Everything had a cost. This time the price didn't matter. "Fine."

"Dinner with me. Tomorrow night."

Blackmail. It was my turn to be silent.

"I'll pick you up at seven."

"Fine."

What had I done?

I had a date with Hunter Tafft. If Mother found out, she'd do a very staid version of a happy dance. If Libba found out, she'd smirk. If Grace found out, she'd wonder what in the world had induced me to go out with one of the men I'd spent an entire European vacation refusing to discuss.

I just had to make sure none of them found out.

EIGHT

Libba squinted at herself in the restaurant's gilt-edged mirror—the bathroom was as dim as the dining room. Whose bright idea was that? She mashed her lips together and the *Plum Crazy* she'd just applied obliged by spreading itself more evenly over her lips. "I'm sorry about him."

Upson? "Don't give it a second thought." To say Upson, the blind date, was boring was like saying a golf course in summer was green. He'd said ten words all night. I'd counted. Two of those were *nice dress*. It was. Chanel. Black. Demure. Utterly perfect. Aside from the dress, he obviously found me uninteresting. Far more compelling were the stingers he ordered, one after another.

Libba pulled her compact out of her purse and squinted again. Between her terrible eyesight and the dim lighting in the ladies' room, she had no hope of actually seeing herself.

"You might be able to see if you wore your glasses."

She stopped squinting long enough to roll her eyes then recited the only poem she knew. "Men seldom make passes at girls who wear glasses."

Dorothy Parker. Short. Witty. Not necessarily correct. On the other hand, maybe I should start wearing glasses. They might scare off men like Quin Marstin.

Maybe if Libba wore glasses she'd see her date more clearly. There was something off about him. Although, he did at least talk.

"What do you think of Charlie?" she asked. It was as if she could read my mind.

I swallowed and patted a stray strand of hair back into place. "He seems nice enough."

"Nice enough?" She leaned closer to the mirror then touched the end of her nose with a satin-backed puff. "That makes him sound as boring as Upson." She wrinkled her freshly powdered nose. "I thought Charlie would have more interesting friends."

I shrugged. "It's one night." I hoped wherever she was, Grace was having as awful of an evening as I was, so awful she'd never go near Jack McCreary again. Did it make me a horrible mother to hope my daughter was having a bad time? Maybe—but I still hoped for something to keep her away from Jack.

Libba mashed her lips again. "So, Charlie. Nice enough?"

I blinked away thoughts of Grace and Jack. "What do you want me to say? I've known him for an hour and a half." I smoothed my hair. "He's very handsome." True, if you liked men with cheekbones so sharp they were almost delicate, piercing blue eyes, and ridiculously long eyelashes.

"He is dreamy, isn't he?"

"Dreamy." Libba didn't hear the sarcasm in my voice. That or she ignored it. Just like she ignored the weird vibes from Charlie.

"Are you ready?" she asked.

There wasn't much point in primping for a man I didn't like. There was no lipstick on my teeth and my hair was combed. That counted as ready. I nodded.

The men stood as we wound our way through the restaurant. Charlie glanced at his watch. "The floor show starts at a quarter to nine. If we hurry, we can still get a good table."

"What's the name of this club you're taking us to?" Libba asked.

"The Jewel Box." Charlie's long elegant fingers closed around her elbow and he guided her toward the door.

She fluttered her lashes. "If you're taking me, I'm sure I'll like it."

"I hope so." Charlie spoke so softly I could hardly hear him, but he sounded sincere, as if he *cared* that she like the club.

Maybe he wasn't as bad as I thought.

* * *

Charlie parked his Mercedes on the street, not far from a marquee with "Jewel Box" and "Cocktail Lounge" spelled out in neon. The building itself was painted blue and the glass of the front window had been replaced with frosted glass bricks, making it impossible to see what was happening inside.

Not that much was happening inside. The tables created a semi-circle around a raised wooden platform that served as a stage. They were half-full. The floor was so scuffed it was hard to make out its tiles, and the wood paneling on the walls looked dingy with accumulated cigarette smoke. *This* was the club Charlie wanted Libba to like? It was a good thing she wasn't wearing her glasses. If she was, she'd turn on her heel and walk out. I was tempted to do just that, but the neighborhood seemed sketchy and the likelihood of me getting a cab seemed slim. I claimed my seat between Upson and Charlie at a table next to the stage.

Even without her glasses, Libba could tell the club wasn't up to her usual standards. "This is an...interesting place. Do you come here often?"

Was that a blush staining Charlie's cheeks? He nodded. "I do. Upson's been wanting to come and see the floor show."

"What's it like?" Libba asked.

Charlie rubbed the back of his neck. "It's a burlesque revue."

"Really? I can't wait to see it."

Charlie waved over a waitress.

"A vodka martini, please," said Libba.

"Dewars with a splash." Hopefully the scotch would sterilize the glass. Given the looks of the place, I had no faith in the thoroughness of their dishwasher.

"Stinger." Upson was up to eleven words, if I allowed for repetition.

Charlie looked up at the waitress and said, "A Singapore sling."

Really? There was definitely something odd about Libba's new boyfriend.

"How did the two of you meet?" I asked.

"On a plane from New York." Charlie reached across the table and took Libba's hand in his. "We were seated next to each other."

"Libba tells me you're researching a book."

Charlie nodded.

"About what?"

He rubbed the back of his neck again. "I don't want to bore you by talking about research. Libba says you're an artist."

Why didn't he want to talk about his research? "I am."

"A painter, she says."

My turn to nod.

Libba's nearsighted gaze, which had been traveling the club, settled on me. "I think we're underdressed."

Libba wore a black cocktail frock with a revealing neckline. I wore a black dress that revealed I had a neck.

I glanced around the club. She was right. A buxom redhead in an emerald-hued mermaid gown stood at the bar next to a platinum blonde wearing a fitted crimson gown with a side slit that reached for her waist. The blonde had a white fur stole wrapped around her shoulders. Both women dripped with rhinestones.

A brunette in a pink gown with a marabou hem sat at the table next to ours. She stared at me for a moment then whispered to a friend who wore a low-cut gold lame gown and evening gloves that covered most of her arms. They both giggled.

They wore more makeup than I wore in a week—long fake eyelashes, arched brows so perfect they had to be drawn, bright lipsticks and heavy powder.

The waitress put my scotch in front of me. I looked up to thank her. The words died on my lips. Our waitress, a slender young woman with a bouffant updo, had a five o'clock shadow.

I blinked and looked more closely. A five o'clock shadow? Check. Her hands, despite the long red-tipped nails, looked mannish. Her shoes, pointed, kitten-heeled and totally wrong for a waitress, were the size and color of one of the blue kickboards they used at the club to teach children to swim. She was a he.

If my perusal bothered her—or was it him?—she (or he) didn't show it. Instead, she put the rest of the drinks on the table and returned to the bar.

With a sideways glance, I looked again at the women at the bar. They were lovely, with strong jaws and broad shoulders. Men. The women at the table next to ours giggled again. The sound was too low, too masculine to belong to anyone but men.

I settled my gaze on Charlie. "Interesting place. You say you come here often?"

He nodded, and I had a vision of Charlie's cheekbones dusted with rouge, his eyelashes curled and darkened with mascara, his navy blazer replaced by a navy gown. Who was I to judge? My late husband had engaged in much stranger things than dressing like a woman.

Poor nearsighted Libba had no idea her boyfriend had brought us to a bar for crossdressers. Then again, she had eyes only for Charlie. Googly eyes.

I lifted my scotch to my lips and drank. Deeply.

The woman wearing the pink dress at the nearby table stood, swayed slightly, then focused her gaze on me. "I could fix your face. A bit more makeup and you'd be fabulous."

Next to me Upson guffawed into his stinger.

"Five minutes in the bathroom and you'll turn every head in the place."

Heat rose to my cheeks. "I...um. I'm a woman."

"Oh honey, we're all girls here. Come on."

"Thank you for your offer but I believe I'll stay here."

"Don't be silly." A very firm grip closed around my arm and lifted me from my chair.

Upson rose too. "She said she'd prefer to stay here."

The man in the pink dress had a good six inches and probably thirty pounds on Upson. My blind date stepped forward anyway. Maybe he figured at least three of those inches came in the form of stiletto heels.

They stared at each other for a moment—the cold stare that

men give each other when they're daring someone to cross a line.

The man in the pink dress blinked first. He released my arm, smoothed the seams of his dress and sashayed away without a word.

"Thank you," I said.

"You're welcome." That brought the word count to nearly twenty. He leaned toward me and with a whisper the floodgates opened. "Just because a man dresses like a woman doesn't mean he's gay." He glanced around the bar that had become crowded with men in dresses. "Most of these guys are straight men who find wearing women's clothes erotic."

"So the guy in pink wasn't interested in my makeup?"

"Doubtful."

I swallowed. "Do you ever wear dresses?"

He didn't respond. His silence was as good as a yes.

"Charlie?"

Upson's chin bobbed—infinitesimal but a bob all the same.

I sank into my chair.

Libba hadn't heard Upson's whisper and her refusal to wear glasses meant she probably didn't realize there were only a few women in the bar who actually had real women parts. "What was that all about?" She tore her googly-eyed gaze away from Charlie. "Are you all right?"

"Nothing. I'm fine."

She nodded. "Charlie says the show will start in five minutes."

"Can't wait." Not only is Libba blind without her glasses, she's deaf to all sarcasm. I'd bet every canvas in my studio that Libba had no idea Charlie liked to dress up in women's clothes. If a trip to The Jewel Box was how he planned to tell her, the man had rocks for brains.

Somewhere behind us a camera flashed.

A rumble went through the bar and someone yelled, "No photos!"

The camera flashed again.

I glanced over my shoulder. The tables were filled with men

dressed as women with varying degrees of success. Really, the man with the olive complexion had no business wearing an orange gown, and someone ought to tell the pale blonde that dove gray washed her out. For heaven's sake, I was a *woman* and someone gave me makeup tips—couldn't someone tell the man in the strapless gown to wax his back?

"You're staring," said Upson.

I was and I couldn't help it—especially not when my gaze lit on a man in a brocade cocktail dress. It suited him. The soft blue looked good with his tan. Heavy ropes of pearls circled his neck and in their center hung a cameo. I narrowed my eyes. I could almost make out frolicking cherubs on the pin's lapis background. I knew that cameo.

I raised my gaze to the face above the pin. Square jaw, brown eyes, powdered cheeks flushed with excitement or liquor. Howard Standish.

He looked up from his drink—something pink with a straw and an umbrella—and caught my gaze. The color drained from his face. His eyebrows raised and pulled together. His lips stretched back toward his ears. For an instant, the poor man looked terrified, then his brows and lips returned to the places they belonged.

Was this why he'd had makeup on his collar at CeCe's? I'd assumed he had a mistress. Was this why his wife drank like a goldfish in a leaky bowl?

Howard stood.

Idiot man. I knew a little something about keeping secrets. Libba, on the other hand...well, if Libba recognized him, everyone at the country club would know that Howard Standish looked lovely in a dress. She wouldn't tell his secret to be malicious—she'd be having drinks with friends and it would be a funny story.

I waved him away but he ignored me, waiting for a heavyset man in rose tulle to pull in his chair so he could pass.

"Someone you know?" Upson asked.

"Yes. It would be better if he didn't come over here."

Couldn't Howard see Libba?

The camera flashed again. This time, someone responded with a string of obscenities. There was a shuffle of bright dresses near the back of the room and the sound of breaking metal and glass.

A man in a flamingo pink gown raised his fist and threw it at the heavily powdered jaw of a man in a canary yellow mini-dress. The sound of knuckles meeting bone quieted the bar—for about a quarter second.

In the next instant, half the patrons tried to push their way through the front door. The bottleneck was rainbow hued. The rest of the patrons picked sides.

Charlie grabbed Libba's elbow and yanked her from her chair. "This way." He lifted her onto the stage then clamored up himself. He scurried toward the beige curtain, calling to Upson and me over his shoulder. "The back door is this way."

My date leapt onto the wooden riser then reached down to help me up. A hand closed on my upper arm.

Upson grabbed my hand. Howard Standish tightened his grip. They both pulled.

The distant wail of police sirens was discernible above the sounds of breaking furniture, ripping satin and fists meeting skin. The bottleneck at the door exploded into the street.

Upson pulled harder. So did Howard.

"Howard! Have you lost your mind? Do you want to get caught here?"

Howard looked over his shoulder at the melee then back at me. His face registered the blare of police sirens with slack-jawed horror. He abruptly released my arm.

Upson, who still pulled on my other arm, fell. I flew onto the stage and landed on top of him. Howard Standish leapt over us—well, as much as a man wearing a tight skirt and heels can leap—and disappeared through the curtains.

I tried to push myself off Upson but we were a tangle of legs and arms, and my injured wrist hurt worse than when I'd injured it the first time. Blood soaked the bandage. Somehow I'd torn the stitches.

Beneath me, Upson still struggled. I rolled off him, sat up and cradled my wrist.

Upson pushed himself onto his hands and knees and then his feet. He leaned down to help me. "We've got to go!" His eyes widened. "Is that blood?"

I nodded.

My date, who had risen leaps and bounds in my estimation over the past several moments, promptly fainted.

Oh. Dear. Lord.

I couldn't leave him, not after he tried to save me. I sat up straight, brushed my hair away from my face with my uninjured hand and waited for the police to arrive.

The few people left in the bar were too intent on their fights to notice a woman and an unconscious man. Two men who must have been sewn into their dresses circled each other, fists raised as if they were Ali and Foreman. Another set of combatants degenerated to hair pulling—well, wig pulling.

The police burst through the front door and the combatants looked almost relieved. The fights ended.

A uniformed police officer who looked only a few years older than Grace approached the stage. "Are you all right, ma'am?"

I held up my bloodied wrist. "I think I've torn some stitches. My friend needs help too." Upson hadn't moved.

The policeman disappeared for a moment. When he returned, he said, "We've called an ambulance. You want to tell me what happened?"

"He fainted when he saw my wrist bleeding."

"Did he hit his head?"

"No." Fortunately, when Upson fainted his head landed in my lap instead of the floorboards.

"What happened in the bar? To start the fight?"

"As far as I can tell, someone was taking photographs then someone else broke his camera."

Broken chairs and tables, torn bits of fancy gowns and even a few wigs littered the floor. Somewhere in the mess lay parts of a camera. Bits of feathers and sequins and the remnants of cigarette smoke filled the air.

Something like a smile flitted across the policeman's face. "Cameras are against the rules in bars like this one. Not everyone wants proof they dress up like a woman." He pulled out a small notepad. "Can I get your name, please?"

"Ellison Russell."

"And him?" He jerked his chin toward Upson.

"Upson Smith."

"Come here often?"

I offered him a wry smile. "First time."

He grinned back at me. "Last time?"

"Definitely."

"You take it easy, ma'am. The ambulance will be here soon."

I breathed in a huge sigh of relief. I wasn't going to be arrested and neither was Upson. I was exhaling when Anarchy Jones stalked through the door.

NINE

Silhouetted by the lights in the street, Anarchy Jones was still identifiable. He reminded me of a sheriff in a western who's just pushed through the swinging doors to the saloon. One who doesn't much care for what he sees.

My hands—even the bleeding one—shook. How could I explain away a comatose date, a crossdressing brawl and a bloody wrist?

Anarchy crossed the room in a few strides. He stared at me for a moment, his eyes scrunched as if he was trying to find answers without actually speaking to me. His gaze shifted to Upson. "Is he dead?"

"No."

"Are you sure? Usually when I see you, someone's been murdered."

The man had a point.

"I'm sure." I folded my hands in my lap. "He's not dead."

"What happened to him?"

"He fainted."

Anarchy's upper lip curled slightly.

The Jewel Box might well be outside Anarchy's parameters of acceptable places, but he shouldn't sneer at Upson. "He protected me."

"From the combatants?"

The blonde in the dove gray dress wore handcuffs, her makeup was smeared and her hair no longer cascaded in ripples down her back. Instead, her wig was off-kilter. The man in the strapless gown sat in one of the few remaining chairs with his face buried in his hands. They didn't look as if they'd ever been dangerous.

I didn't care to explain about the man who offered to fix my makeup. Time for a change of subject. "Why are you here?" I asked. "Is someone dead?"

"I heard Jenkins on the radio talking about a blonde who'd torn stitches in her wrist. I thought I'd make sure it wasn't you."

For a moment neither of us said a word. Instead, we listened to one of the handcuffed men sob. The lights from the police cruisers sent flashes of red through the front window's glass bricks. A turquoise feather floated by and I blew it away from my face.

Anarchy rubbed his hand across his eyes. "Who's the not-dead guy?"

"Upson Smith."

He crossed his arms and waited for more.

Let him wait. The ambulance would be here soon, then, no doubt, I'd be loaded in it. A nice doctor with a shot of novocaine would fix my wrist and I'd go home to find out what happened on Grace's date with Jack.

He shook his head as if amused by my little I-can-be-silent-longer-than-you game. "Does this have anything to do with my investigation?"

"No."

"Why are you here?"

I might as well tell him. "I went to see CeCe Lowell yesterday."

His eyebrows rose and his lips thinned.

I swallowed. "Don't look at me like that. This has nothing to do with your investigation. I went to offer my condolences and there was a girl there—Alice Standish. She wouldn't leave. CeCe called her mother and the mother arrived but she was soused and the daughter ignored her. I called Mother to track down Howard Standish to come get them both. Mother found him. He came. Alice and her mother left. So I owed Mother a favor."

"Are you saying your mother set you up with sleeping beauty there?"

"No. Mother set me up with Quin Marstin. Brunch. At the country club. I walked out. Libba called me. Apparently everyone and their brother were talking about my exit so I asked her to tell everyone I felt ill. I owed her a favor."

Anarchy's lips quirked. He was definitely amused. "So Libba set you up?"

"Double date. Upson isn't from here and they needed a fourth."

He glanced around the bar. "Where's Libba?"

"She....um. She left."

"She left you here? Bleeding in a bar?"

"She didn't know I was bleeding. She probably thought I was right behind her."

"So where is she now?"

Charlie would have mowed down both his grandmothers not to get caught in The Jewel Box. They weren't coming back. Libba was probably—right now—sitting in his Mercedes telling him he had to turn the car around. She'd be loud and insistent and persuasive.

That they weren't here told me just how important it was to Charlie to keep his secret.

Howard Standish probably felt the same way.

I shivered.

"Where is she, Ellison?"

I shrugged. "She's gone."

The tone of his voice softened. "Would you like me to take you to the hospital?"

My wrist throbbed and I blinked back a tear. I *hated* when Anarchy was nice. It made me want to melt into his arms and let him handle all my problems. "No, thank you. I can't leave Upson."

"Your hero." Was that amusement or sarcasm?

"He helped me. I'm not leaving him."

Anarchy's lips curved into a delicious half-moon. A dimple formed in his cheek. His eyes twinkled as if he approved of my decision not to abandon Upson. Looking at him, I couldn't breathe. How embarrassing if I fainted too. At least I could claim blood loss.

A medic pushing a gurney saved me. He parted the sea of cops and crossdressers and enlisted Anarchy's help in lifting Upson onto the gurney.

"Do you need help to the ambulance?" Anarchy asked.

I gave him what I hoped was a withering stare and pushed myself to my feet. Blood loss? Proximity to Anarchy Jones? That damned smile? Who knows why I staggered? I did. Anarchy caught me, swept me into his arms and carried me outside where camera bulbs flashed and the lights atop the cop cars cast everything in a red hue.

Mondays are dangerous days. Sure, they dawn in fifteen lovely shades of pink. The birds sing. The sun shines. Mr. Coffee works his magic before you even get to the kitchen. And you know, with absolute certainty, that today you will not be injured in a brawl at The Jewel Box.

That's just Monday lulling you into a false sense of security.

I followed the scent of fresh-brewed heaven to the kitchen where Aggie whisked batter in a creamware bowl. "Good morning," I said. "You're here early." Not that I was complaining. I poured myself a cup of coffee and settled onto one of the stools that surrounded the kitchen island.

"Good morning." Aggie's muumuu was nearly as violent an orange as her hair. She put down the bowl, repositioned the coffee pot onto the exact center of Mr. Coffee's burner, straightened the tea towels that hung from the oven handle then ran a hand through her hair. "You haven't seen the paper?"

I sipped my coffee. "No."

Slowly, as if I was a snake and her hand was a mouse, she pushed a folded copy of the morning paper across the counter toward me.

The headline read "Socialite Injured in Brawl at Notorious Nightclub."

Sweet nine-pound baby Jesus.

Beneath the headline was a picture of a blonde woman whose

pearls hung askew. She wore a fabulous black dress but the hem had inched up, revealing entirely too much leg. A handsome man cradled her in his arms. Her mulish expression communicated how very little she wanted to be there. At least I hoped it did. His expression was softer.

One of last night's camera flashes must have belonged to a reporter.

Oh. Dear. Lord.

The phone rang.

"You want me to get that?" Aggie asked.

I wasn't going to answer. "I'm unavailable."

"Even to your mother?"

"Especially to my mother."

She answered the phone, listened, then said, "I'm sorry, Mrs. Russell is unavailable. May I take a message?"

She picked up a pen and jotted something on a piece of paper. "No, ma'am, I can't promise she'll call this morning. I'll give her the message." She hung up the phone then pushed the note toward me. One word. Libba. As if a phone call could make everything better. Libba had some serious groveling to do.

The phone rang again almost immediately and Aggie repeated almost verbatim her conversation with Libba—except this time the caller was Howard Standish.

No sooner had Aggie hung up the phone than it rang a third time. Mother's voice boomed through the line.

"I'm sorry, Mrs. Walford, but Mrs. Russell is resting. May I have her call you when she gets up?" Aggie deserved a raise. A large one.

I heard Mother tell Aggie to get me out of bed. Immediately.

"I'm sorry, Mrs. Walford, but I promised Mrs. Russell that I wouldn't disturb her."

Mother hung up.

I gulped at my coffee. "She'll be here in an hour. Maybe sooner."

Grace chose that moment to walk into the kitchen.

"Good morning, honey." I manufactured a smile. "How was last night?" Hopefully her evening hadn't been quite as eventful as mine.

"Fine."

A one-word answer. She was still angry with me. Just wait. I handed her the paper. Better she see the picture now than hear about it at school.

She looked at it for a minute then tossed the paper onto the counter. "And you didn't want me going out with Jack?"

"I thought I was going out for dinner and a drink."

"So how did you end up in Detective Jones' arms?"

"That's a long story."

Grace snorted. "Yeah, right."

Where had the attitude come from? In Europe, we'd been fine. Now that we'd come home, Grace had started acting like a resentful, rebellious...teenager. I forced a smile. "Where did you go last night?"

"Winstead's. Then we went for a walk in Loose Park." She reached past me, picked up the paper and read. With each line, her expression darkened.

Damn Monday straight to hell. I should have stayed in bed.

The telephone jangled.

"Should we unplug the blasted thing?" I asked Aggie.

Grace sneered at me over the top of the paper.

"That's enough out of you, young lady." I already dealt with Mother's regular, deep-seated disapproval. I didn't need Grace's too.

"I didn't say anything."

She didn't have to. Grace dropped the paper onto the counter, tossed her hair and headed toward the door.

"Don't you want breakfast?" Aggie asked.

"I've lost my appetite."

Teenagers.

Aggie picked up the phone, listened for a moment then said, "I'll see if she's available."

She covered the mouthpiece with the palm of her hand. "One of Grace's friend's mothers. She says it's an emergency."

I nodded and Aggie handed me the phone.

"Hello."

"Ellison, thank God I caught you. India Hess calling. My daughter, Donna, spent the night at your house on Friday."

"We enjoyed having her." Well, except for the nightmare and the stepfather.

"My husband left town on business yesterday. New York. His taxi was in an accident and..." her voice quavered, "he's in the hospital with serious injuries. I have to fly out there and I was wondering if Donna might be able to stay with you for a few days."

"Well..." I'd met the girl exactly twice. Didn't India have anyone else she could call?

"I'd take her to my mother's but her health hasn't been good. Donna and Grace seem to be getting on so well that I thought perhaps you'd be willing to take her."

"Um—"

"Really, they have. Donna had such a grand time last night with Grace and her boyfriend."

What? "I—"

"I'd be forever in your debt. I don't want to leave her home alone and I simply have to get on a plane for New York this morning. Please?"

"India, I—"

"She won't be any bother. I promise."

Maybe having a friend around would put Grace in a better mood. "Fine." I didn't try to say more. Chances were good she'd just interrupt me.

"Thank you! I can't begin to tell you what a help this is to me. Jonathan would be so angry with me if he thought for a second I'd left Donna unsupervised. He even suggested I bring her with me, but I don't know how long I'll be gone and I didn't want her to miss school."

Oh dear Lord. What had I done? She didn't know how long

she'd be gone? What if her horse's ass of a husband couldn't travel for weeks? I grimaced and gulped at my coffee.

"May I drop her things off this morning? My flight leaves at eleven."

"Of course. If I'm not here, Aggie will be."

"Thank you, Ellison. I owe you an enormous favor."

How novel and delightful to have someone owe me for a change. Although I couldn't imagine a circumstance in which I'd ever collect. "Not a problem." I scratched my nose. "We're delighted to have her."

A few more gushing thanks, then I hung up the phone and turned to my housekeeper. "We're going to have a houseguest."

Aggie nodded. "I guessed as much. Blue room?"

"Fine."

The phone rang again and I answered. "Hello."

"Ellison? Hunter Tafft here. I'm calling to confirm tonight. I'll pick you up at seven. We have a lot to talk about."

Like I said, Mondays are dangerous days.

TEN

Mother was on her way. India was on her way. I was on my way too—except I was on my way out.

I hurried upstairs, donned pearls—necklace and earrings—a wrap dress and shoes that didn't pinch my toes, then I climbed into my convertible and pointed the wheels toward downtown.

Manicured lawns gave way to overgrown yards, then the yards gave up entirely, replaced by weed-choked lots. Finally, the dandelions ceded to concrete surface parking manned by bored attendants. A twenty-minute trip from affluence to urban decay.

Downtown was dying. Women's favorite shops had moved south to the Country Club Plaza. Only a few restaurants remained and those catered to a lunch crowd. Men drove to their offices and then they drove home. The only people who spent any real time downtown were winos, burlesque dancers and beat cops.

I parked, paid and picked my way up a crumbling sidewalk to a skyscraper in need of a shower. A security guard looked up from his paper and beeped me in.

"I'm here to see Howard Standish."

The guard glanced at the front page of his newspaper then at me. He narrowed his eyes, focused on the paper, tilted his head and opened his mouth as if he intended to ask me a question.

"Howard Standish," I repeated. Men who'd just triple bogeyed a par three use nicer tones than I did. Those men weren't on the front page of the paper.

The guard grunted. "Eleventh floor." He pointed to a pair of elevators then went back to examining the photo of a socialite injured in a brawl at a notorious nightclub.

When I pushed through the doors of Standish & Co., the receptionist's desk sat empty.

I glanced at my watch and sat. Five minutes later with no receptionist in sight, no offer of coffee and only a folded copy of the Kansas City Times to read, I stood.

A short hallway ran to the left of the receptionist desk, a long one to the right.

I went right. After all, there was no way the short hall led to a corner office. My shoes sank into expensive carpet. Too bad. I'd have preferred the sharp click of my heels against hardwood. A purposeful sound. A sound with a mission. A sound that telegraphed my annoyance to all the people working behind closed doors. Monday might be a dangerous day but this particular Monday, I was dangerous too. I'd find out who Bobby loved, tell the girl, then focus all my attention on keeping Grace out of trouble. Being nice wouldn't get me an answer. Being dangerous might.

A woman exited an office. She blinked when she saw me. "May I help you?"

"I'm here to see Howard Standish." I spoke with the triple-bogey tone.

"Do you have an appointment?" she asked with the prim assurance of someone who knew I didn't.

"No. But Mr. Standish will see me."

She lifted her nose—a we'll-just-see-about-that tilt. "Your name?"

"Ellison Russell."

"One moment." She marched down the hall and disappeared through yet another closed door.

She reappeared almost immediately. "Mr. Standish will see you."

As if there'd ever been any doubt. I offered her a sugary smile.

She led me down the rest of the hallway then opened an oak-paneled door. The office on the other side smelled of leather and cigar smoke and ink. Manly smells. The opposite of blue brocade frock smells.

Howard stood when I entered. He straightened his tie. He cleared his throat. He even offered me a grimace of a smile.

His square jaw worked as if he was chewing. A bitter pill? He glanced at the woman who still lingered in the doorway. "Thank you, Ann."

Ann cast me a curious look—I guess municipal bond underwriters don't get a lot of drop-ins—then disappeared.

"Welcome," Howard croaked. "Coffee?"

"That would be lovely. With cream."

He picked up the phone on his desk, spoke into the receiver, then realized I was still standing. "Please..." he waved toward one of a pair of wingback chairs, "...sit."

I sat. I placed my handbag on the rug next to the chair's ball and claw foot. I crossed my ankles. I directed my attention to the man across the desk.

Howard hung up the phone and stared at me. His skin looked grey, maybe even green, and despite the steady breeze from the air conditioning vent, sweat broke out on his upper lip. He wiped it away. "How may I help you?"

"I have a few questions." More than a few, and given what I knew about Howard's predilection for dresses, wigs and frosted eyeshadow, I figured he'd answer them all.

"Questions?" Howard's skin tone went from green to dead white. "About what?"

Had someone been blackmailing him? Did he think I was after money? Or did he think I had some prurient interest in hearing about his dresses? "About Bobby Lowell."

His skin tone improved from dead to dying. "What about him?"

Someone tapped on the door then opened it. Ann appeared carrying a tray with two coffee mugs.

"On the desk," Howard instructed.

With a sideways glance at me, she did as he asked.

When she was gone, he pushed the mug with cream toward me. “What are your questions?”

“Tell me about Alice and Bobby Lowell.”

Howard’s mug froze halfway to his lips. His eyes narrowed. “Your questions are about my daughter?”

“She loved Bobby.” Not a question.

He nodded. “She did.”

“Bobby loved someone else.” Also not a question.

“I don’t know anything about that.”

“I think you do.”

Howard put his mug down in the center of a leather-edged blotter. “Why would you think that?”

“Because I think Alice talked of nothing but Bobby and if she believed that Bobby was involved with another girl I think she’d tell you and Kizzi.”

“Maybe she just told her mother. Not me.”

I didn’t believe him. He might not be scratching his nose but the bridge between his brows wrinkled and his fingers twitched.

“Bobby’s dying words were, ‘Tell her I love her.’ I’m trying to find the girl. Do you have any idea who she is?”

“Maybe he loved Alice.”

I didn’t dignify that with a response. The idea sank below the surface of possibility faster than a lounge chair tossed into a swimming pool. I waited.

Howard squared himself in his chair. The knuckles of the hand that held his coffee mug whitened. His lips thinned. “I can’t help you.”

“Can’t or won’t?”

Howard glared at me then his gaze dropped and he took a sip of his coffee.

All things being equal, I preferred not to bring up the blue brocade dress or Howard’s heavy hand with eyeshadow, but I wanted answers. “Did you hear about what happened at the school? At the stands? Someone wove the word ‘slut’ into the fence with red ribbon. Who do you think would do such a thing?”

We both knew the answer to that.

Howard's shoulders slumped. "I don't know who she is. Alice never referred to her by name."

I leaned forward. "Will Alice tell you who she is?"

"No."

I crossed my arms over my chest and attempted menace. "I'd really like to tell that girl that Bobby's last thoughts were of her."

Howard shook his head. "I'm not even sure Alice knows the girl's name."

I raised a brow. We lived in a world where everyone knew everyone. Alice had to know—unless Bobby had gone beyond the confines of the country club or Suncrest to find a girlfriend. If that was the case, I might never find her. Pish. If the girl didn't go to Suncrest, why bother writing 'slut' in the fence? "Alice needs to give you the name."

He ran a finger around the inside of his collar. "Alice is troubled."

Howard was a master of understatement—at least when it came to describing his daughter. Last night he'd applied makeup with a trowel. There was nothing understated about a man with sky blue shadow on his lids. "Do you think she had anything to do with Bobby's death?"

Howard half-rose from his chair. "Of course not!"

Liar, liar, pants on fire. "Did you have anything to do with the murder?"

He sat—more of a collapse, really. "How can you suggest such a thing?"

I tilted my head. I narrowed my eyes. I might even have pursed my lips. Did I need to say out loud that Alice might have told Bobby about her dad's dresses? "People will kill to keep secrets." I knew firsthand.

"Not me." He rubbed his face with his hands, mussing his thinning hair.

A man who wore satin probably didn't have the...gumption to commit murder. Howard probably hadn't killed Bobby. Alice might have. It seemed as if he thought so too—he'd responded with anger when I suggested she might be involved, while aspersions on his own innocence were met with bewilderment.

"Is there something I should know about Alice? Where was she on Friday night?"

Howard's lips thinned and he turned his head and directed his gaze out the window.

"Alice is troubled." My voice was soft, barely louder than a whisper. "You said so yourself."

He looked at me then. "She didn't kill that boy."

"Are you sure?"

He rose completely from his chair. "Of course I'm sure. How dare you come into my office and suggest my daughter's a killer?"

I dared because he'd given me the power to ruin him by going out in a dress. I dared because I was positive Alice had embellished the fence at Suncrest. I dared because Bobby was dead.

I stood too. "I made Bobby a promise, Howard. Get me the name." I put my coffee on his desk, turned on my heel and walked out his door. Hopefully he didn't notice I couldn't meet his gaze.

I straightened my shoulders. A boy was dead and it was up to me to carry out his dying wish. I couldn't afford to feel guilty about how I went about fulfilling that wish.

Once, I won a round with a PGA golfer at a charity auction. He accompanied me to the ladies tee and watched my backswing. I whiffed. Heat rose to my face and—embarrassed—I swung again too quickly. I sliced the ball into a stand of pines. He laughed at me. Hard. All things being equal, I would have preferred to relive that moment over and over again rather than go out with Hunter Tafft.

I don't pick my moments. They pick me.

At precisely five minutes to seven I descended the front stairs. My hair was up in a smooth chignon. My dress was a Missoni purchased in Italy. My necklace, a hammered gold choker, I'd bought at a jewelry store across from the Ritz in Place Vendôme. I needed every bit of confidence I could borrow from wearing the right clothes and jewelry.

I wandered into the kitchen where Donna and Grace sat at the counter finishing a pizza.

"You look nice, Mrs. Russell."

"Thank you, Donna."

Grace looked me up and down and frowned. "I thought you weren't ready to date."

I wasn't. But I couldn't exactly explain that I was going out with Hunter as payment for having one of his investigators follow her.

The doorbell rang.

My stomach completed a triple flip.

No more favors. They cost too much. "Don't stay up too late. It's a school night."

Donna offered me a polite smile. Grace crossed her arms and tilted her chin. She might have mumbled something about staying out of the papers. I pretended not to hear.

The sight of Hunter Tafft on their front steps might make some women's hearts flutter. He is, after all, tall and tan and more polished than my grandmother's silver tea service. He's also charming and ruthless. The perfect lawyer? Definitely. The perfect date? I wasn't so sure.

Hunter smiled at me and my heart fluttered—just a little bit. Such is the power of his thousand-watt smile.

He leaned forward and gave me a chaste kiss on the cheek. "You look lovely."

"Thank you." My damned heart needed to settle back down to a steady beat.

"Shall we?" He held out his arm.

My fingers closed on the fine wool of his sports coat. He led me down the steps to his Mercedes, opened the door, and made sure I was safely tucked inside before he closed it. Then he climbed into the driver's seat and started the car.

"Where are we going?" I asked.

"The American."

The best restaurant in the city. Where else?

"I don't often dine with a celebrity." He was mocking me.

"Everyone but Mother will have forgotten all about that picture by the end of the week." She'd never forget. Mother was a firm believer that one's name should appear in the newspaper only once. In the obits. I'd made the front page. Worse, I'd made the front page in the arms of a mere policeman. She'd pulled out words like *shameful* and *disgraceful* to describe my behavior. She'd called my inching hemline indecent. She'd called Anarchy, who was blameless, an intemperate gigolo.

"How did you get there?" Hunter asked.

"Libba." Five letters spelled a four-letter word.

"I figured as much."

Mother hadn't. She'd let me know in no uncertain terms that as a woman approaching forty I was accountable for my own actions. True. Also true—I wasn't accountable to her. When I told her so, she got very quiet. Quiet before a storm quiet. Not being a fan of storms, I quietly hung up the phone. She probably wouldn't speak to me until Thanksgiving. I shifted in my seat, suddenly uncomfortable in glove leather luxury.

"Tell me about Europe." One thing about Hunter, he reads people, can tell when a subject is bothering them. He'd changed the subject. He wanted me at ease. That in itself was enough to make me nervous.

"It's old and full of art."

"So you loved it."

I nodded. "Every minute."

"I was worried you might not come back."

He was worried? I swallowed, stared through the windshield at the world whishing past. "The thought crossed my mind."

"I'm glad you came home."

Grace and I had only been home for two weeks and already I'd found a dying boy, hosted an impromptu slumber party, dealt with a crazy girl and a daughter with an attitude problem, been injured at a bar for crossdressers, made an appearance on the front page of the morning paper and threatened a family friend. Hell, I'd done all that in a matter of days. "It's been more fun than a barrel of monkeys."

Hunter chuckled and slowed the car for a red light. "How's the wrist?"

I glanced at my bandage. "It hurts."

"Tearing stitches will do that."

How did he know about my torn stitches? Aggie. "My housekeeper needs to remember who signs her checks."

"She has your best interests at heart."

I knew she did, but that didn't mean I liked her sharing details of my life with Hunter.

"Before I forget..." Hunter reached into the inside breast pocket of his sports coat, withdrew an envelope and handed it to me. The only marking on it was Grace's name, typed neatly and centered.

I closed my eyes, swallowed, battled the competing urges to rip it open and rip it in half.

"Nothing exciting," said Hunter. "Grace and Jack sat in the parking lot by the football stands at Suncrest for thirty minutes or so, then they went to Loose Park and walked. Jack smoked a joint."

"Grace smoked pot?" I squeaked.

"No. Jack did. Grace sat with him while he smoked. Then they picked up another girl and went to dinner at Winstead's. Grace was home by nine."

For all my worry about my daughter, I was the one who'd gotten into trouble. I waited for Hunter to point that out.

He didn't.

I slipped the envelope into my purse. "Thank you."

He glanced at me, gave me a half-smile that made me think I'd amused him in some way. "You're welcome."

We pulled up to the valet, got out of the car and Hunter whisked me into the restaurant.

Slender gold columns opened into elaborate fans where they

met the vaulted ceiling. Fuchsia velvet banquettes waited for bottoms. Walls of windows allowed evening light inside. The best wall—the wall where we were seated—offered a view of downtown. From this distance, the skyline looked almost pretty.

The sommelier presented a wine list to Hunter. A waiter presented us with menus then unfolded my napkin and let it float into my lap.

"Red or white?" Hunter asked.

"Red."

We ordered. A steak for Hunter. Grilled salmon for me.

We sipped wine. We watched the sky fade to lavender and the lights begin to turn on in the buildings downtown. We chit-chatted.

We did not talk about blackmail or my dead husband or the things that Hunter said to me before I left for Europe. Instead, we lifted forkfuls of four-diamond food to our lips and talked about other meals, other bottles of wine, travel.

Slowly—very slowly—I let myself relax.

"Did you go to Harry's Bar when you were in Venice?" he asked.

"I thought going was a requirement."

"And you drank bellinis?"

I nodded. "Of course."

"I love Venice." He leaned toward me as if he meant to tell me something meaningful. He smelled of soap and leather and fresh linen. His eyes sparkled. His lips parted. My heart fluttered again and for a half-second, I half-hoped he'd ask me to run off to Venice with him. "Did you have coffee at Caffe Florian?"

So much for our Venetian tryst. "Every day we were there."

A waiter appeared at the table and waited for Hunter to acknowledge him.

Hunter stared at me, smiling as if he was rethinking that Caffe Florian question.

The waiter shifted his weight from one foot to the other and cleared his throat. "I'm sorry to interrupt, Mr. Tafft, but there's a call for you."

Hunter's brows rose. "For me?"

"Yes, sir."

"Excuse me, Ellison." Hunter stood, dropped his napkin into his chair, and strode toward the maitre d' stand. I couldn't help but notice that most of the women in the restaurant watched him pass.

Hunter. Venice. It might be nice to go to a romantic city with a man instead of a teenager. I conjured up images of us holding hands in a gondola on the Grand Canal, strolling across the Rialto bridge, enjoying an opera at La Fenice. It would be lovely, maybe even magical, and definitely romantic, until I remembered my terrible taste in men. Then I'd start wondering if Hunter was an accomplished liar or indulged in kinky sex.

I shook my head. No trips to Venice for me. Well, not with Hunter Tafft.

At the maitre d' stand Hunter raked his fingers through his silver hair and hung up the phone. If he'd strode away from the table, he practically ran coming back. He didn't sit. Instead, he reached into his pocket, pulled a hundred from his money clip and threw the bill on the table.

"Ellison, we have to go. That was my secretary. Aggie had her track us down. There's a problem at your house."

My heart stopped its foolish fluttering. My heart stopped entirely.

ELEVEN

Hunter drove fast—white-knuckle fast—and I was grateful.

A traffic light turned yellow. I pushed my right foot against an imagined gas pedal and muttered, "Run it."

He did. Good man.

"They didn't say what was wrong?" I asked for the umpteenth time.

"No. But if Aggie called, it's serious." A red light stopped our progress. He looked both ways, saw no cars and drove through the intersection.

Very good man.

He pulled into the driveway and I flung open the car door.

"Ellison, let me stop the car."

He applied the brakes, the car stopped and I ran to the front door.

SLUT.

The sconces that flanked the front door had been turned off, but the light from the street lamps and my neighbors' houses illuminated ugly crimson letters across the formerly pristine white of my door and the mellow red of my bricks.

I stumbled to a halt and stared, slack-jawed.

This was what I'd sped home for? Please let this be all.

The front door opened and Grace rushed outside. Alive. In one piece. Apparently unharmed.

I drew my first deep breath since Hunter and I left the restaurant. I opened my arms and my little girl ran into them. She shook. Holding her to me, I smoothed her fruit-scented hair and inhaled. She'd been a tad heavy-handed with the Tame crème rinse and she smelled like a child. I squeezed her tight against me as if she was still six and not sixteen.

Hunter tapped me on the shoulder. "If you'll let me use your phone I'll get a painter over here. He can power wash the bricks and paint the front door before the sun rises."

"I...um. Just a minute, Hunter." I smoothed Grace's hair again. "Are you okay, honey? What happened?"

She pulled away—just a little—then said, "Someone rang the bell. When I opened the door no one was there." She shuddered and tears formed in the corners of her eyes. "But I saw the paint. I didn't know where you were so I called Aggie."

On cue, Aggie pulled her ailing VW Beetle into the driveway and parked behind Hunter's Mercedes. Her car emitted its usual death knocks and she climbed out.

She looked at the painted door, at Grace, and at Donna, who stood wringing her hands on the front stoop. "Inside, girls, cookies and hot chocolate." Then she took Grace by the hand and led her inside. Donna followed.

"Should I call the painter?" Hunter asked.

"Give me a minute." My legs felt like a Jell-O mold, one without even fruit or marshmallows to give it form. I shuffled back to Hunter's car and leaned against the hood.

Grace was unharmed. As was Donna. Meanwhile, I'd been frightened near to death by a prank. The bones in my legs firmed. The ones in my spine solidified. Anger will do that for you.

That little bitch. "I'm thinking I should call the police."

"Why?"

"Because someone defaced my house. That same someone wove the word 'slut' into the fence where Bobby was killed."

"Who?"

"I'd bet money on Alice Standish." I'd challenged Howard Standish to get information from Alice and twelve hours later my house had been vandalized. I'd bet *big* money on Alice.

"Think about that, Ellison. If we call the police, this..." He nodded his chin toward the ugly word. "This will still be here in the morning."

Hunter made an excellent point. I knew from experience exactly how long the police took to process a crime scene. They'd be here all night.

What's more, the neighbors didn't need any new reasons to talk about me or Grace. I'd already been branded a killer. The neighborhood would positively buzz over this latest title. Just the word "SLUT" emblazoned across our door might convince some of them that Grace or I had done something to deserve it. We'd be modern-day Hester Prynnes for whom a mere A wasn't good enough. With gossip that juicy, our innocence wouldn't matter.

On the other hand, if I called the police, they might arrest Alice. The girl had lost her mind entirely if she thought I'd let her get away with terrorizing my daughter or vandalizing my home. Put that in the plus column.

Also, if Anarchy Jones ever found out I'd destroyed evidence...I shuddered. His imagined scowl was fearsome. If he found out I'd had the paint removed, the scowl would be real. He might actually arrest me.

The upstanding, law-abiding, moral thing to do was call the police. I gazed at the mulched beds where my hostas should be. They hadn't recovered from the last time the police investigated a crime at my home. I rubbed my eyes with my uninjured hand. Grace's eyes had just recently lost the injured, haunted look they'd acquired when her father was murdered. No way was I welcoming another three-ring circus of police to our front yard. I wouldn't put Grace through that. Not for a few letters on my front door. "Call the painter."

I didn't sleep. A mish-mash of memories kept me staring at the ceiling. The strength of Anarchy's arms when he carried me out of The Jewel Box mished. The lingering softness of Hunter's goodnight kiss on my cheek mashed. Plus there was the indelible picture of the word "SLUT" painted in red on my door. It mished. It mashed. It picked up a mallet and pounded on a kettledrum hidden behind my temples.

It had to be Alice who defaced my home.

What if I was wrong?

If not Alice, who?

Max's pacing didn't help. Every so often he'd whine softly, presumably begging for permission to go and chase away the men on the front stoop who disturbed his rest.

Since the men were washing my bricks, painting my door and making Tuesday bearable, I ignored his whining.

I thumped my pillow, tossed from side to side, told Max to go lie down, then thumped again.

I must have slept somehow. The alarm woke me. I glared at the clock for a moment as if the balefulness of my stare could somehow turn back time and allow me more than a few hours rest. It didn't work.

Defeated, I lay there for a moment, gathering the strength of will to separate from the sheets. I swung my feet to the floor and forced myself out of bed.

Max lifted his chin off his paws and tilted his head as if to say, *Now? You're getting up now? I wanted to go out all night long. The men are gone. What's the point in getting up now?*

Max was onto something. Maybe I should stay in bed—maybe all day.

Instead, I pulled on a robe, jammed my feet into slippers and made my way downstairs. I opened the front door, admired its white expanse, and stepped outside. The birds were singing, the sun was shining and the newspaper lay neatly folded on the stoop.

I picked it up then turned and examined the bricks. If anything, they looked too clean. An envelope protruded from under the front mat—the painter's bill. I opened it and gulped. Was he kidding?

Probably not. He'd spent the night at my house.

His midnight visit was costing me a fortune. In cash, and probably in favors too.

I shrugged, stuffed the bill in my pocket, the paper under my arm, and went inside. I had a steamy rendezvous planned with Mr. Coffee.

I'd just brought a hot, fresh cup of ambrosia to my lips when Grace appeared.

"Did you sleep?" she asked. "You don't look like you slept."

I sipped my coffee, ran my fingers through my hair—perhaps I should have brushed it before I came downstairs, seeing as we had a houseguest—then tightened the belt of my robe. "Not much. The door is white again and the paint is off the bricks."

Grace poured herself a cup of coffee. "Who do you think did it?"

"No idea." My nose itched. I ignored it. I'd be taking my suspicions and the astronomical bill to Kizzi and Howard as soon as Grace and Donna left for school. In the meantime, Grace didn't need to know that Alice Standish had targeted our house because I'd challenged her father.

She stared at me a moment. "Maybe it has something to do with that picture in the paper."

I choked on a sip of coffee. When had Grace become so resentful? We'd gotten along so well in Europe, but now that we were back, things seemed to be going downhill fast. When our houseguest went home, Grace and I were going to have a long talk. "I doubt it. Where's Donna?"

"Blow-drying her hair. May I take your car today?"

I arched a brow. "What's wrong with yours?"

"Nothing. It's just that Donna has never ridden in a convertible and it looks like it's going to be a gorgeous day."

There was no reason Grace shouldn't drive my car. I could take Henry's. "Fine. The keys are in my purse next to the bed. What do you want for breakfast?"

"Cereal is fine." She put her foot on the first riser of the back stairs. "We'll grab some before we go."

Perfect. Cereal was one of my specialties. I opened the pantry, took out boxes of Life, Cheerios and Shredded Wheat and put them on the counter. Two bowls and two spoons later, breakfast was complete.

I grimaced. We had a guest. I ought to make more of an effort. I sighed and added a banana and a knife.

I was contemplating my third cup of coffee when Grace bellowed, "Mom!"

The Call of the Mom. There are a million variations. The please-take-me-shopping *Mom* has a pleading quality. The you're-embarrassing-me *Mom* requires a drawn out *ah* sound. The I-need-you *Mom* turns one vowel into two syllables. There's outraged *Mom*. This call of the Mom was definitely outrage. Short. Terse. Loud.

Had Max eaten her favorite shoes? Chewed his way through a belt or a purse strap? Nested in her bed while she was getting coffee?

I hurried up the stairs.

She met me at the top with something crumpled in her hand. "What's this?" She shook an envelope at me.

"What's what?"

She shook the envelope again and I recognized her neatly typed name.

Lord love a duck. She'd found Hunter's report when she searched for keys in my handbag.

"How could you?" she wailed.

"Grace, calm down. We have a guest."

"Donna should know about this. The whole world should know. My mother hired a spy to follow me around."

"Grace, if you'll just calm down and let me explain."

"How could you, Mother? I thought you trusted me."

There it was again. *Mother*. "I do trust you. I do not trust Jack."

She shook the report at me. "What now? Are you going to turn Jack into the police for smoking pot?"

"Of course not. I don't care if Jack fries every brain cell he has. Although I wish you had the sense to stay away from him while he does it."

"It was just pot. It's not like he was dropping LSD."

What did Grace know about LSD? Cold seized my spine as if I'd been shoved into an icy swimming pool. "They're drugs. They're illegal. And I thought you had better sense than to hang out with boys who do them."

My daughter rolled her eyes. "Get with it, Mother. Everyone does drugs. Besides, I'm an adult. I should be able to make my own decisions."

If you live in my house, you live by my rules. The thought bubbled up from some cave hidden deep inside my soul. I pressed my lips together, fisted my hands, counted backward from twenty. Anything to keep the words locked tightly inside my mouth.

Four, three, two, one...I risked parting my lips. "We can discuss this later."

"That's right, Mom. Just pretend things you don't like haven't happened and they'll go away." Her lips curled into a sneer. "How did that work out for you with Dad?"

I was thrown off a horse once. I landed with a thud on rain-parched ground. I lay there, staring at the stars revolving around my head and struggling to fill my empty lungs with air. I couldn't. All I could manage was one tiny wheeze, enough to keep the stars spinning, not enough to allow me to sit or speak or even move. Grace's words hit me with the same force.

I used the wall to keep me upright.

She turned on her heel, marched down the hall to her bedroom, and slammed her door with enough force to make the house shudder.

I didn't move. I couldn't.

A moment passed, then another and another. Finally, I pushed away from the wall. My legs shook. I forced them to carry me to my room. I needed a shower, two aspirin and a primal scream. Not necessarily in that order.

* * *

The house had an empty feeling when I got out of the shower. Grace and Donna were gone and I had thousands of very private square feet to scream or cry or stomp my feet, but I didn't have the energy.

My limbs felt heavy, as if I'd lost something effervescent and replaced it with lead. Exhausted, I sat on the edge of the bed and stared at my bare feet.

I couldn't do this. Couldn't sit and wallow in self-pity just because my daughter didn't respect me. I pushed myself to standing, stumbled toward my closet and picked out an outfit. I put it on, made a half-hearted attempt at hair and makeup, then went downstairs for another cup of coffee.

The cereal boxes, bowls and banana were untouched. I poured myself another cup of morning magic and put them away.

Max sat and stared at me, his doggy face sympathetic. We might have stared at each other all morning, but the phone rang.

I answered it with a dull *Hello*.

"How does it look?" Hunter asked.

I blinked, then traced a mental path back to what he meant. SLUT. The door, the bricks, the painter. "It looks like new. Thank you."

"Are you all right?" he demanded. "You don't sound like yourself."

"I didn't sleep well last night."

"No. It's more than that."

God save me from perceptive lawyers. "No, it's not." He wasn't there to see me scratch my nose.

Maybe he guessed I was lying. He answered me with silence. That wouldn't work. A full fifteen seconds ticked by before Hunter said, "I called because Lyle said he left his bill at your house."

"I found it under the mat."

"I'll pay it."

"Why would you do that?" I asked.

More silence. Only Hunter could make silence charming and

electric. His silence was an eloquent offer to take care of me.

This time I squirmed before I ceded defeat. "I'll pay the bill." I tucked a strand of hair behind my ear. "Or, better yet, I'll get Howard Standish to pay it."

"Do you want me to send him a letter? Legal stationery might make him more likely to pay."

"I can handle this on my own." God, that sounded bitchy. But my wrist ached and grit from an unsettled night scraped my eyes. Besides, Howard paying for the painter came second to finding the name of the girl Bobby loved. A letter wouldn't get me that name nor would it give Howard control over his wayward daughter. The man needed a spine for that, and last time I checked that particular body part was made of bone, not paper.

"I'm here if you need me." More charm. Damn him.

"Thank you. I have to run." I scratched the tip of my nose. "Goodbye."

I hung up the phone and looked at the clock. It was early enough that I might yet catch Howard at home. I searched through a stack of directories until I found the Junior League's, located Kizzi's number and dialed.

"Hello." Kizzi sounded slurry already.

"Kizzi, it's Ellison Russell calling. I need to speak to you and Howard about Alice."

"Whash she done now?"

"I'd really like to speak to you both in person. Is Howard there?"

"No. You mished him but you can come tonight."

It wasn't like Howard would be able to extract a name while Alice was at school. "Fine," I said. "Seven o'clock?"

"We'll see you then. We'll have a drink."

As if she needed another one. "Seven o'clock," I repeated. I'd present Howard with the bill, get the name, track down the girl, give her Bobby's message and move on.

Amazing how wrong I can be.

TWELVE

Playing bridge held less appeal than dissecting my life choices with Mother, but I'd promised and it was too late to find a substitute. Besides, when you are a sub, you shouldn't find another—not according to Hoyle or Mother.

I showed up on time, decked out in a linen camp shirt and a pair of wide-leg trousers I'd bought in Italy. And pearls. For bridge at the country club, pearls are *de rigueur*. Sally Montgomery had found a sub too. Amy McCreary, wife of John, mother of Jack, sat in Sally's usual chair.

I smiled at her. A real smile. If I directed the table talk, maybe I could learn something useful—why Jack acted so strangely on Sunday, what drove his sudden interest in Grace and, most importantly, if he'd shared with his mother the name of the girl his best friend loved.

"Ellison, how are you? How's your wrist?" Amy asked. "John said he saw you at brunch and that you looked a little peaked."

Who wouldn't look peaked having lunch with Mother? "Thanks for asking." I held up my bandaged wrist. "It's on the mend."

"You do lead an exciting life." Peazey Moore occupied her favorite seat. Its view of the hallway meant she could see everyone passing. She manufactured a smile—at least she tried. The corners of her mouth twitched.

The woman was fishing for gossip. She had as much chance of getting gossip from me as she did catching a catfish in a swimming pool. "Europe was exciting," I said blandly.

"I meant this past weekend." The corners of her lips forced

themselves further toward her nose. Not exactly a smile but as close as she ever got. The expression was catty? Bitchy? Pure Peazey? All of the above?

Amy patted my good hand. "It must have been horrible. Jack is still beside himself. He went to the game with Bobby, you know." She sipped iced tea garnished with fresh mint. "They sat together until Bobby got the note."

"What note?" I asked.

"Someone passed him a note right before half-time. Jack said Bobby disappeared after he got it."

I'd found Bobby shortly after the second half began. Had there been a crumpled note in Bobby's pocket? Perhaps trapped beneath his body? Did Anarchy know to look for it?

"Jack ought to tell the police."

Amy shook her head. "His father thinks not. He doesn't want Jack to get involved." Amy held out her left hand and inspected the shine on her wedding ring. "I think John is being silly. The only thing Jack did was sit with Bobby in the stands." She looked me in the eye and shrugged. "What can I do?"

She could tell me, knowing that if Jack wasn't going to the police about the note, I would. Telling Anarchy might help catch Bobby's killer. It would definitely assuage my guilt about destroying potential evidence by repainting the front door.

Tibby Davis rushed into the ladies' lounge. "Sorry I'm late, girls. The school called and Beth forgot some assignment that she simply *had* to have so I ran it up there. While I was there, Annie Pendleton asked me to work on the carnival committee and *insisted* on showing me the file. Then I ran my stockings and had to go home. On the way over here, I realized there was no gas in the car so I stopped. Do you realize gas is up to nearly fifty-five cents a gallon? I swear the price goes up every time I drive by the station." She paused for breath. "But I'm here now." A triumphant smile lit her face. Having conquered errands, she collapsed into a chair and waved a waiter over. "I believe I'll have a glass of Blue Nun."

Peazey glanced at her watch. "A little early in the day, isn't it?"

She turned toward me. "Was it awful? Finding him, I mean."

Of course it was awful, I'd found a dying boy. "It was. Were any of you there?"

Amy shook her head. "I only go to games where Jack is actually playing. Believe me, I'll go to plenty of games come basketball season."

Peazey pursed her lips and looked down her long nose. "You just have a girl, Ellison. You have no idea how boys' sports can take over your life."

Tibby, the mother of three daughters, scowled. "Really? Try ballet lessons and art lessons and tap lessons and piano lessons. Missy—took up the violin." She shuddered. "Besides, they do have sports. My girls all swim and play golf and tennis."

Amy looked from Tibby to Peazey then offered up a conciliatory smile. "Shall we draw for dealer?" She fanned the cards across the table.

Peazey drew the ace of spades.

Amy handed her a made deck then cut. "Thin to win."

Tibby shuffled the second deck.

I thought about Bobby. If Jack was telling the truth about the note, the murderer had lured Bobby under the stands. Had Anarchy found the note? I hadn't noticed one. I'd been too focused on the boy and the blood and his last words to notice much else.

Peazey cleared her throat. Everyone else had picked up their cards. They'd caught me wool-gathering.

"Sorry," I muttered. I gathered, sorted and counted in record time. Then—to make up for my lapse—I introduced a new topic. "Do any of you remember India Easton—India Hess now? Her daughter is staying with me."

"How did that happen?" asked Tibby.

I explained.

"India was in my sister's class," said Amy.

"No, she wasn't. She was in mine." Peazey moved a card from the left side of her hand to the right. "One club."

Amy passed.

Tibby glanced at her cards. “One heart.”

I studied my hand. “One spade. What did you think of her?”

Peazey caught her upper lip in her teeth and pinched the end of her pointy chin. “Three hearts.” She looked at me then crinkled her nose. “Quiet girl. Kind of a doormat.”

Peazey had managed a zinger? “Quiet” and “doormat” exactly described me for most of my marriage to Henry. I pretended not to notice. “Oh?” The woman who’d foisted a girl I barely knew on me for Lord knew how long hadn’t struck me as a doormat.

Peazey nodded. “She’d do *anything* to fit in.”

Amy said, “Pass.”

Tibby held her cards in her right hand and counted points with her left. “Four hearts.” She arched a brow. “*Anything*?”

My hand wasn’t good enough to go to game without help. I passed.

“Not *that*. It was the fifties. Not like today. You wouldn’t believe the way girls throw themselves at my boys.” Peazey closed her cards with a snap. “Pass.”

Who was she kidding? When Peazey was in high school someone coined the term Easy Peazey just for her. The lemon-squeezy part came later. None of us were foolish enough to remind her.

“Speaking of girls and boys, was Bobby Lowell dating anyone?” I played the ace of spades.

Peazey laid down her cards in neat rows. “Not that I know of.”

Tibby pulled the low spade from the dummy. “I haven’t heard anything.”

“Me either.” Amy threw the nine of spades. “Why?”

Tibby pulled the two of spades from her hand and Amy swept the trick.

“No reason.”

Peazey cut her gaze toward me. “Ellison, you simply must tell us about the picture in the paper.”

I should have known we couldn’t get through an afternoon without discussing my trip to The Jewel Box. “It’s boring, really. I went there with Libba. There was a...kerfuffle and I ripped my stitches."

She sent one of her almost-smiles my direction. "What about that gorgeous man who carried you out?"

"Detective Jones?" I returned her almost-smile and raised her narrowed eyes. I ignored the way my stomach quivered whenever I thought about Anarchy's arms around me and played the king of spades.

Tibby pulled the low spade and Amy discarded a club.

I hid a smile. Peazey could ask all the uncomfortable questions she wanted but she—and Tibby—were going down.

I arrived home at two to find a lonely Max and a handwritten note on the kitchen counter. An enormous bouquet of Stargazer lilies sat next to the note.

I gave a poor-poor-pitiful-me-eyed Max a dog biscuit. Read the note—Aggie had gone to the supermarket. Then I eyed the lilies, my favorite. Already the kitchen smelled like my version of heaven. A sealed card peeked out from between the petals.

I reached for the tiny envelope with shaky fingers. What if Hunter had sent them? Was I ready for a man who sent me flowers?

I slid my finger under the flap.

Forgive me? Libba

She'd left me in a bar filled with crossdressing men intent on pulling off each other's wigs and tearing each other's dresses. She'd left me with a man I barely knew. If she thought that I would forgive all that just because she'd sent me a bunch of flowers, she was as nutty as Alice Standish. Forgiveness would require serious groveling.

I crumbled Libba's note and tossed it in the trash.

Max, who'd finished his biscuit, tilted his head and raised his doggy brows as if questioning my hard line stance.

"Give her an inch and she'll take a mile," I told him. "I've known her for almost forty years. She never changes."

He yawned and directed his amber gaze at the telephone.

"I'm not calling her." I crossed my arms.

He whined softly.

"I'd rather call Anarchy Jones than Libba."

Woof.

The dog had a point. I ought to tell Anarchy about the note. I dug his card out of my billfold, picked up the phone and dialed.

"Jones."

Why had I thought this was a good idea? "It's Ellison," I squeaked.

I could almost see him in his office with his long legs stretched out, his feet crossed, maybe propped on his desk, the receiver held carelessly against his ear. "What is it?" His voice held an edge.

I'd never called him without a problem.

I swallowed. "I played bridge today."

He didn't respond to this exciting news.

"I talked to Amy McCreary."

Still no response.

"Her son Jack went to the football game with Bobby Lowell."

"We talked to him."

"Did Jack tell you about the note?"

"The note?" A bang carried through the phone lines. Anarchy's feet hitting the floor? "What note?"

"Bobby got a note just before half-time, then he took off. I just thought you should know." Anarchy was more than smart enough to count the minutes. I'd found Bobby just a few minutes after the second half started. It seemed likely the note was from the murderer.

"What else did you talk about?"

"Declining morals."

The police detective snorted. "Thank you, Ellison. We'll look into this right away. Anything else you want to tell me?"

My thoughts flew to my perfectly white front door. "No. Nothing." I scratched my nose.

"You're sure?"

Was I sure I didn't want to explain why I'd eradicated potential evidence in a murder investigation? "Positive."

"Any idea where I might find Jack McCreary?" Spoken like a man without children.

"At school."

Anarchy said goodbye and presumably hurried off to track down Jack and the note. I inhaled lily-scented air then went upstairs to put on paint clothes. Too much time had passed since I picked up a brush. Lord knows I'd tried, but my hands reached for dark colors and my brushes created brooding swirls heavy with pent-up emotions. The exact opposite of the colorful, hopeful canvases my customers demanded.

Perhaps I *needed* to paint something dark, work the negativity out of my system with a paintbrush, a primed canvas and tubes of carbon black, dioxazine violet and old Delft blue deep. I painted, let my frustration with Grace and Mother and Libba bleed onto the canvas. My confusion with Hunter and Anarchy shaded amorphous shapes. Henry's betrayals were reduced to dark slashes.

When I looked up, the afternoon was gone and the slam of the front door reverberated through the house.

"Mom!"

There it was again. The outraged Mom call. Loud enough to reach my attic studio. What had I done now?

I wiped off my hands and descended two flights of stairs.

Grace stood in the foyer; she'd dumped her backpack on the floor and her hands were planted on her hips. The dropped pack was pure teenager. The pose was reminiscent of Mother. Grace saw me and narrowed her eyes. "What did you do?"

I drew a deep calming breath. God save me from dramatic teenagers. "I have no idea what you're talking about."

"Yeah, right." Grace lifted the corner of her upper lip. Her dismissive tone and her sneering expression made her opinion clear. I was a bitch beyond measure.

Donna, pale as early April, stood behind her looking as

horrified as a romantic heroine from a gothic novel who's just discovered the lonely castle where she cares for children of questionable parentage is haunted.

I shook my head. "No idea what you're talking about."

"You sent the police to get Jack."

"I told the police what Jack told his mother. Someone passed Bobby a note shortly before half-time."

She crossed her arms over her chest. "Well, they don't believe him."

"Why not?"

Again with the narrowed eyes. "They didn't find a note."

My jaw dropped—just a little. Had Jack lied? Had the murderer taken the note? More likely Bobby just threw it away before he went under the stands. I snapped my lips closed.

"Just because you don't like him doesn't mean you frame him for murder."

"I'm not trying to frame anyone for murder. Don't you want Bobby's killer caught?"

Her fingers bent as if wrapped around someone's neck. She shook them and growled. "You don't get it."

"I get that Bobby's dead and that if the police are going to catch his killer they need everyone to tell the truth."

"Like you did last night?"

I'd had the door painted to protect her. Rather than appreciate the gesture, she'd thrown it in my face. "That's enough out of you, young lady."

Behind her, Donna dropped her backpack and clutched her stomach as if she was in pain.

"Are you all right?" I asked.

Donna nodded. Weakly.

"I apologize, Donna. Normally Grace and I can control our tempers." I glared at my daughter.

She glared back.

"We'll discuss this later. Perhaps you'd like to get Donna a drink?"

Grace flounced off to the kitchen. Just last night she'd run into my arms like a child. Where had that girl gone?

The phone rang. I went into my late husband's office and answered it. "Hello."

"Ellison? This is India Hess. I'm so glad I caught you. We've had the best news! Jonathan's injuries aren't as serious as originally thought. The doctors will release him by the end of the week. We'll pick Donna up on Friday. Is she there? I'd like to tell her."

"We've loved having Donna, but that is wonderful news." Poor kid. She'd put up with vandalism, all-night painters and far too much drama. She'd be thrilled to get home even if her stepfather was a jackass. "I'll get her for you."

I hurried down the hall to the kitchen. "Donna, your mother is on the line."

A bit of color had returned to her cheeks. "Thank you, Mrs. Russell." She picked up the phone.

Grace cast me a dirty look.

I didn't want sticking my nose in Donna's business added to my list of sins. I yielded the field—for now—and returned to the study. When Donna went home, Grace and I had a few issues to work out.

I picked up the phone lying on the desk.

"Don't be silly, darling," India snapped. "You can't impose on the Russells forever."

"I wasn't planning on it, Mother." There it was, the teenage tone that encapsulated embarrassment, superiority, attitude, and need. Nice to know it wasn't just Grace who spoke that way.

"Stop being so dramatic," India chided.

I was all too familiar with drama. Drama flowed through my house like a river out of its banks. I hung up the phone before Grace rightly accused me of eavesdropping.

It was hardly surprising Donna didn't like her stepfather. I barely knew him and I didn't like him. Who could blame her for not wanting him home? Not me.

THIRTEEN

That evening, I drove to Kizzi and Howard's with the top down. The wind grabbed strands of my hair and wrapped them around my neck in a blonde noose.

The painter's exorbitant bill, tucked into my pocketbook, fueled my anger with one Miss Alice Standish.

I parked at the curb, maneuvered the uneven bricks of their front walk—thank God I hadn't worn heels—and rang the bell.

Kizzi answered the door and stared at me as if she couldn't place who I was or why I might be standing on her front stoop.

"You told me to come at seven."

She blinked and wiped at one of her blurry eyes with the back of her hand. "I did?"

"You did."

"I suppose you'd better come in." She opened the door wider and stepped aside.

I followed her into a living room with walls paneled in recovered wood and a floor covered in tiles. A long, black, tufted leather sofa ran the length of one wall. In front of it sat a white shag area rug topped by a glass coffee table. It matched the end tables that held brass lamps and crystal ashtrays. Club chairs upholstered in a black and white floral print sat at right angles to the couch.

It was all very trendy, and Kizzi had probably paid her decorator a fortune. I didn't like it. It felt more like a stage set than a home. The only personal touch in the whole room was the highball on the coffee table. Kizzi had marked the glass with her lipstick, a frosted pink half-moon hanging above a veritable sea of gin.

"Please, Ellison, have a seat." She'd finally remembered my name. "May I get you a drink?"

"No, thank you." I didn't plan on staying long enough to finish it. I sank so low into the couch that my knees were higher than my seat.

Kizzi, better acquainted with the hazards of her furniture, sat in one of the club chairs. "Howard will be right in. He's just making sure Alice is doing her homework."

I nodded.

Kizzi patted her hair then glanced around her living room. "What brings you here?"

"Shall we wait for Howard?"

She scrunched her nose. "Everyone always wants to wait for Howard. What's happened?"

If she wanted the bill, she could have it. I pulled the flimsy piece of paper with the astronomical number written on the bottom from my purse and handed it to her. "I think Alice vandalized my house."

"Alice?" She held the painter's invoice at arm's length and squinted. She saw the total and rubbed her eyes. "Why would you think that?"

"I think it has something to do with Alice's fascination with Bobby Lowell."

She stilled, then lifted her drink to her lips. "Poor boy."

"Bobby was seeing another girl and I don't think Alice much liked it."

Kizzi leaned forward and lowered her voice. "I hope you won't hold this against her." She fingered the bill. "She went a little crazy over Bobby. When he started seeing someone else, she was distraught." Kizzi hiccupped. The smell of gin made my eyes water. She lifted her glass, drank, then leaned closer still. "Alice said if she couldn't have him, no one could."

"That's enough!"

Our heads swiveled toward the door. Howard stood at the room's entrance. His face flushed, his arms crossed, his chin lowered.

Kizzi waved the painter's bill. "Ellison says Alice vandalized her house."

Howard stepped into the antiseptic decorator's delight of a living room and took the bill from Kizzi's hand. When he saw the total, the flush ran away from his cheeks. "What happened, Ellison?"

"Alice painted on my door."

He regarded me with an arched brow.

"Someone painted the word '*slut*.'"

The brow rose higher and his mouth formed the beginnings of a smirk.

A smirk? Surely he wasn't suggesting...I'd been with one man my entire life. And even when Henry cheated on me, I'd kept my vows.

As for Grace, I'd bet her trust fund that she hadn't done anything to deserve having such an ugly word written about her. I tilted my head slightly, pursed my lips and raised my own brow. "The same word that was woven into the fence at the school. Near where Bobby died."

Kizzi hiccupped. "We know. A policeman came by to ask us about it."

I offered her an encouraging smile. "And?"

"Alice said she didn't have anything to do with it."

Alice said, not Alice didn't—it seemed as if Kizzi doubted her daughter. "You didn't believe her?"

Kizzi glanced at her drink, her husband, then me. "Um..."

"That's enough." Howard was repeating himself. He crumpled the bill in his hand, stepped outside the door and yelled, "Alice!"

When Alice appeared, she wore enough black for two funerals. Also, she'd taken black eyeliner and circled her eyes. She might have been going for a haunting look. What she got was demented raccoon.

She stared at me with narrowed, kohl-rimmed eyes and I straightened my shoulders to keep them from shaking. Looking at her, it seemed all too possible that she'd killed Bobby.

"What?" she asked.

Howard shook the painter's bill in her face. "Did you deface Mrs. Russell's property? Did you paint on her door?"

She shrugged—a classic, world-weary teenage shrug. "What if I did?" She leaned against a wall and crossed her arms.

"And the fence at school?" I asked.

The corner of her upper lip lifted slightly. "I haven't been painting any fences."

I sat a little straighter on the uncomfortable couch. "The fence wasn't painted."

"There you go. I didn't do it." Something flickered in her ebony-ringed eyes. Madness? Murder? Teenage angst?

"Didn't do what?" Kizzi asked. She clutched her drink as if it was a lifesaver keeping her from drowning in deep waters.

Alice's sneer became more pronounced. "I didn't paint the fence."

"Did you paint the door?" Howard demanded.

"Maybe. Maybe not. What are you going to do about it?" The challenge in her voice was unmistakable. Her mother drank. Her father wore frilly dresses. Alice did whatever she wanted.

I levered myself off Kizzi's ridiculous couch. "I'm going to call your grandmother."

The direness of my threat hung in the air like a lobbed tennis ball, and the next few seconds ticked by in slow motion.

The ball landed. Kizzi dropped her drink, Howard clutched his chest and Alice's rebellious posture collapsed. They all breathed a collective "No!" Tossing a live grenade would have made less of an impression. Interesting. Alice Anne, the Dragon of Drury Lane, terrified her family too.

"I'll pay the bill." Howard held the crumpled paper in his left hand. It shook. "I'll write you a check right now."

Kizzi dropped out of her chair and began daubing at her white carpet with a cocktail napkin. She needn't have bothered—straight gin doesn't stain.

Alice stared at her shaking father, her daubing mother, then at me. "You're a bitch."

Her parents gasped.

Alice and I stared at each other. She'd thrown a gauntlet and now she waited to see what I would do. I borrowed one of Mother's insincere smiles and said, "He didn't love you."

She winced. My barb had hit close to home. Then she shrugged as if she didn't care that Bobby Lowell had loved another girl. "I guess we'll never know."

Damn. While she'd removed all doubt as to who'd woven and painted the word "slut," I'd removed any possibility she'd ever tell me who Bobby loved.

I opened my front door and called, "I'm home."

No one answered except for Max. He trotted down the stairs, rubbed his face against my leg and wagged his stub of a tail.

I scratched behind his ears. "Nice to see you too, fella."

He followed me up the stairs, sat beside me when I tapped on Grace's door and tilted his head when I cracked the door and yelled over ear-splitting decibels of a very apropos Elton John song, "I'm home."

The girls sat cross-legged on Grace's bed. My daughter ignored me—didn't even turn her head to acknowledge me. Donna offered me a tremulous smile.

At least our guest was behaving like a human and not a teenager. I closed the door and continued down the hallway with Max at my heels.

When I reached the sanctuary of my bedroom, I took off and hung up my clothes and donned a soft blue caftan. Maybe Aggie was rubbing off on me. Then again, maybe not. Aggie's caftans are usually brightly colored and embellished with embroidery or beads or spangles. Mine was just...soft.

I curled up in the armchair near the window to think. Alice had woven ribbon into the fence and painted my door. I was sure of it. But had she killed Bobby? I shook my head. Finding Bobby's killer was Anarchy's job. Mine was to find the girl Bobby loved and share his last words with her. Alice knew who I was looking for. Fat lot of good that did me. I had a better chance of getting Elton John to serenade Grace and Donna in person than I did of getting a name out of Alice Standish.

I abandoned the chair and wandered through the room. I pulled the loose hairs out of my brush and threw them away. I positioned the crystal jars on my dresser just so.

I picked up my copy of *Watership Down,* stared at the rabbit on the cover, then put the book back on the nightstand. The wandering rabbits would have to solve their problems without me. I couldn't solve my own.

Finally I jammed my feet into a pair of slippers and climbed the stairs to the attic. If my bedroom couldn't calm my thoughts, maybe my studio could.

Donna's sketchbooks sat on the worktable where they'd languished since she'd dropped them off. The girl hadn't mentioned painting or lessons since she'd arrived. Remarkable patience for a teenager. I picked them up, settled onto the chaise in the corner and opened the first one.

Donna's drawings weren't exactly hearts and unicorns, but they came close—flowers and small, furry animals frolicked across her pages. They were good, but they were bunnies. I closed the book and looked at the date on the front. It was almost four years old. I put it down and searched for the sketchbook with the most recent date.

I found one that was eighteen months old and opened it. No frolicking in this book. The drawings—again, very good—were somber, filled with sadness.

I counted back in what I knew of Donna's history. Her father had died—that explained the numerous portraits of the man with her nose and the kind eyes. It explained the sketch of India crying.

It explained the drawings of graveyards. It explained the self-portrait of a girl ravaged by grief. Looking at the sketches was like looking into her soul.

Did Grace feel such grief over her father's death? She'd been in shock at first. We'd whisked her away to my parents' place in the country. Then I'd whisked her away to Europe. We'd traveled to sunny, happy places—Italy and Greece and Turkey. I'd avoided the gray skies of London and our trip to rainy Paris had been brief, just long enough to shop and see the Louvre.

Since I hadn't felt a whit of grief when Henry died, I hadn't considered Grace's feelings. Did she feel the same soul-deep grief that Donna did? What kind of a mother was I?

Duh. Henry had been an unmitigated ass but he'd also been her father. I hadn't given her time to grieve. No wonder she was angry and resentful and...awful.

I rested my forehead in my hands. First thing in the morning, I'd find her a psychologist or a grief counselor or someone who could help her. Help us. I'd talk to her about Henry. If she asked, I'd even tell her part of the truth.

I flipped through Donna's drawings until the lines blurred from fatigue. Then I padded downstairs and went to bed.

Max's whine awakened me.

I pried my eyelids open and asked, "What time is it?"

He scratched on the door.

"Seriously?"

Max whined again.

Seriously.

I dragged myself out of bed, grabbed my robe and followed Max down the stairs.

The hallway that led to the back of the house should have been dark. It wasn't. Light spilled out of the kitchen. I tiptoed forward and peeked through the door.

Donna stood at the counter with a jar of Sanka and a coffee filter in her hand. The girl was about to violate poor Mr. Coffee.

I cleared my throat.

She startled as if I'd caught her with her hand in the drawer where I kept the sterling.

I stepped into the brightly lit kitchen. "That's instant coffee."

"I hope you don't mind," she said. "I wanted a cup of decaf." She tugged at the opening where Mr. Coffee accepts offerings of coffee grounds.

"Donna, put down the filter and step away from the coffee machine." Mr. Coffee had endured enough abuse in his short life—too many filters, too many coffee grounds, no filter—he didn't need Sanka running through his innards.

She blinked, then did as I asked.

"For instant coffee, you use hot water, not a coffeemaker."

"Really?"

"Really." I picked up the kettle from the stove, went to the sink and filled it with water. "What are you doing up?"

"I couldn't sleep."

I replaced the kettle, lit a burner, and asked, "Why not?"

"Tomorrow—" She glanced at the clock on the oven. "Today is Bobby Lowell's funeral."

Guilt tightened my neck and shoulders. Bobby was being buried and I still hadn't found the girl. "Did you know him well?"

She ducked her head. "A bit. Our houses are nearby and, of course, in school."

"You might not have met him at his best. And now—"

"What do you mean?"

"I mean Bobby had a rough time after his parents split, but deep down he was a good kid."

A single fat tear ran unchecked down Donna's cheek. "It's so sad when good people die."

The sketches of her father and the kindness in his eyes came to mind.

"It is." I patted her back.

When she didn't flinch, I draped my arm around her shaking shoulders and squeezed.

A tear plopped onto the kitchen counter.

Donna parted her lips and drew a ragged breath. "I'm sorry. It's just that since Daddy died..." She stepped out of my half-embrace then raised her chin. "I'm sorry. I shouldn't be all teary."

"It doesn't bother me a bit." I scratched the end of my nose—just a little.

Donna pulled a paper towel off the roll and wiped her face. She gulped for breath. "Do you remember what it's like to be sixteen?"

"I'm not *that* old."

She shook her head, apparently annoyed with my flip reply. "Do you remember?"

Why would I remember that? It was a time best forgotten. The emotions, the hormones, the way every little thing *mattered* so much. "I remember parts of it."

"Which parts?" she demanded.

"Wanting to be grown up. I wanted lipstick and high heels and dates. But when Mother gave my stuffed animals to charity, I cried for a week." Mother had not been sympathetic.

"I don't want to grow up. When you're sixteen you *know* things. I liked not knowing a lot better."

"What things?"

The kettle whistled. Of course it did—right when I was about to get real insight into how a teenage girl thought. I lifted the kettle off the heat and set it on a cold burner. I spooned Sanka into a cup for Donna, found myself a bag of chamomile tea, and poured hot water over both. Max lifted his head and grumbled so I tossed him a dog biscuit.

I dropped the spoon into Donna's mug then pushed it across the counter toward her. She wrapped her hands around its sides as if she was cold, caught her lower lip in her teeth, and chewed. "Have you had time to look at my sketchbooks?"

Thank God I had. "You're very talented. If you're still interested, I'd be happy to work with you."

"That would be great," said the girl who'd begged me for lessons. Her voice was flat. Then she picked up her mug, a white one with Wile E. Coyote on the side—Lord only knows how the hideous thing found its way into my cupboard. "I think I'll go upstairs now. Thank you for the coffee."

Somehow, I'd expected more enthusiasm.

If I live to be a thousand years old, I'll never understand teenagers.

FOURTEEN

Mr. Coffee was full and hot and he looked happy, almost jaunty. It could only mean that Aggie was around somewhere. I'd overslept—completely forgotten to get up and fix breakfast for two teenage girls. I probably wasn't going to be nominated for the world's greatest hostess.

Or mother.

I poured myself a cup of heaven, topped it with a splash of cream, settled onto one of the stools that surrounded the kitchen island and planned my day. Find a psychologist for Grace, go to a funeral and cook something decent for Donna's last night at our house. I boiled a mean noodle. Spaghetti? I reached for a pad of paper and wrote out a quick grocery list—pasta, pasta sauce, parmesan. Did we need a salad? I added romaine and croutons to the list. Max nudged my leg as if reminding me to add treats. Dutifully I wrote down dog bones.

Aggie bustled in with a basket of laundry in her arms. "You slept in."

"I did. Donna got up in the middle of the night and woke me. I had trouble going back to sleep." An understatement of epic proportions.

"What's that?" She jerked her chin toward my grocery list.

"I thought I'd make dinner."

Aggie's eyebrows rose.

"I can make pasta," I insisted.

She muttered something about mushy noodles.

"I can!"

Her lips primmed. "Let me get this in the washer, then I'll see what I can come up with." She pushed through the swinging door that led to the butler's pantry and the small room that housed the washer and dryer.

I sipped my coffee and waited to be upstaged—or at least out-cooked. Aggie can whip up better meals than spaghetti with her eyes closed.

The door swung again. "I could make veal piccata."

"I can make spaghetti."

We stared at each other. Both stubborn, both determined, both ignoring the cartoon bubble above Aggie's head that said, "Can and should are not the same thing."

"Fine," I ceded.

She had the good grace not to gloat when I tore my list in half.

Max grinned. Traitor. He'd rather eat leftover veal than leftover spaghetti.

I took another sip of coffee. "I've been thinking maybe Grace and I should see a psychologist or a counselor."

"You think?"

I don't usually associate Aggie with dead-pan sarcasm—something to do with her purple muumuus and red hair seems straightforward, incapable of wryness. With Aggie, appearances are deceiving. She dresses as if she just escaped a commune for crazies but she's the wisest person I know. Grace and I are blessed she took us on.

"Do you know anyone?" Everyone I knew sent their kids to Stan Sheridan. In my humble opinion, he didn't seem to be helping much.

"Mary Stevens. I can call for you if you'd like."

I suspected Grace wasn't going to be pleased. I nodded anyway.

"I'll take care of it. Are you painting today?"

If only. "I've got Bobby Lowell's funeral."

"Such a tragedy."

I nodded. "I just wish I had been able to find the girl he loved."

She stared at me. Goggled, really. "You're kidding."

"What?"

"You haven't noticed the girl moping around here like the world has ended?"

"Grace?"

Aggie shook her red head so hard her curls sproinged. "Donna."

"Donna?" Aggie was way off-base. "I asked her if she knew Bobby and she said a bit."

"And teenagers never, ever lie."

Oh good gravy. Donna? It would explain why Alice had painted "SLUT" on my door while Donna was in residence. It would explain her nightmares the night Bobby died. I put my coffee down, planted my elbows on the counter, and let my head fall into my hands.

Aggie patted my shoulder. "I wouldn't have known for certain if I hadn't found her sketchbook when I was picking up Grace's room."

"Her sketchbook?" I had her sketchbooks.

"I found it under Grace's bed. There are lots of pictures of a boy named Bobby."

Head still in hands, I groaned.

"You should take a look at it. There are some...interesting drawings."

I lifted my head. "Is it still under Grace's bed?"

Aggie flushed. "No. I...I put it away."

"Away where?"

"The linen closet." She smoothed a neatly folded tea towel.

"Why?"

"I really think you should look at the drawings."

Max rose from the floor, his too-long nails clicking against the hardwood. He started toward the foyer, pausing only to see if someone was following him.

The doorbell rang. I swear that dog is psychic.

"I'll get it," Aggie offered.

A moment later her voice floated down the hallway. "Mrs. Russell, you'd better come."

Libba, a wrapped gift clutched in her hands, stood next to Aggie. Neither was looking toward me. They both stared outside, and something about their postures—a certain tightness in the shoulders, a tautness near their necks—suggested disaster.

"What?" I demanded.

As one, they stood aside and I saw my car in the driveway. Red letters augmented its British racing green paint. BITCH. I stumbled outside and touched one of the letters. The paint had dried.

Holy Mary and the ass she rode in on.

I drew a deep breath and counted to ten. It didn't calm me. Fire had replaced blood in my veins and marching over to the Standish house and throttling Alice seemed a reasonable, *desirable*, plan of action. I counted again. "Aggie, would you please get Howard Standish on the phone? If you can't get him, call his mother."

She scurried inside.

Libba stood alone on the front stoop with her damn package. Her mouth opened then closed. Repeatedly. "Alice Standish did this?"

"She did."

She descended the stairs and shoved the package into my arms. "It's for you. I...um...I'm sorry about Sunday night. I shouldn't have left you."

The package weighed more than I expected and it sloshed. Liquor. Libba was trying to earn my forgiveness with a bottle. Then again, compared to the violation of my car, being abandoned at The Jewel Box was nothing. "Don't worry about it."

"You know Charlie likes to dress up as a woman? So does Upson."

"I gathered that."

"I can't date a man who might borrow my clothes." She shook her head. "I have the worst taste in men. I swear I'm going to become a nun."

"You're not Catholic."

"Is that a requirement?"

I nodded.

"Well, maybe I just won't date. Worst. Taste. Ever."

I could have argued. And won. After all, I married a philandering blackmailer who enjoyed acts so kinky my mind shied away from thinking of them. But Libba had just apologized and there was no need for another argument.

"What are you going to do about your car?"

I tightened my grip on the bottle she'd given me. "Howard Standish is going to have it repainted for me."

My poor, poor car. I couldn't zip around town with "BITCH" painted across the passenger side—people might believe it was true. I traced my fingertips along the defaced racing stripe. "I'll drive Henry's car until it's painted."

Aggie appeared in the front door. "I have Mrs. Standish on the phone."

"Kizzi or Alice Anne?"

She grimaced. "Alice Anne."

I straightened my shoulders, drew my robe tighter around me and prepared for battle.

Bobby Lowell's funeral promised to be packed so I arrived early. No sooner had I stepped foot in the church's nave than Mother grabbed me. She reviewed my black Chanel suit, Ferragamo pumps and pearls and silently deemed me acceptable.

"Go sit with your father. I'm making sure there are enough cookies for the reception." Mother takes her altar guild duties seriously.

Daddy stood when I reached his pew. He kissed my cheek then shifted to his right so I could sit on the aisle.

"Should we save a seat for Grace?" he asked. The church was already half-full and forty-five minutes remained until the service started.

"I bet she'd rather sit with her friends." A very safe bet given her recent anger with me.

I sat.

"How are you, sugar?" Daddy asked.

I was tempted to tell him about my problems with Grace, about Alice Standish's campaign against my property, about Donna and Bobby. I was tempted, but church pews aren't the best place to share private problems—too many ears, too much interest. Instead, I said, "Fine. And you?"

We whispered banalities. Every few minutes I snuck a peek behind me to locate Grace.

Daddy chuckled. "Don't let your mother catch you doing that."

Mother disapproved of peering in church. It was fine to eyeball those who sat in front, but those seated behind were to remain a sacred mystery until the service ended.

Of course, Mother caught me with my head swiveled. "What are you doing?" she demanded. "Move over." She scooched me down the pew.

"Looking for Grace."

She sniffed her disapproval. Tardiness at funerals was even worse than swiveling to stare at rear pews. "I haven't seen her."

A moment later, CeCe and her sisters filed into the first pew and Bobby's father, looking like a haggard ghost of his former self, claimed his seat in the second.

As a rule, funerals are either dreadful or lovely. Bobby's was lovely. The priest had actually known Bobby and filled his eulogy with funny stories from Bobby's childhood. There were no maudlin remembrances from friends designed to elicit tears. At the end, Reverend Trentham invited the congregation to pay their respects in the Walford Room (my grandparents provided a generous gift during the last capital campaign).

The ushers dismissed the pews one at a time. Because we were near the front, Mother, Daddy and I were among the first to stand. I walked up the aisle and scanned the packed church.

Three generations of Standishs sat together. Alice Anne was

rigid with disapproval. Next to her, Alice's eyes were nearly swollen shut with tears. Howard's brows were drawn, his lips flat—he looked angry enough to commit murder. All three of them glared at me.

I hoped Alice Anne had given her son, daughter-in-law and granddaughter absolute hell. Maybe that explained Kizzi's absence. Then again, maybe she'd gotten too cozy with a gin bottle. The woman needed help. They all did.

My gaze skipped away from the Standish clan and their poorly controlled emotions. Where in the world was Grace?

Mother, Daddy and I paid our respects to CeCe and Robert. She looked more brittle and delicate than a bit of decades-old newspaper. Robert looked stoned. Mother muttered something under her breath about Robert's state then disappeared to manage cookie consumption. Daddy spotted a few of his cronies. I was left to my own devices.

I looked for Grace and Donna but couldn't spot them in the crowded room. If Donna felt for Bobby what he'd felt for her, she was probably nearly as upset as CeCe. I listened for the sound of teenage sobs.

Nothing.

Meanwhile, half the congregation seemed to think that Bobby's funeral was the appropriate place to ask me about his death.

It wasn't.

The other half asked about my unfortunate trip to The Jewel Box.

It was none of their damned business.

I settled into a conversation with Amy McCreary. She already had the answers the rest of the congregation wanted.

"I thought it was a lovely service." She patted under her eyes with a lace-edge handkerchief.

"It was."

"I worry about Jack driving. I worry about him doing something stupid like swimming alone." She cut a quick glance my way, flushed, then hurried on. "Or tipping a canoe on the float trip he takes with his dad every spring. There are so many accidents that take children." She shook her carefully coiffed head. "I never worried about murder."

Since my husband's murder, I'd given murder a lot of thought. Yes, there were random victims—people who were in the wrong place at the wrong time—but I suspected most murder victims knew something or did something to get themselves killed. "I wonder why Bobby—"

"I've wondered the same thing. Endlessly. The only thing I can come up with is the—"

John McCreary dropped his hand on his wife's shoulder hard enough to make her buckle slightly. He bared his teeth and said, "Ellison."

"John."

"Amy, there's someone I want you to meet." His hand closed on his wife's elbow, then he pulled her away from our fascinating conversation. "Ellison, if you'll excuse us."

What was it John McCreary didn't want me to know?

I wandered over to the buffet table where Mother monitored the number of cookies teenagers put on their plates as if their rapacious appetites might singlehandedly cause a worldwide oatmeal-raisin shortage. "Have you seen Grace?" I asked.

"No." She narrowed her eyes and glared at Tuck Whitaker, who'd dared reach for a third piece of iced shortbread. His hand shook but he claimed his prize. He scurried away as if he was a hungry ground squirrel and Mother was an eagle swooping out of the skies. "You'll never find her in this crowd."

She was probably right.

I drove home in Henry's staid Cadillac and missed my Triumph with every mile.

Max and a ringing phone met me at the back door. He wove between my legs, making my trip to the phone a veritable obstacle course.

"Hello."

"Mrs. Russell?"

"Yes."

An institutional sort of voice said, "This is Angela Mayer from Suncrest. I'm just calling to verify that Grace stayed home sick today. You're supposed to call if your child won't be at school."

"I'm afraid there's been some mistake. Grace went to school today." She had. I knew it. I'd sent notes with her and Donna excusing them for the funeral.

"No, ma'am. She did not."

My heart skipped so high it bumped into my throat. "I see. Well, thank you for your call."

I hung up the phone with a shaking hand. Where the hell was my daughter?

FIFTEEN

"Grace!" I marched up the stairs, down the hall to Grace's room and flung open the door. If Grace thought, even for a second, that I'd put up with her cutting school, she had another thing coming.

A Chris Evert poster hung on the wall next to Elton John. Chris clutched a tennis racket and looked determined. Elton wore a white suit, a panama hat and rose-colored glasses. They both stared at me. Their eyes said it all—I was doing a terrible job dealing with this new defiant Grace. I glared at them. Just let them try handling a teenager.

Tab cans—presumably empty—crowded everything but the lamp and a clock radio off the bedside table. One of Grace's tennis rackets lay on the unmade bed. Another racket, this one in a case, hung from the closet doorknob. Clothes littered every surface—the bench at the foot of the bed, the chairs, the dresser and even the floor. A stack of dog-eared magazines cascaded under the dust ruffle. No wonder Aggie had declared Grace's room a disaster area and asked for hazard pay.

When I found my daughter, we had lots to talk about.

I turned and faced the hallway. "Grace!" This time I yelled louder.

Who knew silence echoed?

Where was she? If she and Donna wanted to skip school to get ready for Bobby's funeral they need only have asked. Except—I hadn't seen either one of them at the funeral.

I crossed the threshold into Grace's room, bent and looked under the bed. Joining the magazines were a plate, shoes, boots, a bra, several books—the latest Victoria Holt, *The Other Side of*

Midnight by Sidney Sheldon and *Fear of Flying* by Erica Jong—and an empty space the size of a suitcase. I couldn't catch my breath.

She'd probably stuck her suitcase in the closet.

I hauled myself off the floor and looked.

More clothes. More shoes. No suitcase.

Where could it be? And where was Ducky, the stuffed bear that lived on her bed? My heart thudded. Huge knocks against the side of my chest that sent blood rushing to my ears. I was being silly. Given the mess in her closet, she'd probably stowed her suitcase in the guest room.

I stumbled into the hallway, knocked on the door to the guest room and didn't wait for an answer.

The guest room was empty.

No suitcase flowered with bright daisies sat in the middle of the floor waiting to reassure me.

With the exception of Max, who looked at me with a quizzical expression—*has she finally gone round the bend?*—I was alone.

Sandtraps on July afternoons had more moisture than my mouth. I crossed the room and opened the door to a cavernous closet. Where were Donna's clothes? Her suitcase? Gone.

My legs, usually such reliable holders of my body, quit working. I collapsed onto the edge of the bed.

Grace and Donna had run away.

Because Grace was mad at me? Because Donna was upset over Bobby's death? I shook my head. The reason didn't matter. The important thing was getting them safely home—so I could kill them.

How dare they pull this kind of a stunt? My jaw tightened. My hands fisted. If Grace thought she was getting away with running away to punish me for telling the police about a note or for getting Jack McCreary in trouble, she had a lot to learn. Grounded. No allowance. No phone. School and home. Period.

I pressed my fist into my thigh.

No tennis lessons. No television. No car. No radio.

By the time I was done, Alcatraz would look like a spa.

I pushed up from the bed and paced.

No magazines. No stereo. No leaving the house. No...

What if something happened to her? Grace lived in a shiny bubble of privilege. The closest she ever came to privation was when we ran out of cream for her coffee. No way could she make it out in the real world. She was still a child. Alone—or as good as. My baby had run away.

I crumpled to the floor and stared up at the ceiling as if God might appear. He didn't. It was, after all, my guest bedroom, not the Sistine Chapel. Still, I whispered, "Keep her safe. I'll do anything, just keep her safe."

Max nudged me and whined—*You're freaking me out! Get off the floor and track her down.*

I had to find her.

The doorbell rang and I flew down the stairs. It was all a misunderstanding. Grace and Donna were home.

I fumbled with the lock and opened the door, ready to encompass both girls in an enormous hug.

Jane Addison stood on my front stoop. "I just heard!"

"Heard what?" How could Jane have learned Grace was gone before I did?

"That Libba and you are at odds. I'm here to tell you to make up. Nothing is worth losing a best friend."

I blinked. Once. Twice. Three times. Jane and her best friend had nearly come to blows over the listing for Thelma Harrison's home. To my knowledge, they hadn't spoken since. Right now, I didn't care if they ever did.

"Libba and I are fine. Really." My relationship with Libba was nothing compared to my need to find my daughter. "Thank you so much for your concern." I inched the door toward its frame.

"You're sure?"

I nodded with feigned enthusiasm. "Positive." Another inch closer to closed.

"I'm so glad to hear that. What a relief. As long as I'm here, why don't I take a look around? You should know I've got the perfect buyer for this place." Her foot crossed the threshold.

Oh dear Lord. I didn't have time for this. I stood firm, not moving, definitely not letting her into the house. "It's not for sale."

"All this space for just the two of you? Are you sure?"

"Positive." I nodded so hard I was in danger of giving myself whiplash. "I love my studio and we're not moving."

"Grace will be going to college in a few years."

Not if she got herself murdered and left in a gutter. My stomach twisted. "Jane, it's dear of you to stop by, but I need to change." My nose itched as if dive-bombed by a swarm of mosquitoes. "I...um, I'm going out this evening."

Jane liked acquiring information almost as much as she liked acquiring listings. Her eyes gleamed. "Really, with whom?"

I pretended not to hear. "Truly, it's dear of you, but—" I waved a hand over my dark suit. "I need to start from scratch." Would the woman never leave?

"I understand." Her blue eyes twinkled.

She might understand, but she wasn't leaving. According to Mother, it's easier to get rid of wood rot than a pushy real estate agent. Much as it pained me to admit, Mother was right.

Jane winked. "I saw you having brunch with Quin Marstin the other day."

I lifted my still-bandaged hand and covered my mouth. Oh dear Lord. She couldn't seriously think—I suppressed a shudder. It didn't matter what Jane thought. I had far bigger problems than Jane Addison's propensity for gossip. I swallowed the bile at the back of my throat and said, "Thanks for understanding. Toodles."

I closed the door and leaned against it.

For the millisecond it took me to blink, I missed Henry. Not the cheating, lying barnacle on the ass of humanity who'd been my husband; I missed the man who'd been a doting father. If that man was here, he'd be wild with worry, then decide on a plan.

I needed a plan. My own plan. I needed to think. Trouble was, I couldn't. The jumble of random thoughts, feelings and adrenaline swirling through my brain were the opposite of rational. No way could I formulate a plan while in a panic.

I held a deep breath in my lungs until they ached then exhaled slowly.

Think! Where would Grace go? I had no idea. When she was six and I made her eat Brussels sprouts she packed a bag and moved to the tree house in the backyard. That didn't seem likely.

Where would Donna go?

Donna.

Unless I found the girls quickly, I was going to have to tell India Hess that Donna had run away. I gulped. Not just India, I'd have to tell Donna's bully of a stepfather too.

The phone rang and my heart ricocheted around my chest like a golf ball driven into a stand of oaks. Could it be Grace?

A spike of hope sent me running to the phone, desperate to hear my daughter's voice. "Hello." The edge of hysteria in my voice lent the single word importance.

"Mrs. Russell, it's Jack McCreary calling."

Hope is cruel. It allows your lungs to inflate and your heart to race with anticipation before it pulls out a meat cleaver and beats you as if you're a bit of veal Aggie's transforming into picatta. "What?" I didn't even try for politeness.

"Um...Grace...um..."

"Grace isn't here."

"I know."

He knew? How did he know? What did he know? Hope re-inflated my lungs and started my heart beating again. I squeezed the coil of the phone cord—unstretched since Grace hardly ever used the phone in what had been Henry's office—and asked, "Do you know where she is?"

"Not exactly."

"What exactly do you know?"

"She asked me to tell you she's safe."

"When did you talk to her?"

Jack paused. Was he considering his answer? A lie? The truth?

"Please, Jack, I need to know."

"Last night."

"And?"

Another pause.

If I could have crawled through the phone lines to shake the boy silly, I would have. "And..." I prompted.

"She's safe."

"Safe where?"

"I can't tell you."

I thought flies. I thought vinegar. I thought honey.

I kept my voice pleasant. "Please? I'm worried sick. Where is she?"

"I'm sorry but I can't..."

Jack McCreary, the dope-smoking boy who might or might not have killed Bobby Lowell, was refusing to tell me where my daughter was. I bit my lip hard enough to draw blood. I tasted the salt on my tongue. A voice that wasn't mine said, "I want to speak with your mother. Now." How had Frances Walford's voice of doom ended up in my body?

The voice must have scared the pants off Jack. He hung up.

Well, if he thought I was frightening over the phone, he'd be truly terrified when he saw me in person.

The McCrearys lived ten minutes away. I made it there in five. Henry's stodgy Cadillac never moved so fast.

I pulled into the driveway, parked behind a Jeep that was surely Jack's and clambered out of the car.

I jabbed at the doorbell with such force I bent my finger backward. When no one answered immediately, I lifted the brass knocker and banged the ring in the lion's mouth against its base.

A little girl answered the door. Her curly hair was tied into pigtails with rainbow-striped ribbons. Her face scrunched with what was probably annoyance—I had been trying to dent the door. With her huge brown eyes and frizzy red hair, she looked like a troll doll guarding its toy bridge.

"Is your mother home?" I asked.

Those enormous eyes stared up at me and she crossed her arms over her six-year-old chest. "No."

"How about your father?"

She shook her head. "Nope."

"Your brother?"

She turned and bellowed with a voice worthy of a real troll, "Jack, there's a lady here to see you."

When he failed to materialize, she shook her head, rolled her big brown eyes and said, "Boys."

Clearly she understood them better than I ever had.

"I really need to talk to Jack."

She stepped away from the door and I stepped into the McCrearys' foyer.

My hostess proceeded to the bottom of the steps. "Jack!"

Jack's voice floated down the steps. "I told you to send her away."

"May I?" I asked her.

She nodded.

I joined her at the bottom of the stairs and called, "It didn't work."

I heard a few words an older brother had no business uttering within hearing distance of his younger sister, then silence.

"I'm not leaving until you tell me where she is," I yelled up the stairs.

"Did you lose someone?" the little girl asked.

I nodded and swallowed an unwelcome lump. "My daughter."

She raised a disbelieving brow. "How do you lose a person?"

The lump rose again. "She ran away."

"Why?"

"I don't know."

Jack's sister stared at me, measured my worthiness as a mother, or maybe my bravery at attempting to cross her bridge. "What's your name?"

"Ellison Russell. What's yours?"

"Betty. I bet your daughter is fine."

"I hope so. I think Jack knows where she is."

"He won't tell you?"

"No."

Betty planted her six-year-old hands on her six-year-old hips and yelled in a voice loud enough to shake the house off its foundations, "John Wilson McCreary, Junior, get down here."

Jack appeared at the top of the stairs.

At the bottom, Betty tapped her toes on the Oriental rug.

Jack descended. "I told you, I don't know anything."

Breathe in. Breathe out. "She confided in you. You knew she was running away before she did it." He had to tell me. I had no other ideas on how to find her.

"Maybe. But I don't know where she went."

I stared at the boy on the stairs. His gaze was fixed on the risers and a flush pinked his cheeks.

Like Betty, I planted my hands on my hips. "I don't believe you."

Standing next to me, Jack's sister nodded as if she agreed. "He lies."

"Shut up," Jack snapped.

Betty's response to such verbal mastery was to stick out her tongue. "I can say what I want. You're not the boss."

"Am too. Mom left me in charge."

Not since the Scopes trial had such sparkling rhetoric been on display. Like William Jennings Bryan and Clarence Darrow, the McCreary children cut to the quick of the matter. Truth versus lies. Power. Rebellion.

Fascinating as it might be, I didn't have time for their rhetorical wrangling. "Jack," I pleaded, "please, tell me."

Behind us, the front door opened. Betty and I turned.

"Daddy!" Betty ran toward her father.

The flush on Jack's cheeks faded until he looked almost chalky.

I squared my shoulders.

John McCreary looked at me and narrowed his eyes. "What the hell are you doing here?"

SIXTEEN

John McCreary stood just inside the front door and regarded me with a look of distaste, the same look Mother reserved for people who wore white after Labor Day.

Betty wrapped herself around her father's leg. She turned, smirked at her brother and mouthed, "You're going to get it."

Jack clutched the banister. His gaze shifted from me to his father to the door as if he was weighing his chances for a successful escape.

As long as I drew breath, his odds weren't good.

"What do you want, Ellison? Why are you here?" So rude. He sounded as if he'd like nothing better than to toss my Chanel-covered fanny out the front door.

I didn't like his odds of success either. I wasn't leaving until I found out where Grace was. When Jack told me what I needed to know—then I'd be on my way.

I shifted my gaze to the boy on the stairs and counted to ten, giving him the opportunity to explain my presence to his father. Jack wouldn't meet my gaze and his mouth twisted as if he was sucking on his teeth. He said nothing.

So be it. If Jack wouldn't tell his father, I would. "Jack's keeping a secret."

John's cheeks, already flushed the same deep red shade as an American Beauty rose, took a turn for purple.

Jack looked as if his hold on the railing was the only thing keeping him upright.

"I wanna know the secret," Betty insisted.

John pulled Betty off his leg. "Sugarpuss, you go outside and play."

The child's little brows drew together and her lower lip thrust forward into a quivering pout.

"I'll take you for an ice cream later."

She batted her eyelashes. "Any kind? Even Daiquiri Ice?"

John nodded.

"Two scoops?"

"Sure, Betty."

"In a waffle cone?"

"Anything you want, sugar."

Her expression cleared. "Okay, Daddy." She stuck out her tongue at Jack, who presumably would not be getting any ice cream, and skipped out the door.

"Jack." I opened my hands in a pleading gesture. "Some secrets are too important to keep. You have to tell me."

"He does not."

I narrowed my eyes and redirected my gaze toward John. With his frightening expression and his skin mottled red and purple by anger, the man looked like a monster. Any man who kept me from finding Grace was a monster.

"Dad, it's not what you think."

The scowl John directed at me grew more fearsome. He lifted his arm and pointed toward the door. "It's time you left."

No. Not without a truthful answer from his son. I crossed my arms and lifted my chin. "He has to tell me."

"He doesn't have to tell you anything."

"So, if Betty was missing, you wouldn't want the kid who knew where she was to tell you?"

His scowl slipped—a fraction. "What?"

I stepped toward him. "My daughter ran away and your son won't tell me where she went."

"I don't know where she went," Jack insisted.

I turned to face Jack. "I don't believe you. She told you she was leaving."

The boy looked down at the Oriental runner covering the stairs as if the rug's pattern held the answers to the mysteries of the universe. That or he'd developed a sudden fascination with his Jack Purcell sneakers. "Doesn't mean she told me where she was going."

The clock chimed the quarter hour.

"Please," I begged, "if someone you loved went missing, you'd do everything possible to find them." Including, but not limited to, threatening teenaged boys.

Jack lifted his gaze from his shoes to the grandfather clock that marked each minute my daughter was gone. "I care about Grace."

Behind me, John McCreary snorted.

Obviously something at the McCrearys' had caused a deep rift. Maybe Amy and John knew their son was smoking pot. I didn't give a damn what personal baggage they stuffed into their closets or what Jack smoked, I just needed help finding my daughter. "Please, Jack. You have to tell me."

The boy shook his head. "I don't know."

John cleared his throat. "Why?"

"Because she didn't tell me!" Jack cried.

"No. Not you." John rubbed the back of his neck and glared at me. "Why did she leave?"

"I have no idea," I lied. No way, no how, was I telling the hulking man standing just a few feet from me that I'd had our children followed. His face was still flushed. Perspiration dewed the skin between his nose and his upper lip. Jimmie Walker might be Kid Dy-No-Mite, but it was John McCreary who looked ready to explode.

John's glare shifted to his son. "Did she tell you?"

For a half-second Jack's gaze returned to the door. The boy bounced on his toes as if he meant to take off running. He knew something. "No."

"And you have no idea where she is?"

"No! Why don't you believe me?"

Jack sank onto the step and lowered his head into his hands.

Despite the hand-stitched needlepoint belt that looped through the waistband of his khakis, despite the trappings of wealth that surrounded him and despite the presence of his father, Jack looked lost and alone.

The clock ticked off another minute.

Jack lifted his head and stared at me with red-rimmed eyes. "I don't know where she is or why she left. I'd tell you if I did."

Damn. I believed him. Mostly. "What exactly did she say when you talked to her?"

Jack cut a glance toward his father and mumbled, "Shashed me to gowim."

What? "Pardon me?"

"She asked me to go with them," he blurted.

"Why?" John asked. He asked that a lot—especially when the important question was *Where?*

"Because we're friends," Jack muttered.

"No." John crossed his arms over his chest and squeezed his biceps, wrinkling his suit. "Why didn't you go?"

No teenager should ever wear an expression as bleak as Jack's. "I wasn't ready to give up on being a part of this family."

Grace was ready to give up on me. I squeezed my eyes shut, pressed my lips together and ignored the need to curl into a ball, wrap my arms around my knees and keen.

The McCrearys didn't see my pain. That or they didn't care. They kept talking. "Seems to me you gave up a while ago." John's voice was as bleak as Jack's expression.

"Sometimes things just...happen. They're not the way you—" Jack snorted. "Definitely not the way *you* planned them. They just happen."

Holy Mother of mystifying men, what were they talking about? Had Jack killed Bobby? Was the note a fabrication meant to send the police scurrying down the wrong rabbit hole? I opened my eyes.

Jack removed his glasses and dashed away a tear.

John loosed his hold on his arms and used the heel of his right hand to rub his chest.

I found my voice. "What happened, Jack? Is this about Bobby?"

"Lately, everything's about Bobby."

"That's enough!" John scowled at us both.

I ignored him. Jack could have run. Teenagers ran away every day. Most of them were never found. Oh, God. While the McCrearys argued, an invisible sword had sliced me open. I crossed my arms over my stomach to keep my intestines inside. I was in danger of bleeding out on their parquet floors. I gritted my teeth. "Why did you stay?"

"Because you can't run from what you are." Guilt, misery, anger—they all skittered across his face.

Was Jack a murderer? Huddled on the steps, he didn't look like one. Then again, murderers don't exactly wear sandwich boards proclaiming their sins.

"Why'd you do it, Jack?" What if he hadn't? Open mouth, insert foot.

He lifted his gaze to me. "Do what?"

I swallowed. "Kill Bobby."

His jaw dropped. "I didn't."

"Then what—"

"Jack!" John raised a clenched fist. He even waved it. "Not another word."

Wearing an expression that managed both sadness and defiance, Jack turned his gaze on his father. He straightened his shoulders, lifted his chin and said, "I didn't kill Bobby. I loved him."

The silence that followed possessed an eternal quality, as if none of us would ever find our voices again. Even the clock muted its infernal ticking.

Tears streamed unchecked down Jack's cheeks. My face, reflected in the mirror hung above the bow-front table, was whiter than a new golf ball. A sheen of sweat glistened on John's face and he'd advanced from rubbing his chest to clutching it.

"Daddy!" Betty barreled into the front hall. "I want my ice cream."

John staggered when she hit his leg. "Not now," he croaked.

"Why not?" She stomped her little foot.

John's right hand still clutched his chest. His left hung limp at his side. His color had faded to celadon green. He looked like death.

Oh. Dear. Lord.

I pushed past her, grabbed John's elbow and led him to a chair. "Jack, call an ambulance."

He didn't move.

"Now! Your father's having a heart attack."

I went to the hospital. What choice did I have? I loaded Jack and Betty into Henry's Caddy and followed the ambulance to St. Mark's.

Jack sat mute and frozen in the front seat. I've spent time with more animated dead people.

From the back, Betty babbled. "He's going to be okay. I know he is. The doctors will take extra-special care of him."

That much was probably true. John sat on the hospital board.

"You left a note for Mommy, didn't you, Mrs. Russell?"

"I did."

"Then Mommy will come and Daddy will be fine."

Oh, to have the faith of a six-year-old.

We pulled into the hospital lot, I parked the car and the three of us hurried inside to the emergency room.

The woman at the reception desk with her heavy eyebrows and pursed lips looked about as approachable as Brezhnev. She peered over the top of her glasses and waited for me to say something.

"John McCreary was brought in."

"And you are?"

"A friend of the family. These are his children."

She eyed us with mild interest. "Where is Mrs. McCreary?"

"At a party," Betty offered.

The woman's brows rose. They looked like caterpillars inching across her forehead.

I leaned forward to read her nametag. "Please, Sue, how is Mr. McCreary? His children are very worried."

Well, maybe Jack was. Betty climbed into a chair then swung her feet into Sue's desk. Repeatedly.

Sue glowered.

I leaned forward and inserted my arm in front of Betty's legs. "Don't do that, sweetie."

"Why not?"

"It might scuff the desk," I extemporized. The desk was well past worrying about scuff marks, but Betty annoying the woman who sat behind it was counterproductive.

I turned my attention back to Sue. "If you'd just check on Mr. McCreary for us."

"I can't do that."

"Why not?"

"You're not his wife."

Thank God for small favors. "These are his children."

"So you say."

"So I say." I didn't have time to spend the night arguing with a mulish receptionist who borrowed her manners from the politburo. My daughter was missing and I had to find her. I glared at Sue, even raised an eyebrow, daring her to continue defying me.

She took the dare. "I'm afraid I won't be able to help you until next of kin arrives."

"You're sure?"

She answered with a tight smile and lowered her gaze to the paperwork in front of her.

"I'm afraid that won't do."

She looked up from her papers with narrowed eyes. "Oh?" Not the politburo, the KGB. The woman definitely wanted to send me to a work camp in Siberia.

"I'm Ellison Russell. My mother, Frances Walford, is the chairman of the board of this hospital. Mr. McCreary, whose status you've declined to share with his children, is also a board member." I smiled at her—a crocodile smile. "Shall I call my mother? I'm sure she'd like to know how John is doing. She'll probably even come down here and check on him in person."

Throwing Mother's weight around wasn't exactly my favorite thing to do, but it got Sue moving. She stood so suddenly the papers on her desk cascaded to the floor. She ignored them. "One moment, Mrs. Walford...I mean, Mrs. Russell." She disappeared through a swinging door.

"Wow," said Betty. "Is your mother scary? Is she like the chainsaw guy?"

"The chainsaw guy?" I asked.

Betty nodded. "In the movie Jack and his friends saw. Mom said he couldn't go but he went anyway. I heard them talking after."

I'd read about that somewhere...something about a massacre in Texas. "She's scarier."

Betty's eyes grew round.

"My mother is real." Just tossing her name across a desk produced results in the form of a doctor.

He strode through the swinging door, leaned across Sue's desk, and shook my hand. "I'm Doctor Connor, the cardiologist on call tonight." He glanced at the children. "Mr. McCreary is stable. We're admitting him and monitoring his condition." The doctor checked his watch. "We should have him in a room within an hour or two. I believe the snack shop is open if you'd like to wait there."

"Do they have ice cream?" asked Betty.

"They do."

"Daiquiri ice?"

"Maybe not that flavor, but they do have vanilla with hot fudge and nuts. If you ask, they'll give you extra cherries."

Betty considered this, then shrugged. "I guess I can eat vanilla this one time."

"If anything changes I'll have someone come find you."

"If Mrs. McCreary arrives, would you please have her sent to the snack shop?"

"Of course, Mrs. Walford." The doctor flushed. "I mean, Mrs. Russell."

Mother can be controlling and interfering and difficult but, to her credit, she did teach me how to get things done—throw her name around.

I led Betty and Jack to the snack shop.

Betty looked longingly at the counter with its stools that spun in place and impressive pie case. I ignored her, found a table next to the windows and collapsed into a chair.

A waitress deposited a glass of water in front of me.

It's a crying shame hospitals don't serve wine.

"One ice cream sundae." I nodded toward Betty.

"Extra cherries, please." The child smiled up at the woman with the order pad. Two dimples pierced her six-year-old cheeks.

"Jack, are you hungry? Do you want anything? People who don't have to come to the hospital come here just for the pie." I glanced up at our waitress. "The best kind is coconut cream, right?"

She nodded.

Jack didn't respond.

"Two ice cream sundaes," I told the waitress, then I turned my fractured attention on the boy who wasn't talking. "You haven't said a word since you called for the ambulance."

Jack shook the crushed ice in his water glass until it fully submerged then he shrugged.

I dug a few dollars out of my purse and handed it to his sister. "Betty." I pointed to the gift shop. "Would you please buy me a copy of the evening paper? And why don't you get yourself a comic book?"

She rose from the table. "Don't let Jack eat my sundae."

"I won't let him touch it," I promised.

I watched her until she disappeared inside the shop then I turned to Jack. "Tell me what's wrong."

Another shrug.

"You aren't thinking this is your fault, are you?" I pretended not to see his wince. "Because it's not. Heart attacks don't work that way."

"How do you know?"

"I know because the cause of heart attacks is heart disease and you didn't give your father heart disease. He did that himself."

The dark cloud on Jack's face lifted slightly. "But—"

I waved a finger at him. "No buts. Not your fault. Your father loves you."

"Does not," Jack muttered.

"Does too. Parents love their children—even when those children do things we don't much like."

"Not Dad. If I'm not just like him, he doesn't want me around."

"You don't believe that."

"I do."

"You don't. If you did, you'd have run away with Grace and Donna."

The tight line of his lips softened; he ducked his head and audibly swallowed. "About that..."

"Yes?"

"Grace only ran away to help Donna."

SEVENTEEN

Betty sat at the formica-topped table, swung her legs, devoured her sundae and read her comic. Only a few moments passed before she dropped her spoon in her empty dish, turned the last page and commenced twiddling her thumbs, large enthusiastic twiddles that shouted, *I'm bored and plotting mayhem.* I gave her money for a word search book. She gave me a gratified smile then she skipped off to the gift shop.

Jack sat and stared at his dish of melting ice cream.

"What did you mean?" I asked. "Why did Donna have to leave?"

He shrugged, grunted and lifted a spoon of ice cream soup to his lips.

"You're not going to tell me?"

He answered with a half-shrug. Only his left shoulder lifted.

Fine.

I rose from the table. "I need to make a call."

He didn't lift his gaze from the sundae dish.

The payphones were conveniently located in a spot where I could keep an eye on both the gift shop and the snack shop. With my gaze fixed on the gift shop entrance—who knew how much havoc Betty could wreak if she got loose in the hospital?—I dropped a dime in the phone and dialed Aggie's number.

She answered on the third ring.

"Aggie, it's Ellison Russell calling. When was the last time you saw Grace?"

"Yesterday. Why?"

I swallowed around a lump in my throat. "She and Donna are missing."

A few seconds ticked by. In her former life, Aggie worked as an investigator and silence usually means she's thinking hard. Rather than hurry her, I craned my neck to see Betty. I couldn't spot her but the woman behind the register looked worried.

"Shall I come over to the house?" Aggie's question surprised me—touched my heart.

"I'm not at the house." I explained about John's heart attack and his children. "I can't just leave them here." Although it was very tempting.

"No," she agreed. "I suppose not. Have you called the police?"

I should have done that first—before I rushed out of the house to confront Jack. If not then, I should have called before I loaded John McCreary's children into the car and drove them to the hospital. I definitely should have called before I let Betty natter. No wonder Grace left. I was a terrible mother. "No," I admitted.

Aggie grunted. "Probably doesn't matter. The police won't take a report. Not yet. The girls have to be gone at least twenty-four hours before they're considered missing."

"What if I called Detective Jones?"

"He's homicide. He can't help you with Grace."

I could let my eyes fill with tears. I could dredge up a brave smile. I could beg.

Who was I kidding? I could sob pitifully and it wouldn't make a difference. Anarchy Jones would still follow the rules.

"We have to do something!" My voice sounded unnaturally high.

"I'm thinking, I'm thinking."

I let her think.

"Did they take a car?"

"A car? I don't know." I hadn't thought to look.

"I'll go to the house right now. If Grace's car is gone, we can report it stolen. That way, even if the police won't look for Grace, they'll look for her car."

"Thank you," I breathed. Aggie was a genius.

"We'll find her," Aggie promised. "When you get home, I think you ought to look at Donna's sketchbook."

When I got home, I was going to put all my energy into finding my daughter, not look at sketches drawn by the girl who'd lured her away. "Uh-huh."

"I mean it, Mrs. Russell. You need to look at those sketches."

"Will they help us find the girls?"

A dime's worth of silence passed. "They might." If Aggie said so, it must be true.

Betty stepped out of the gift shop, glanced into the café, presumably saw me missing, then headed across the lobby in the wrong direction.

"Aggie, I have to go. I'll call you at the house." I hung up the phone and intercepted Betty before she disappeared into the patient wing.

We returned to the table, where Jack hadn't moved and my coffee had cooled to the temperature of the crushed ice in the glasses. Betty flung herself into a chair, asked me for a pen, and set herself to circling words. I waved for the waitress.

"Warm that up for you, ma'am?" she asked.

"Maybe a fresh cup?"

"What about you, hon?" She looked at Jack's dish of sugary soup. "You want me to get that out of the way?"

Another shrug. She whisked away the dirty dishes and brought my new cup in record time.

"Ellison!" Amy McCreary flew through the coffee shop holding two four-year-olds in party dresses by the hands. She looked at our table, covered with newspapers and a comic and a word search, then dropped her daughters' little hands. "How can I ever thank you?"

She could let me leave. I stood.

Standing, I was easy to hug. Amy took full advantage. Her arms circled my shoulders and she squeezed. "Thank you."

"You're welcome," I squeaked, trying to free myself from the vise of her arms. "I need to get home, Amy."

"I'll walk you out." She turned her gaze on her son. "Jack, watch your sisters."

That wouldn't end well.

No longer my problem.

Amy and I stepped outside the coffee shop.

"I talked to the doctor and it looks as if John will be fine." She held her hand over her heart. "You saved his life by getting him to the hospital so quickly."

"Happy to help." I glanced at my watch. "I do need to get home." But...Damn. "Amy, you ought to know..."

"Yes?" She tilted her head to the side, probably waiting to hear that I'd fed her children ice cream for dinner. I had. Or that I'd let Betty read a comic that might give her nightmares. I had.

"Um...Jack feels responsible. He and John were having an argument when..."

"That boy." She shook her head. "Jack always feels responsible. He felt responsible for Bobby's death." She snorted softly. "As if he could have anything to do with that. His father wasn't home so I got to deal with all that angst by myself."

"Where was John?"

"He was at the game for a while. He said it wasn't very good." She lowered her voice. "He left with a few friends and went out for a drink before you found the body."

Even I, who knew nothing about football, understood that all the cheering and the boys running with balls tucked under their arms meant an exciting game. John wouldn't have left. I stared at Amy. Her eyes were wide and honest. She didn't realize she was lying.

Why had John McCreary lied about being at the game when Bobby died?

I drove home with single-minded purpose. Donna's sketchbook. Aggie suggested it might hold answers.

Would it tell me why Grace and Donna disappeared?

What they hoped to achieve?

Where they went?

I parked the Cadillac in the drive and got out, fumbling with the house keys. One second I had them, the next they were airborne, arcing toward the mulch where my hostas should be, were it not for their brush with death and police procedure. Damn it. I hiked up the hem of my suit, fell to my knees and dug amongst the bit of wood.

A car pulled into the driveway and I looked up from the shrubbery. Mother's BMW sat behind Henry's Cadillac.

Perfect. Just what I needed. The extra cherries on my very own sundae.

One black leather pump touched the drive, then the other. "Ellison, what are you doing?"

"I dropped my keys."

"Why didn't you tell me?"

About what? Grace? I could already hear the parenting lecture she'd deliver. She didn't even need to give it. "I just haven't had time yet."

"You didn't think it was something I'd want to know right away?" She smiled at me as if I'd unexpectedly done something right.

I blinked. I was crawling around in the shrubs wearing Chanel. Donna was missing. Grace was missing. None of those things deserved a smile.

"Well," her smile brightened, "I'm here now. Tell me all about it."

Mother was unbelievable. There! I snatched up the house keys and struggled to my feet. "You'd better come inside." I'd tell her, then I'd send her back to central command. From the comfort of her Sister Parish-designed sitting room Mother could wage any battle, win any war, maybe even find a couple of missing teenage girls.

I opened the door. Max waited on the other side. He saw Mother and backed away, whining softly.

Not even the sound of a car in desperate need of a new muffler could lure him forward.

Mother's smile only faltered a bit when Aggie parked her ailing Bug, Bessie, behind the BMW. The smile lingered when Bessie emitted her usual death rattle. The curve of her lips even held steady when Aggie stepped out of her car wearing a retina-burning orange muumuu.

"Are the cars here?" Aggie called across the drive.

“I haven’t had time to look.”

Aggie nodded then disappeared around the corner of the house.

Mother’s smile finally gave out. “Are you quite sure about that woman?”

I was sure. Aggie was better than an early morning swim followed by the perfect cup of coffee. She was better than shooting a hole-in-one. She was better than bidding and making a vulnerable, doubled grand slam. But my opinion mattered little—at least to Mother. I played my trump card. “Hunter recommended her, remember?”

Mother might argue with me but Hunter’s opinions were above reproach.

She blinked away any lingering Aggie doubts and followed me through the foyer, down the hall and into the kitchen.

In a half-second, Mother inventoried the room’s cleanliness, organization and general appeal. Thanks to Aggie, she was unable to find fault. “I wish you wouldn’t keep the coffeemaker on the counter.”

Well, almost unable.

“I use it every day.”

She sniffed.

Enough. Grace was missing. I didn’t have time to debate where Mr. Coffee spent his nights. “What is it, Mother? What do you want?”

She smiled at me—a high-beam smile. “Tell me all about it.”

Mother’s smile didn’t look brave in the face of adversity, it didn’t even look like a don’t-let-the-neighbors-see-the-cracks-in-the-façade expression. Mother’s smile looked happy. Had she downed a few martinis to deal with the worry?

I dropped my handbag on the counter. “As far as we can tell, she’s been gone since this morning.”

She blinked. “Who?”

Who did she think? Faye Dunaway? “Grace.” I rubbed my eyes. “Donna is missing too.”

She stared at me, her expression fading to a more familiar expression. Utter disapproval. “My granddaughter is missing?”

“Yes.”

“Since this morning?”

"Yes."

"And you're just telling me now?"

Mother in a nutshell. Not *where did she go?* Not *have you called the police?* Not *have you called all her friends?* Instead, she offered up implicit criticism on my timing.

A key turned in the back door and Aggie blew into the kitchen like an orange tornado. "The car is gone. You can call the police and report it."

"Report what?" Mother asked.

"We're going to report Grace's car as stolen," I explained.

"If she gets pulled over, she'll be arrested."

Exactly. I picked up the phone and dialed the operator. "Would you please connect me with the police?"

"Ellison, this is a mistake."

I narrowed my eyes and glared at Mother. Must she question all my decisions?

"I'll connect you now," said the operator.

Mother ignored my glare. "Grace could be arrested."

Max whined and Aggie sidled toward the door to the back stairs.

I'd understood the first time she said it. Grace could be arrested and found. "It's not like I'd press charges. This way the police will look for the car even if they won't look for her."

"I don't think—"

"Hunter's idea," I snapped. A lie, but a lie that would buy me Mother's silence. I turned my back on her and listened to the woman on the other end of the phone line. "I need to report a stolen car."

She connected me to another woman who offered to take my information. I gave her the make, model and license plate number of Grace's car as well as my name and phone number. She read everything back to me. I thanked her and hung up.

Mother glared. Aggie opened the door to the stairs, mimed drawing, and slipped away. Max followed her.

Great. Left alone with Mother.

The phone saved me. It rang. I reached for the receiver and the doorbell gonged. "Would you get that?" I asked.

Mother huffed then disappeared down the hall.

I snatched up the receiver. “Hello.”

“Ellison, it’s Amy McCreary calling.”

What now? “Is John all right?”

Mother’s voice floated down the hallway. Who was at the door?

“No change,” said Amy. “Listen, Jack told me Grace is missing.”

My throat tightened. “Yes.”

“I wanted to let you know, I saw her this morning at the service station on Broadway.”

“Broadway?”

“Just north of Westport.”

Nowhere near school. Nowhere near home. Nowhere near her mother.

“What time?” My voice hardly broke.

“That was the odd thing. It was eight thirty, and I remember thinking she and her friend ought to be in school.”

Mother’s voice got louder and her heels clicked on the hardwoods.

“Thank you for calling, Amy.”

“Are you kidding? John owes you his life. You let me know if I can help.”

I thanked her again and hung up the phone—just in time to look up into Hunter Tafft’s concerned face. He brushed past Mother, closed his hands on my shoulders and pulled me into a hug. Then he kissed me. On the lips.

I froze, too stunned to move.

He released me, stepped back and said, “Ellison, what can I do?”

From her vantage point near the door, Mother smiled brightly. Beamed. How quickly she forgot the bigger picture. Grace was missing.

I focused on that picture and not the firmness of Hunter’s lips or the comfort of his arms—certainly not on what had possessed him to kiss me.

Aggie swung the door to the back stairs open and stepped into the kitchen with Donna’s sketchbook clutched to her tangerine-clad chest.

Mother raised a brow at the intrusion. Hunter stepped farther away from me. I turned my back on both of them and held out my hands for the book. Finally, I got to see what was inside.

EIGHTEEN

Aggie extended Donna's pad slowly, as if it was a box and I was Pandora.

Ding-dong. The doorbell. Again. What now?

Mother glanced at me then Aggie. It was almost too easy to read her mind. I showed no signs of moving, which left Aggie and her orange muumuu. Hardly the ensemble Mother would pick for someone answering her daughter's door. "I'll get that." She disappeared through the door to the front hall.

"What's in there, Aggie? You look almost sick." Hunter offered her an encouraging smile.

My fingers closed on the pad's edges.

"Ellison!" Mother's voice carried down the hallway. Her tone was unmistakable. I hadn't heard it since my sister Marjorie's father-in-law had one too many and spilled a black Russian down Mother's new cream dupioni drapes. The tone meant trouble. Capital T trouble.

Were the police at my door?

Had something happened to Grace?

My stomach completed not one, not two, but three flips—all high, all worthy of Olga Korbut—then sank somewhere lower than my knees. Breathing was an impossibility.

The pad slipped through my fingers. With the last bit of air in my lungs, I called, "Coming!" I shoved through the door and rushed down the hall through a cloud of oxygen-deprived stars.

Mother stood at the front door. She glanced over her shoulder and I searched her expression. No horror. No grief. Nothing but disapproval. Deep disapproval.

This one time Mother's disapproval was a comfort. If something awful had happened Mother would look appalled or horrified. She didn't.

My stomach returned to its customary position in my midsection. Air whooshed into my lungs. The stars disappeared.

Mother moved aside and I saw who stood on the other side of the door.

India and Jonathan Hess waited on the front stoop. Chances were good they were waiting for their daughter.

My heart didn't quit beating. Instead, it raced. My feet slowed to a stop. Holy Mother of disappearing daughters, what was I going to tell them?

"You're here," I croaked. Nothing like stating the obvious. "Won't you please come in?"

They stepped into the foyer and I searched my feeble brain for some sort of explanation. How had I overlooked explaining their daughter's whereabouts in my planning?

Because I'd hoped she'd be safely tucked in the guest room bed before her parents returned.

"You're home early." My voice still sounded as if it belonged to an ailing frog. I cleared my throat. "I wasn't expecting you until the end of the week."

India smiled brighter than a hundred watt bulb. "Jonathan was desperate to come home."

Jonathan looked pale and clammy and ill. "Where's Donna?"

The wattage on India's smile flickered and she patted his arm as if he was a fractious child and not a man.

He swatted her hand away. "Where is she?"

"Um..." I glanced at Mother, half-hoping she'd interfere and say something—anything. She crossed her arms over her chest and watched me struggle for words.

"Won't you sit down?" I said. "You look..." *Like hell* didn't seem terribly polite. "Tired from traveling." I waved an arm in the general direction of the living room.

Mother was at least willing to help me insofar as she led the way into the living room. Bless her. I pretended not to see her run a finger across a table to check for dust.

India brushed past me and the scent of Shalimar assaulted my nose. Shalimar with a hint of nervous sweat. Nerves I understood. My frayed nerves were bumping hips with panic.

But what about India? She didn't know Donna was missing—yet. Did traveling make her nervous? Maybe it was Mother. That too I understood.

Mother possessed an expression that said she knew every bad thing you'd ever done or thought of doing and she didn't approve. She wore it now. Then again, maybe it was India's bully of a husband who made her nervous. Who could blame her if that was true?

I smiled at her. "Would you care for coffee? Maybe tea?"

She glanced at the bully as if waiting for his approval.

He shook his head.

"No, thank you." India's voice was soft, regretful.

"It's no trouble," I insisted.

"I find a cup of tea restorative." Was Mother helping India or hinting that I should fetch her a cup of darjeeling? She inclined her perfectly coiffed head toward India and smiled. Helping. If Mother wanted tea herself, the hint would be underscored by a stare that bored straight through me.

Jonathan's chin jutted forward and he leveled his gaze at me. "She said no. We'll just collect Donna and be on our way."

No wonder India was nervous. I tugged at the collar of my suit and repeated, "Won't you sit?"

Rather than ease his frame onto the couch, Jonathan Hess stepped toward me. "What's going on here? Where. Is. My. Daughter?" Not a subtle man, India's husband. He also wasn't Donna's father. I decided not to point that out.

A few seconds ticked by. India's hands fluttered like butterflies. Jonathan drew closer to me. "Well?"

"Donna and Grace are missing." I spoke too loud, too fast, the verbal equivalent of a running cannonball jump into an icy pool.

India staggered, raised a shaking hand to her throat, then sank onto the settee.

Her husband paled to a heretofore unimagined shade of white.

Mother tsked, over the news or my delivery, I wasn't sure.

"What do you mean missing?" India's voice was as brittle as the little melba toast rounds they serve before dinner at the club. Exert any pressure and you're left with nothing but crumbs.

Perhaps I should have found a way to break the news more gently. "I mean—"

"She means they ran away." Jonathan narrowed his eyes and color climbed up his neck, painting his face in ruddy shades. "We trusted you with our daughter."

I searched for something to say and found only trite and meaningless words. I said them anyway. "I'm sorry."

"What's being done to find them?" India asked.

"They haven't been gone long enough for the police to take a report, but we've reported Grace's car as stolen."

"When did they leave?" Jonathan demanded.

"They didn't go to school today." Just thinking about it made my stomach renew its efforts to flip like an Olympic gymnast.

He glanced at his watch. "When did you discover they were gone?"

"This afternoon."

"And all you've done is report a stolen car?"

"I...um..." I glanced at my black pumps.

"Flyers!" India clasped her hands together. "We'll put up flyers. All around the neighborhood. All over the city. And maybe we can call the newspaper and the television stations."

Mother raised a brow. "There's no reason to panic."

India and I gaped at her. There was every reason to panic.

"They're two bright girls." Mother smoothed a strand of hair that had dared stray. "They're in a vehicle. Presumably they have cash. Ellison did the right thing asking the police to look for the car."

My jaw dropped. Frances Walford had ceded a point.

Somewhere in hell, the damned were having a snowball fight. Heck, they were probably building a fort. Maybe even sledding.

Mother lowered herself into an armchair and leaned back as if it was a throne. Ensconced, she crossed her ankles and surveyed the three of us as if we were less than desirable subjects. "I hardly see the need to advertise their lapse in judgment with...flyers or newspaper or television." She sniffed and allowed her shoulders a delicate shudder.

With the exception of the society page, Mother believed the people written about in papers were crooks or politicians. Lately she'd been hard-pressed to tell the difference. As for television, newscasts covered nothing but the same crooks and politicians, that and the weather—and everyone knew the weatherman was a liar.

A moment passed before India found her voice. "You haven't talked to their friends?"

"I talked to Jack McCreary. He knew they were running away but doesn't know where they were headed."

India's hand still hovered near her throat. "What about their girl—"

"Who's Jack McCreary?" Jonathan Hess' face mottled carmine red and stark white.

"Won't you please sit down?" I'd already been through one heart attack, I didn't need a second.

He ignored my question. "Who is he?"

The man might look flushed and sick, but his tone was as bossy as ever.

"A friend."

His upper lip curled. "What kind of friend?"

"A friend who's a boy."

Somehow the bigger picture had passed Jonathan by.

The girls were missing and all he cared about was whether or not one of them had been interested in Jack McCreary. I shifted my gaze to India and lied without so much as a scratch near my nose. "I was just getting ready to call Grace's girlfriends when you arrived."

"Why didn't you call them first?" Jonathan glowered at me with what appeared to be barely contained fury.

What an ass. A heart attack would serve him right.

Just not in my house. "Grace and Donna have been spending a lot of time with Jack this week. I started with him."

"You let my daughter spend unsupervised time with a boy?"

An unmitigated ass.

He turned to his wife, raised his brows, crossed his arms. "I cannot believe your poor judgment. You left our daughter with this...woman?"

Her poor judgment reached its apex when she married him. India paled and her hands resumed their fluttering. Fool woman.

The asinine man returned his gaze to me. "You'll be hearing from my lawyer."

Mother snorted—a soft, exquisite snort, worthy of a queen. The snort said, *Bring on your lawyer. Ours will eat him for breakfast.*

She was right. Hunter would dispatch the Hess' lawyer faster than a plate of blueberry pancakes. Then he'd wipe his lips with a linen napkin, take a sip of his coffee and ask for seconds.

Jonathan ignored the snort and all that it meant. He jabbed a finger at me. "You are responsible for this."

I should have seen his accusation coming. Then again, I should have worked things out with Grace so that when she had a problem she ran to me instead of away from me. I should have paid more attention to the pain in Donna's eyes. I should have kept better tabs on both of them.

I opened my mouth to respond then closed it. Jonathan Hess was right. The girls had disappeared on my watch.

But Jack's words still echoed in my brain—*Grace only ran away to help Donna.*

Those words burned my throat. They singed my tongue.

If I said them aloud Jonathan would ask what they meant. I'd be forced to guess. My guess? Donna preferred the streets to living with him. I might even express my agreement with her decision.

Poor India looked miserable enough. Her shoulders hunched. Her hands fluttered. Her lips had disappeared. I couldn't add to her misery. I had to figure out what Jack meant before I started tossing accusations like hand grenades.

I went to the couch, sat, caught one of India's fluttering hands in mine and said, "I'm doing everything I can to find them. Like Mother said, they're bright girls. We'll get them home safely."

She stared at her lap, nodded slowly, then raised her watery gaze to her husband. "Are lawyers really necessary?"

Hunter chose that moment to enter the living room. "Problem?" His tone was polite but his eyes narrowed to chips of mica-flecked granite when he saw Hess looming over India and me on the couch.

Of course Hunter entered without knocking. He'd kissed me without asking. A little thing like barging into a private conversation was hardly a speed bump on the fast track of his life.

Mother didn't see his entrance as barging. She bestowed a smile upon her favorite subject then glanced toward Jonathan Hess. Her expression hardened to imperious disdain. "Hunter, we were just telling the Hesses that the police are looking for the car. Ellison will call Grace's friends..." She looked at me expectantly.

"Kim, Debbie and Peggy," I supplied.

She acknowledged my contribution with a small wave of her fingers. "Yes. Kim, Debbie and Peggy and ask if they know where Donna and Grace might have gone."

"That sounds like an excellent plan, Frances. If I may, a question?"

Mother inclined her head, giving him permission to continue. It wasn't as if he needed it. Didn't she remember the barging—or the kissing?

"I don't suppose either of you have any idea why Donna ran away?"

"None." India gave my hand a small squeeze.

I squeezed back.

Hunter is charming. Hunter is urbane. Hunter is a man who

keeps his emotions well-hidden. But when he turned his gaze on Jonathan, I would have sworn Hunter was a man about to throw a punch.

Maybe Jonathan sensed it too. He puffed up his ailing chest and asked, “Who exactly are you?”

“Friend of the family.”

“What makes you think it was Donna’s idea to run away?”

Hunter raised an eyebrow. “Call it intuition. I look at things and draw—” He made the word *draw* last longer than the previous eight. “Conclusions.”

Intuition, my fanny. Mother’s golden—well, silver-haired—favorite had looked at Donna’s drawings without me.

A few seconds passed, the only sound the ticking of the grandfather clock. Hunter stepped further into the room, closer to Jonathan. “You didn’t answer my question.”

Jonathan shrugged. “I have no idea why Donna left. I wasn’t even here.”

“No idea?” Hunter’s eyebrows were drawn, his lips pulled back from his teeth. It was an expression I never thought to see on his face—taut, angry, almost feral.

“What the hell is that supposed to mean?” Jonathan fisted his hands and stepped toward Hunter.

Hunter squared his shoulders and stepped further onto my Oriental rug.

Perfect. They were going to brawl in my living room. I glanced at a side table where pieces of my great-grandmother’s collection of crystal hand coolers rested. If anything happened to them, if they were broken or chipped, I’d be eating at the kids’ table at holidays for the rest of Mother’s life.

I had to do something. I gave India’s hand another quick squeeze. “Both you and Jonathan look exhausted. Maybe you should go home and rest. We’ll call if we hear anything.”

Mother cleared her throat and shifted on her throne. “Ellison’s right. You do look tired. We can continue this in the morning.”

Jonathan shifted his gaze from Hunter to Mother.

"You ought to go home." Like an actual queen, she expected her suggestion to be taken as writ. She stared at Jonathan and India as if waiting for them to bow and curtsy before taking their leave.

They didn't disappoint. While they didn't bow or curtsy, India did stand and Jonathan loosed his fists.

I stood too. "I'll see you out."

"I'll do it." Hunter's expression was grim.

At least there weren't any heirlooms in the foyer.

India gave me one last desperate look then followed Mother's silver-haired courtier out of the living room.

When the unmistakable sound of the front door closing reached us, Mother lowered her head and squeezed the bridge of her nose. "That awful man is going to be a problem."

I hate it when she's right.

NINETEEN

The grandfather clock gonged nine o'clock.

Mother folded her hands in her lap. "Are you going to call them?"

I blinked. "Call who?"

"Kim and Debbie and Peggy." She counted the girls' names off on her fingers.

"Later." I stood, ready to send Mother on her way. After all, I had a sketchbook to review.

Mother settled in her chair and narrowed her eyes. The corners of her mouth drooped as if she despaired of me ever amounting to anything. "How could you let Grace spend time with their daughter? Welcome that girl into your home?"

More criticism in the form of questions.

Hunter stuck his silver head into the living room, caught sight of Mother's expression and mine—deeply disapproving and plotting matricide, respectively—and withdrew, muttering something about checking on Aggie in the kitchen.

"Ellison," Mother enunciated carefully, "those people are simply not our kind."

Oh merciful Lord. I set my tone to spun sugar on the sweetness dial. "What kind is that?"

Mother pursed her lips and wrinkled her nose as if she'd bit into a particularly sour lemon. "There's no need for sarcasm."

So said she. "Mother, I have better things to do than argue with you." I had to look through Donna's sketchbook. I had to drive aimlessly down dark, graffiti-marked streets, peering past dented trashcans and wind-borne bits of flotsam for the sight of two desperate girls, huddled and freezing despite Indian summer weather. I had to call Debbie and Kim and Peggy. And when I hung up the phone, I had to pray.

Ding-dong.

We both glanced at our watches. It was far too late for unannounced arrivals. I left Mother in her chair with her back ruler straight, her ankles properly crossed and her expression more dire than a hanging judge's.

Ding-dong.

I hurried through the foyer and pulled on the door's brass handle. The light from the sconces that flanked my once-again-pristine door revealed Alice. What in the name of painted porticos had brought her back to my house at this hour?

She glanced up through the fringe of her bangs then thrust an envelope at me. "It's a check for the damages."

I raised a brow.

She mumbled...something.

"I didn't hear you. What did you say?"

"I said I'm sorry," she snapped.

She didn't look sorry. She looked more annoyed than Mother when I left her in the living room.

"Who made you apologize?"

"My grandmother."

Alice Anne. Alice's grandmother and my mother were of the old-school, iron-willed women whom others dared not cross. I reached for the envelope in Alice's outstretched hand. "Since you don't mean it, should I accept it?"

For a half-second something like amusement flashed across Alice's face. "The check or the apology?"

Alice had a sense of humor lurking somewhere within. Who would have thunk it?

"Are you? Sorry?"

She studied her shoes—clunky platforms that made her skinny legs look like sticks. A half-smile played on her lips.

"Why did you do it?"

She lifted her gaze from her footwear, brushed aside her bangs and looked at me with eyes glowing with conviction. “I had to do something. People had to know.”

“Know?”

She nodded. “I’m supposed to apologize to Donna too.”

To Donna? I blinked. Duh. How was it I’d missed that? Donna and Bobby. Duh, duh, duh. “She’s not here.”

“She went home?” Something dark and sly slithered across Alice’s face.

I crossed my arms over my chest, suddenly cold despite the warm night. Did Alice know something? Had Alice done something?

“If Donna’s not here, I guess I’ll be going.” She turned her back on me and descended the first step.

“Alice.”

She paused and looked over her shoulder. “What?”

“Is there anything you want to tell me?”

“About what?” She sounded too innocent.

“About Donna or Bobby.”

“Anything I want to tell you? About them?” She snorted. “I don’t think so.” She stepped away from my door.

Merciful Lord. Had she killed Bobby? What if Grace and Donna hadn’t run away? What if Alice had done something to them?

“Alice,” I called.

This time when she paused, she didn’t look over her shoulder.

“Do you know where Donna is?” My voice was too high.

“Nope.” Her voice was too low, as if it held a rumble of laughter, as if she was laughing at me.

I watched her get in her car. I watched her drive away.

When she rounded the corner, I closed the door. I really ought to call Anarchy. And tell him what? That Alice seemed guilty of...something? Yeah, right. Teenage girls regularly murdered their would-be boyfriends.

I hurried past the living room and the gorgon within. Why

borrow trouble? Besides, Donna's sketchbook waited for me in the kitchen.

The pad lay on the counter, spiral-bound with a brown cover and corners softened by use. Aggie and Hunter regarded it with distaste.

I reached for it.

"Aren't you going to call Grace's friends?" Mother asked from the doorway.

Why couldn't she stay ensconced in the living room? Better yet, why couldn't she climb into her car and drive home?

"Later." My voice brooked no arguments.

Or so I thought.

"You said you'd call."

"I will." I drew a breath. "Later."

Mother glanced pointedly at the kitchen clock. "It's after nine now." The *tsk* in her voice set every one of my nerves on edge and tightened all the muscles in my neck and shoulders.

I gave her the scrunched up smile Grace shared with me whenever what I've said doesn't deserve a response, then I flipped open the book.

The first drawing was a picture of Donna's father, her real father—not the jackass masquerading in the role. He'd had kind eyes and a gentle expression. I touched the paper and sensed the grief Donna had poured into each line of his face.

I turned the page.

India stared back at me, her lip caught in her teeth, sadness and indecision alive in her eyes. She held a younger Donna's hand.

Mother glanced over my shoulder. "The girl has some talent."

The girl had loads of talent.

The first sketch of Jonathan depicted a self-important man with a puffed chest and frightening eyes.

The drawings turned darker. Dread leapt off the page while demons danced their way through fiery backgrounds. One demon with a puffed chest and frightening eyes jigged on a chintz couch. In another drawing he lurked in the shadows of a grandfather clock. In yet another, the demon trapped Donna's chin in his claws while his forked tongue tasted her tears.

My hands shook and I rested the pad against the edge of the counter and turned another page.

Each drawing was worse than the last—the demon grew more terrifying and Donna grew up. Gone was the little girl who'd held her mother's hand. Instead the Donna on the latter pages looked like a sex kitten. Barbarella with dark hair.

Bile rose in my throat.

Mother stiffened to her most disapproving self. "That man..."

Hunter nodded. "It looks that way."

Tears stood in Aggie's eyes. "That poor, poor girl."

"I can't believe you let him in your house," said Mother.

It wasn't as if I knew he was a character from a Nabokov novel when I offered him coffee. The buzzing in my brain was near deafening. I searched for a response anyway.

Hunter found one for me. "Monsters don't wear signs, Frances." His lips curled into the wry approximation of a smile. "They look just like everyone else."

Mother sniffed. "Be that as it may, I told Ellison they weren't our kind of people."

Rich coming from Mother. My sister married the rubber king of Ohio. As for my late husband—well, the less said about his predilection the better. But what Jonathan Hess had done to Donna went beyond selling King Cobra condoms or cheating on your wife with a woman who enjoyed being tied up and flogged. What Jonathan Hess had done was pure evil.

Mother pointed at the sketchbook. "That family has always been trouble. India's mother was a gold digger, India hasn't the sense God gave a goat and this girl...Well, you know she's the reason Grace is gone. Grace helped her escape."

The buzzing in my head grew louder and I gripped the edge of the counter.

Mother encompassed us all with her glare. "The question is, what are we going to do next?"

"Ellison needs to lie down," said Hunter.

I opened my mouth to argue but my skin felt flushed and frigid at the same time. The act of forming words was more than my tongue could handle and my stomach seemed to have completed yet another flip and lodged itself near my throat.

Mother narrowed her eyes and examined me. She unclasped her handbag, withdrew a bottle and shook out two pills. "Take these, Ellison. I'll call Grace's friends."

I didn't move.

She thrust her hand toward me. "You're no good to anyone in the state you're in. I'll call Kim and Debbie and Peggy and tomorrow we'll find Grace."

I couldn't. I couldn't just go to bed when my daughter was missing. I couldn't climb into a comfortable bed when Lord only knew where she was sleeping. If she was sleeping. I couldn't ignore what Jonathan Hess had done to Donna. I couldn't rest not knowing where they were.

I shook my head. "No."

"Are you planning on driving around like that? You look like you've already taken half a bottle." She shook the pill bottle for emphasis. "We can't find them tonight. We can tomorrow. Besides, you need some rest. Tomorrow morning you're going to have to tell India Hess her husband has been molesting her daughter."

Oh dear Lord. She was right. I held out a hand for the pills.

Aggie put a glass of water in my other hand and patted me softly on the back.

"We'll find them tomorrow," Hunter promised.

Tap, tap, tap.

I opened my eyes just wide enough to glare at the door—for half a second—then I remembered Grace was missing. Whoever was knocking might have news. "Come in!"

Aggie stuck her head in my room. "I'm sorry to disturb you, Mrs. Russell."

Aggie? I glanced at the clock on my bedside table. Too early for Aggie. "What are you..."

"Your mother didn't want you to be alone. She asked me to spend the night."

I swallowed my annoyance. In her own bossy, interfering way, Mother cared. "Thank you."

"You're welcome. Um..."

"What is it?" I asked.

"Your friend Libba is here."

Libba? At this hour? I looked at the clock a second time. Libba didn't move this early in the morning.

My housekeeper's brows were drawn and the corners of her mouth sagged. She looked almost apologetic. "She's waiting for you downstairs."

Had Grace gone to Libba's? If so, if my daughter had been there all day yesterday and Libba was just now telling me, Anarchy Jones would have another homicide on his hands. I threw off the covers.

Aggie opened the door farther. "I brought you coffee."

Truly, I don't pay the woman enough.

"Thanks." I crossed the room, accepted the cup and sipped. "Would you please tell her I'll be right down?"

Aggie closed the door behind her.

I let go of my coffee long enough to jam my arms into a peignoir, then followed her downstairs.

Libba perched on a stool at the kitchen island. She'd traded in her usual effortless elegance for jeans and a t-shirt, smudged mascara, red eyes and splotchy skin.

My heart, my stomach—hell, my kidneys—all triple-flipped. Why was Libba crying into her coffee before seven thirty in the morning? "What's wrong?" I squeaked. Two words used up all the air in my lungs.

"I have terrible taste in men."

True, but not news and not worth crying over first thing in the morning.

"You're not here about Grace?"

"I'm here because Charlie asked if he could borrow my earrings." She lowered her head to her hands.

"I thought you were done with him."

"I gave him another chance." She shook her head without lifting it. "Mistake."

"Which earrings?"

She raised her head. "Don't be catty."

"Those sapphire chandeliers would look lovely with his eyes."

"Why do I talk to you?"

"Because I'm your oldest friend and I tolerate your showing up unannounced before I've had my coffee."

"Hhmph."

We both stared into our cups and considered the obvious merit of my words.

"Why would I be here about Grace?"

"She's missing."

"Oh my God! Ellison!" She jumped off her stool as if standing translated into doing or solving or finding. "Why didn't you say something? Has she been kidnapped?"

"No. She and Donna ran away."

Libba lowered her chin and snorted. "Have you called the Alameda?"

"The hotel?" The nicest hotel in the city.

"Grace doesn't exactly enjoy roughing it." Libba regarded me with her raccoon eyes. "You weren't thinking bus terminal?"

That and worse.

"You were!" Her lips curled into an almost-smile. "This is the child who insisted you send softer sheets to summer camp, the child who won't eat store-bought bread, the child who keeps a thermometer in her bathroom to test the temperature of her bath water. She didn't run away. She went somewhere."

Maybe. I put down my coffee mug and rubbed my eyes with the heels of my hands.

"Stop that!"

I stopped long enough to glare at her.

"I mean it. You'll give yourself wrinkles." Libba sipped Arabica-scented ambrosia and stared at me over the edge of the cup until I dropped my hands. Victorious, she asked, "Where would she go?"

"If I knew that she wouldn't be missing."

"Ha. Ha. I'm serious. Where would she go?"

The country. "She might go to Mother and Daddy's place up north." The sheets were soft, the water was hot and there was a good bakery nearby. I'd taken her there when her father died. "But the caretakers would have called me."

"You're sure? Grace can be very persuasive."

"I'm sure." I poured more coffee into my cup, added cream and watched the clouds billow on the surface. "It wouldn't hurt to call."

"Call." Libba crossed her legs and looked at me expectantly.

"Fine." I picked up the phone. My hand hovered above the dial.

Libba wrinkled her nose. "I'm waiting."

I narrowed my eyes. "Did you loan him the earrings?"

She grinned. "Bitch. Just make the call."

I dialed. "Hello, Mrs. Smith. It's Ellison Russell calling. I'm wondering if you've seen Grace?"

"Um..."

"Have you?" My voice sounded as tight as a freshly strung tennis racket.

"Let me put Mr. Smith on the phone, dear."

My heart beat faster. Was Libba actually right?

"Mrs. Russell, you're looking for Grace?"

"Yes." I was afraid to hope.

"I think she might be out at your father's hunting cabin."

For the first time since I'd realized she was gone, my lungs filled fully. "Why?"

"I thought I saw her car yesterday. And this morning, Mrs. Smith accused me of eating half the pie she left in the icebox."

No one made better pie than Mrs. Smith. If Grace was anywhere close to one of Mrs. Smith's pies she'd be hard-pressed not to eat a slice...or three. "Apple?" I asked. Grace's favorite.

"A hunk of cheddar was gone too."

It was her. It had to be. My shoulders lifted as if the weight of three or four full golf bags had disappeared. "Can you keep an eye on her? I'll be up in a few hours."

"I reckon."

"Thank you, I'll see you shortly." I hung up the phone.

Libba smirked at me.

Brrrng.

I picked up the phone immediately. "Hello."

"Ellison? It's India Hess calling. Have you had any news?"

My heart, which had felt almost buoyant, sank faster than a golf ball driven into a water hazard. As much as I wanted Grace safely home, could I send Donna back to her stepfather? I swallowed. "India, we need to talk."

TWENTY

"What's happened? Are the girls all right?" India's voice climbed higher with each word. So high the phone vibrated in my hand. So high that *right* was little more than a squeak.

"I'm sure they're fine." I tried to sound soothing—easier now that I knew our daughters were in the country eating stolen pie rather than dining from a dumpster in a shadow-filled alley.

Libba, always helpful, rolled her eyes, and stared at me over the rim of her coffee cup.

"Have you found them?" India demanded.

"No." It wasn't exactly a lie, but close enough that I scratched my nose anyway.

"Then what do we need to talk about?" she asked.

"We found Donna's sketchbook—"

"She draws all the time. What has that got to do with anything?"

"Yes, well...this sketchbook has some drawings you ought to see."

"Why?"

"They might explain why the girls ran away."

India answered with silence.

"India? Are you there?"

"Jonathan said you'd do this."

"Do what?"

"Blame Donna." The pendulum of her voice swung from treble to bass.

"I'm not blaming anyone," I insisted. "You ought to see her drawings."

"I think we should find the girls before we worry about Donna's doodles."

My mother had dismissed my interest in art as a nice hobby until I found a husband. Her certainty in my inability to succeed still rankled.

"They're not doodles. Donna's very talented."

"Donna needs to give up this crazy idea she's going to be a painter. Jonathan has told her over and over. It's not like a woman can make a living off art."

"I do."

The response earned me more silence.

"India, let's not argue. Meet me at the French bakery on the Plaza. Say four o'clock?" Four o'clock gave me almost all day at the farm. "I'll show you the sketchbook. Maybe by then we'll have found the girls. Maybe they'll be home." I crossed my fingers.

"Fine." A grudging affirmative if I ever heard one.

"I'll see you then." I hung up the phone before she could change her mind.

"What is going on?" Libba put her coffee on the counter, the better to give me the hairy eyeball. "What's in this sketchbook?"

"Cross your heart?" Silly but effective. We started crossing our hearts for silence when we were ten. Still did it now. This was the sort of secret I didn't want her blabbing all over town. I waited.

Libba dutifully drew an x over her heart.

"India's husband molested Donna."

"No!"

"Yes." The mere thought soured my stomach. I put down my coffee.

"I don't believe it."

"It's true." I wouldn't make up something like that. I looked around the kitchen for the sketchpad.

"Oh, I believe he did it. I just don't believe someone has worse taste in men than I do."

I stared at her. "Well, I suppose every cloud has a silver lining, doesn't it?"

Her eyebrows and shoulders rose, her lips pulled away from her teeth and she ducked her head. At least she had the decency to look abashed. “Sorry.” She wrapped her hands around her coffee mug, pulled it closer and stared into its depths. “Molested or molesting?”

“Molesting.”

“So what are you going to do now?

“Drive up to the farm.”

“You can’t send Donna back to that man.”

I scraped a few strands of loose hair away from my face. “I know.”

She released her mug and gripped the edge of the counter. “So what’s your plan?”

“I don’t have one. I’ll figure things out as I go along.”

Normally I enjoy the drive north to my folks’ farm—the hilly landscape, the breathtaking vistas and, in the fall, the splashes of brilliant color from maples and ash and sumac flaming amidst the brown of countless oaks.

This drive, the trees could have worn amethyst leaves with chartreuse polka dots. I wouldn’t have noticed. I sped toward Grace. Neither trees, nor landscape, nor color mattered.

While the weight of my foot on the gas pedal was as heavy and unchanging as lead, my emotions swung from fury to euphoria. Half of me wanted to yell until I was hoarse or Grace was deaf, whichever came first. The other half wanted to hold her forever. Decisions, decisions.

I couldn’t return Donna to a home with Jonathan Hess in it. Would India see her daughter’s drawings and realize her husband was a monster? Would she leave him?

Denial was a comfortable place to live. I knew firsthand. It was safe. It was easy. The storm clouds on the horizon were easy to ignore, plus they added a certain vibrancy to sunsets. I’d known my husband was a heel, but if someone had told me what Henry was up to, I would have laughed in their face. What Jonathan Hess did to Donna was worse than anything Henry ever considered—and he'd considered just about everything.

No way was India going to believe me.

Thanks to my lead foot, the miles sped by, bringing me closer to Grace, Donna and the need for a plan.

What the hell was I going to do?

I pulled into the long driveway to Mother and Daddy's country house without an answer. I parked the car without an answer. I got out of the car without an answer. The front door opened and Mr. Smith stepped outside. I looked up into his weather-tanned face without an answer.

"They're still out at the hunting cabin."

"Thank you, Mr. Smith. I can't tell you how worried I've been."

He offered me a sympathetic grimace. "Don't be too hard on her. She's a good girl." The Smiths have adored Grace since her first toddling steps.

I made no promises. "You're sure they're still there?"

A smile cracked his face and his wrinkles radiated like starbursts. "They're not going anywhere."

"Oh?"

"I disconnected the battery in Grace's car."

Mr. Smith was an evil genius. Good thing he was on my side.

"I won't tell her," I promised.

"She's a good girl," he repeated, as if saying it twice might convince me to go easy, to hug not throttle.

I thanked him then climbed back into Henry's Cadillac and drove down the rutted dirt lane that led to the hunting cabin.

Grace might well be a good girl, but she'd left home without a word. I'd never been so worried in my life. The desire to gather her in my arms and wrap my hands around her teenage neck warred within me.

Hug or throttle? Hug or throttle?

My hands gripped the steering wheel and I guided the car around a particularly deep pothole.

Hug or throttle?

Maybe both?

And what about Donna?

I had no answers.

I parked the car in front of Daddy's cabin and drew clean country air deep into my lungs.

Grace must have heard the car. She opened the door to the cabin, her face a study in *busted.*

At least one answer was easy. The need to hold Grace in my arms far outweighed my desire to choke the life out of her.

I was halfway to the cabin before I even knew I'd opened the car door.

Whatever resentment Grace harbored toward me must have sailed away on the rough waves of sleeping in a cabin without fine linen or hot water. She ran toward me. We hugged.

Who knew the scent of Tame crème rinse in my daughter's hair was sweeter than the purest country air? I tightened my hold around her.

"I'm sorry."

My shoulder muffled her words but not their impact. I hugged tighter. "It's all right." I rubbed circles on her back. "We'll figure this mess out. Together."

She stiffened. "You know?"

"About Jonathan Hess?" I nodded and my chin bounced against her shoulder.

"I'm sorry," she said again.

For running away? For not trusting me enough to tell me about Donna's problem? For putting me through hell?

Now that Grace was safe, now that I could smell her hair, feel the softness of her cheek against mine, hear the quaver in her voice—now I wanted to throttle her.

I didn't let on. One of my hands kept rubbing circles on her back, the other wiped a tear from her face. "You know you're grounded, right?"

Her shoulders shook and she hiccupped a sob. "I didn't think about what would happen after we left. I just knew we needed to get away."

The fabric of her t-shirt felt rough beneath my fingers. I abandoned rubbing circles and smoothed the silky length of her hair.

Grace pulled away and looked up at me with red-rimmed eyes. "We can't send her back there."

"We won't," I promised.

"How?"

"We'll figure it out. Hunter will help. Maybe we can get Donna's grandmother named guardian. Anarchy—" I reached out and wiped another tear from the perfect plane of her cheek. "I mean, Detective Jones will help if I ask him."

Donna appeared in the doorway. Her eyes were enormous and her skin looked loose, draped over her bird-like bones. "I'm sorry, Mrs. Russell." Her voice was little more than a whisper.

I should have been angry with her. I could have blamed her for every moment of worry I'd endured. But—poor kid.

Turns out, I wanted to hug her too.

We sniffled and hugged and wiped our eyes for longer than was strictly necessary.

Then we walked over to the picnic table and benches and sat beneath a stand of sumac with leaves just beginning to flame. Grace sat next to me. Donna sat across.

"You want to tell me about it?" I asked.

The two girls stared at each other, communicating in some silent teenage language I had no hope of comprehending.

"Donna was upset when you told us her stepfather was coming home and I asked her why. She told me he..."

Donna, her eyes still large enough to do a bush baby proud, covered her mouth with her hands.

Speak no evil?

"Donna." I reached across the table, pried one of her hands away from her face and held it. "We're going to have to tell the police."

"No!" Her voice was louder than the last of the crickets. It startled a nearby bird. "We can't," she whispered.

"Why not?"

Her gaze fell to her lap and a flush rose to her cheeks. "He'll tell Mom it's my fault. I'll lose her, too."

She lifted her gaze. Tears overflowed her lashes and streamed down her face. She shook her head. "I didn't start it."

"Of course not." India would believe that. Wouldn't she?

Donna swiped at a tear. "He was nice at first. Whenever he came to pick up Mom, he'd talk to me." She closed her eyes and seconds ticked by—an eon's worth of them. "It seemed like he made Mom happy and she'd been so sad ever since my dad died."

Under the table, Grace took my other hand in hers and squeezed.

"And then?"

"They got married. Jonathan brought her flowers all the time. Whenever he brought some for her, he brought some for me too. Pink roses." Donna wiped her eyes again. "Mom started living again. She went out with her friends. She even got a volunteer job at the hospital on Tuesday mornings. Someone asked if she could switch to Tuesday nights. We had a family meeting about it." With her free hand, Donna rubbed her eyes. "She'd leave something for us to heat up for dinner but Jonathan would scrape it down the disposal, make me promise not to tell, then take me out to nice restaurants."

Nearby a crow cawed.

"He told me how pretty I was and that I was too good for the boys at my high school and that I deserved someone who cherished me."

"How old were you?"

Grace squeezed my hand.

I squeezed back.

"Fifteen." Her voice held no emotion. Either she didn't understand the violation of her childhood or she understood it too well.

My stomach churned.

"One night when he brought me home, he kissed me." She covered her mouth again, paused, let more seconds tick by. "I should have told Mom. I should have. But we'd been lying about the dinners and it was just one kiss and he was so *nice*."

No one said a word.

The leaves rustled.

The birds called.

The crickets sang.

Bile rose in my throat.

Donna pulled her hand free of mine and crossed her arms. Her shoulders hunched. Tears ran unchecked down her cheeks and splashed against the table.

"The next Tuesday he kissed me again." Her body shrank with the memory. "He said he knew I wanted him because I'd kept our secret. Because I hadn't told Mom."

Grace squeezed my hand so hard the bones crunched.

In the sun-dappled light, shadows created a death's head where Donna's face should be. "After that, things...escalated. He told me I'd seduced him. He told me that I'd asked for—" she drew an audible breath, "—his attentions. He told me I wanted it. That I belonged to him. He said Mom would never believe me. If I told anyone about what he did to me, they'd know I was a slut. My life would be hell."

Her life had already been hell. No wonder she ran away.

"I thought when we moved here things would change." She drew another breath—a fractured breath. "They changed all right. Mom was gone more. That gave him more time to..." She shook her head. "It gave him more time. I dreamt about killing him—or myself."

The birds still sang, the sky was still a brilliant blue, and the leaves still looked like jewels, but the day seemed darker, the rustling in the woods full of menace.

"Then I met Kim," she said.

"Kim?"

Donna nodded. "She was cheating on her boyfriend and needed an excuse to go out. I was the excuse. That's how I met Bobby."

"Who was Kim cheating with?"

"One of Bobby's friends." Donna shifted her gaze to her lap. "I didn't like him. He sold drugs."

So Kim had stepped out on Mr. All-American with a bad boy and hidden behind Donna. She'd known about Bobby and Donna all along and said nothing. I could have delivered Bobby's message days ago if only she'd been a bit more forthcoming.

"Bobby loved you."

Donna stared at me.

"The last thing he said was 'Tell her I love her.'" I prepared for a storm of tears.

Donna surprised me. She looked up into the canopy of branches and whispered, "I loved him too."

TWENTY-ONE

No way could I take the girls back to town, not until India understood the monster she married and either kicked him out or left him.

But a cabin in the woods was not an ideal place to leave two teenage girls. "You can't stay here."

Donna's chin wobbled and Grace tensed.

"I'll take you to stay at the farmhouse until we get this sorted."

Donna's chin firmed but Grace squeaked, "Now?"

"Do you want to spend another night in those bunk beds?" The cabin was designed for hunters; describing the accommodations as rustic was kind.

Grace held up her hands, fingers spread, as if a mere gesture could keep me at the table. "Why don't you give us a few minutes to pack and pick up?"

"I'll help." I stood.

"Really, Mom, it's okay. We'll do it."

What was she hiding? I stood, marched across the clearing and yanked open the door.

Holy Mother of God.

I tiptoed through a minefield of discarded shoes. I gawped at clothes draped over the backs of chairs and the couch. Jeans joined the shoes on the floor. A bra hung from a light fixture.

I glanced from the brassiere to Grace and raised a brow.

"I washed it," she said. "I needed a place to hang it while it dried."

Of course. Why didn't I think of that? I'd been underutilizing the crystal chandelier in the dining room for years.

I returned my attention to the cabin. In the course of their time on the run, Grace and Donna had filled the place with empty Tab cans. A forgotten plate of flower-shaped butter cookies half hid beneath the couch. On the oak table sat opened bags of cheese puffs, and one, two, three, four boxes of lemon coolers. I tiptoed through the wreckage and picked up a box. We never had that particular cookie at home; it had to be Donna's favorite.

Given the amount of powdered sugar dusting the furniture, the counters and even the floor, she'd already enjoyed a box or three.

Maybe I should have throttled Grace. Maybe she guessed the direction of my thoughts. She stood in the doorway, gnawing on her lip, waiting for the storm.

"I—" I sealed my lips. As a teenager, if I'd let my room reach this state, Mother's anger would have melted the varnish of the furniture. This wasn't even Grace's room. She was squatting in a cabin that didn't belong to her. But anything I said now would just start another argument.

I opened the tiny supply closet, grabbed a broom and shoved it into Grace's hands. I gave Donna a trashbag and waved at the sea of cans and wrappers. I claimed a rag and a can of furniture polish that promised to dust, clean, shine and protect. Getting rid of the lemon-scented sugar coating most every surface was my goal.

We worked in silence. What was there to say? I'd raised a savage? True. But she was my savage and I loved her.

When the cabin was passably neat, the girls stuffed their clothes into their suitcases and their shoes onto their feet.

I helped them heft their bulging bags into the trunk of Henry's car and drove them to the farmhouse. At least there the possibility existed they might ingest a vegetable. More importantly, Mr. and Mrs. Smith would keep a weather eye on the both of them.

They dragged their suitcases inside then joined me on the front porch.

"Donna, I'm supposed to meet with your mother this afternoon. I'll call you after."

Her eyes filled. Perhaps she suspected as I did that India Hess liked living in denial. Then again, maybe she missed her mother.

"You're safe here. Do not leave." I shifted my gaze between the two girls and repeated, "Do not leave. Promise me."

They both nodded and mumbled their assent. Was crossing their hearts and hoping to die too much to ask?

"I mean it." I treated them to my version of Mother's most severe look.

Grace giggled.

Perfect.

If Grace left the safe harbor I'd found them, I would throttle her.

Aggie stood at the kitchen counter, silver candelabra and blackened cloth in hand. She looked up when I entered. "Did you find them?"

I answered with a relieved smile.

"There's a mercy. You didn't bring them back?"

I explained my reasoning.

Aggie rubbed the tarnish off heirloom silver. "You did the right thing."

"I hope so. I bet I broke some law—aiding and abetting in the delinquency of a minor or kidnapping or something."

"That reminds me. Detective Jones called."

All my organs screeched to a halt. Lungs stopped breathing. Heart stopped beating. Brain went blank. "Why did he call? What did he want?"

"He just asked for you to call him as soon as you got in."

I picked up the phone. "Did he leave a number?"

"It's on the pad."

I squinted at Aggie's tiny writing, dialed, waited, then said, "Detective Jones, it's Ellison Russell returning your call."

"I heard about Grace. Are you all right?"

How to answer? I swallowed and searched for the right words. Seconds ticked by.

"Ellison." The way he said my name felt like a caress.

No man should say my name that way. Ever. I almost blabbed everything. Only the sudden tightness in my throat saved me.

"May I count on your discretion?" he asked.

As long as he never, ever used that tone and *Ellison* in conjunction again. "You may."

"Not a word, Ellison." Thank God he'd switched back to cop mode. "Not a whisper."

"I promise." What had happened?

"The only reason you can know is because your daughter is missing."

"Who told you about that?" I'd reported a missing car, not a missing daughter.

"I spoke with India Hess. She told me." Clipped, cool, cop-like, no extraneous information, no emotion, yet somehow his unspoken disappointment with me spoke louder than words.

I let a few seconds pass looking for a response.

"You could have called me." His tone was softer, more human, too close to the purr that had nearly melted my bones.

"You're homicide, not missing persons."

"True, but I wasn't talking about me with a badge."

Anarchy as a man, one willing to step in and help me, was overwhelming. "I don't like asking for help."

He chuckled.

The sound reverberated down my spine, all the way to my toes. They curled.

"No one likes asking for help," he said. "But life is like that Bill Withers' song."

"What song?" I asked. Anarchy was quoting song lyrics?

"Lean on me. No one can fill the needs you don't let show."

A far too graphic image of Anarchy Jones filling my needs flashed across my brain. I gulped air, choked, waved at Aggie for a glass of water. When my body stopped trying to expel my lungs and I regained the power of speech, I said, "The next time Grace goes missing, I'll call you first."

"Good. Now, do I have your promise?"

"I promise I'll call."

Another toe-curling chuckle. "Do I have your promise of discretion?"

Oh. That. "Yes."

"The accident that landed Jonathan Hess in the hospital wasn't an accident."

Not what I was expecting. "What do you mean?"

"According to the FBI, it was attempted murder."

The FBI? Murder?

"I don't understand."

"There's a chance Grace and Donna have been abducted."

Hell on a stick. What was I supposed to tell him? If I told him where the girls were, would he feel obligated to return Donna to her parents? He would. Anarchy believed in rules. I swallowed.

"Are you there, Ellison?"

"Yes."

"Are you all right?"

"Yes."

"Can you say anything besides yes?"

"No."

He chuckled again. Damn him.

I loosened the tight muscles in my toes. "Why would someone want Jonathan dead?" I wanted him dead and I had a darned good reason, but that was hardly worth sharing with a homicide detective. "Isn't he a tax consultant?"

"Apparently, Jonathan Hess has an unsavory client."

I gulped. "Are we talking waking up with a horse head in your bed unsavory?"

"Yes."

"Maybe I've been watching too many movies, but wouldn't they just shoot him, or blow up his car? Marlon Brando would never abduct someone's stepdaughter."

"This isn't the movies, Ellison."

Anarchy was right. This was much more dramatic.

Ding-dong.

"I'll get that." Aggie put down the silver and the cloth, wiped her hands on the apron that covered a muumuu the colors of autumn foliage, then pushed through the swinging door into the front hall.

"I don't think they've been kidnapped."

"Why not? Because Marlon Brando wouldn't do it isn't a valid reason." Sarcasm? From Anarchy Jones?

"No. Call it a mother's intuition." That and absolute certainty the girls were at Mother and Daddy's farm.

"There's something you're not telling me."

What I wasn't telling him could fill a book—a sketchbook.

Aggie saved me. She pushed through the kitchen door with Amy McCreary at her heels.

Amy ignored the phone receiver in my hand and thrust a bouquet of flowers into my arms. "Jack told me that Grace and Donna ran away but you gave him a ride to the hospital, and stayed with Betty until I got there. You must have been wild with worry."

"Anarchy, I have to go. I'll call you if I hear anything." My nose itched but my hands were too full of flowers and phone to scratch it. "Goodbye."

I hung up the phone, passed the bouquet to Aggie. She disappeared into the butler's pantry with them.

"Thank you for the flowers."

"It's the very least I could do. You stayed. I'll never be able to thank you enough." She patted the skin beneath her eyes, surveyed the array of silver on the kitchen counter, then brought her right hand to her chest. "It hardly seems fair."

That I got the silver instead of my sister? If Marjorie wanted the family sterling, she shouldn't have married a condom maker. "What's unfair?"

She shook her head. "You were nice enough to take that girl into your house, then she convinced Grace to run away."

The blood coursing through my veins chilled by five degrees. "How do you know that?"

"Jack told me." Amy looked at me from the corners of her eyes. She looked...sly. She was up to something. "Well, I think it's just awful. Jack told me it was all Donna's idea but he didn't know why she was so anxious to leave."

I knew. I wasn't telling.

Amy waited for my answer.

I wasn't offering one.

She patted her hair, frowned at a chip in her nail polish, and glanced at the clock. "I can't help wondering if Donna saw Bobby's murderer."

I blinked. That was the question Amy had danced around? If Donna was a witness to murder?

"I think Donna would have said something to the police."

"What if she didn't realize what she saw? What if she only realized that she'd witnessed a murder a few days later? Would she still come forward? Or would she run away?"

Had Donna been under the bleachers when someone shot Bobby? She was a smart girl. If she saw a murder, she'd know it. But would she tell? "I have no idea."

Amy nodded as if I'd made her point for her. "You were there. What did you see?"

"It was dark. Someone knocked me down. I didn't so much see Bobby as hear him."

"Did he say anything?" She looked at me with desperation in her brown eyes. Her shoulders rose and she seemed to vibrate with tension.

"Not about his killer."

Her shoulders relaxed a bit. At least they no longer touched her ears.

"You seem very concerned about Bobby's murder," I said.

"Do I?" Amy's cheeks paled and she shifted her gaze from me to Mr. Coffee. "Well, Jack and Bobby were such good friends. I just want to keep Jack safe."

Everyone was wrong. I was not the world's worst liar. That title belonged to Amy McCreary.

"I wouldn't worry," I said. "I don't think it was a random murder. I think Bobby knew something or saw something that got him killed."

Her pale cheeks blanched the color of freshly painted lines on a tennis court. Stark. White. Vibrant against the red of her lips. "You're sure you didn't see anything that night?"

Just what—or whom—did she think I might have seen? It seemed as if...Did she suspect John? Would he have killed the object of his son's affections? I remembered the mottled appearance of his skin before his heart attack. Damn. Amy was right to worry. "I'm positive. There was just the person at the gate and I can't even tell you if it was a man or woman."

Her mouth thinned. "Why did you go down there?

"I dropped my lipstick."

"You went under the stands for a lipstick?" Amy's tone was frankly disbelieving.

Let her disbelieve. It looked to me as if she purchased her lip color at the corner drugstore.

"I bought it in Paris and paid too much for it. So I went looking for it. I bumbled upon Bobby. If I hadn't dropped my lipstick, no one would have found him for hours."

"Poor boy."

I didn't bother to answer.

"You're sure you don't know where the girls are?"

"No." I refrained from scratching my nose. "Why?"

"You don't look nearly as stressed as you did the other night at the hospital. I was wondering if perhaps you'd found them."

"No," I repeated.

Amy regarded me with narrowed eyes as if she could tell my *Rouge Chaud* lips were spinning lies. She shrugged. "Well, I'm sure you have a million things to do. I won't keep you. Thank you again for what you did for John and the kids."

"You're welcome."

She stepped forward, wrapped her arms around my shoulders and surprised me. No let's-not-wrinkle-our-clothes, ladies-lunching, followed-by-an-air-kiss half-hug for Amy. She squeezed. I raised my arms and hugged her back.

"I mean it, Ellison. Thank you for what you did for my family. If I get anything more out of Jack, I'll let you know right away."

She released me.

Amy McCreary was a nice woman, too nice to go on a fishing expedition. She was lucky she'd thrown her lure into my pond. I stocked my shallows with minnows and tadpoles and bluegill. Other women, women we knew well, stocked their ponds with electric eels and tiger sharks and barracudas. Amy might not have survived it.

TWENTY-TWO

Walking into Le Petit Zinc was like walking into a Paris bistro. Same tile floors, same rattan chairs, same matchbooks jammed under the table legs to keep the tops steady so the coffee didn't spill.

I picked a table in the corner, ordered a café au lait and a palmier (after my day thus far, I deserved a French pastry) and checked my watch—five minutes early, a minor miracle.

At precisely four o'clock, India pushed through the entrance. She scanned the room and I stood and waved. I even managed something of a smile, or maybe a grimace.

She zig-zagged through the tables and claimed the seat across from me. "Have you heard anything?"

I folded my hands in my lap and ignored the sudden outbreak of poison ivy on the tip of my nose. "They're bright girls. They have a car. They have money. I'm sure they're fine." That at least was the truth. I called every hour and talked to Grace just to check.

She raised her brows. "That's all well and good but have you *heard* anything? They could be in trouble or they could be halfway to California."

"California?"

"Or Connecticut."

"You think they're running that far away?" Did India know about Donna and Jonathan? Was that why she assumed Donna wanted to put as much distance as possible between herself and her stepfather?

In French fashion, a waiter deigned to stop by the table. He scribbled India's order for coffee and pain au chocolat on a pad then disappeared.

"There's something you should see." I pulled Donna's sketchpad out of the tote bag I'd carried instead of a handbag and turned to the picture of Donna's dad.

India lifted her gaze from the interlocking Gs on my tote and stared at the page. Her eyes filled and she looked away. "Why are you showing me this?"

Donna's art could do my explaining for me. I flipped to an early picture of Jonathan Hess, one where he looked like a pompous human being and not a demon from hell. Slowly, I turned pages. If India saw the progression from nice man to monster, she might believe me, might believe her husband had stolen her little girl's innocence.

India stared slack-jawed at a drawing of Donna pinned to a bed by the demon. Then her mouth firmed and she straightened her spine. She slammed the pad closed and sent it flying off the table with a sweep of her arm.

It thunked on the floor.

Heads swiveled and eyes stared at us over the rims of coffee cups and croissants half-lifted to waiting lips.

"I can't believe—" India glanced around the room, presumably noticed all the curious stares then lowered her voice to a furious whisper. "I can't believe my daughter drew such filth."

"She drew what was happening to her."

India's lips thinned to a mere line. They matched the slits of her eyes. "How dare you suggest such a thing?"

"Because it happened."

"Don't be ridiculous."

The waiter chose that moment to arrive with India's coffee and pastry. Given India's propensity for flinging things, I wished he'd taken his time. My tote wasn't yet Scotchgarded.

He put India's order down in front of her, bent, picked up the sketchpad and put it in the center of the table.

He might as well have deposited one of Boris and Natasha's bombs. We both stared at it. Both waited for the explosion.

I leaned forward. "You need to entertain the possibility that what Donna depicts in this sketchpad—" I tapped the bomb with the tip of my finger, "—is real."

India's features looked as if they'd been carved in limestone. Cold. Remote. Unmoving. "No, I don't."

"This is your daughter we're talking about."

She lifted her coffee.

I feared for my tote.

India sipped, settled the white china cup back into its saucer then leaned against the woven back of her chair. "Who the hell do you think you are?"

I blinked.

"Who are you to interfere in my marriage, my family?"

"Someone who cares more about Donna than you do." Cruel words. Words I should have swallowed. Damn.

"Mother told me I shouldn't leave Donna at your house. She told me a Walford would never accept her granddaughter. It looks as if she was right."

Any guilt I felt over being bitchy disappeared. "Whatever issue our mothers have with each other has nothing to do with this." I tapped the sketchpad again. "Your daughter needs you."

"She made it up."

"What if she didn't?"

"Donna has too much imagination. Jonathan is always saying so."

I let that comment hang in the air for a moment. Too much imagination? As if there could be such a thing. Jonathan Hess was preparing his defense, denying accusations Donna hadn't even made yet.

"What if Jonathan is raping your daughter and you let it happen because you don't want it to be true?"

She lifted her purse off the floor and stood. "I don't have to listen to this."

"What if Donna ran away to escape him?"

"Lies." She spat the word.

I grabbed her wrist, kept her from walking away. "What if they're not lies? Are you willing to risk Donna?"

She pulled against my hold, looked down her pert nose, narrowed her eyes. "Jonathan would never lay a hand on her."

"India, please sit down."

She didn't move.

"My late husband and I had problems," I said.

She snorted, but stopped pulling.

"He cheated on me. That I believed. I had to. He and Madeline Harper were caught *in flagrante* in the coatroom at the club Christmas party." My head ducked of its own accord from the mere mention of that evening. I bit my lip and forced myself to look up. "The whole club whispered and tittered and rubbed their collective hands with glee. I couldn't deny it. It's hard to deny eyewitness accounts from twenty people."

Mother had sniffed but refrained—almost—from telling me that if I'd been a better wife Henry wouldn't have strayed. Daddy gave me the name of a good divorce lawyer. I should have listened to Daddy instead of Mother.

India's expression softened.

"He did other things too. Terrible things. I'm still coming to terms with what Henry did."

India lowered herself back into her chair.

I released my hold on her wrist. "If I ever trust another man, it will be a miracle."

"Will you live the rest of your life alone?" Her voice fell at the end of her question as if being alone was the worst possible of fates.

"I'd rather be alone than with a man who lied to me or betrayed my trust or hurt my daughter."

India's lips thinned. I'd gone too far. Again.

"You don't know Jonathan."

I bet I knew him better than India did.

"He'd never hurt us." She shook her head. "Never."

"How did you meet him?" It sounded so much nicer than *how did you let this cancer into your lives?*

"At a grief support group. His wife and daughter were killed in a car accident. The poor man was bereft."

So bereft he'd replaced one wife and daughter with another.

My thought hung in the air, nearly tangible, as real as the taste of croissant or coffee. "And I'd lost my husband," she added. "I needed..."

What had she needed that made living with Jonathan Hess bearable? Companionship? Status? Money?

"India, if you need help to get away from him..." I bit my lip. Warmth rose to my cheeks. I'd rather talk about Henry's preference for kinky sex than money.

Apparently India shared my aversion to discussing things financial; her cheeks flushed too. She bit her lower lip. "It's not like that."

What exactly was it like? She was married to a man who molested her daughter. If she had the means to leave him, why didn't she? If she *didn't* have the means to leave him, why didn't she?

Because she didn't believe me.

"He loves me. He wouldn't hurt Donna."

Was it my imagination or did she sound less certain?

"What if I'm right? What if Donna's art tells a truth she couldn't put into words? Are you going to stay with him if there's so much as a chance this happened?"

India's face hardened again. "What happens when she doesn't like the next man, Ellison? Her father's gone. I can't spend the rest of my life alone just because Donna doesn't want me to replace him."

India didn't understand her daughter at all.

Who was I to throw stones? I didn't understand mine either. Maybe that was the way of mothers and teenage daughters.

Then again, I might not understand Grace, but I still believed in her. India didn't even do that.

* * *

I arrived home to a ringing telephone. I picked up the receiver.

"Ellison? It's Amy." Amy McCreary pitched her voice high enough to shatter glass, as if she had an exciting secret to share—that or she'd been sniffing helium.

I held the receiver away from my ear. What fresh hell was this?

"I have wonderful news! I know where Grace and Donna are."

"You do?" She couldn't. The girls were safely hidden. I brought the receiver close.

"Grace called Jack."

Had Grace lost her everloving mind?

"They're at your parents' farm. They're both safe."

I couldn't think of a thing to say.

"You're speechless with relief. I know. That's just what happened when I told Jonathan Hess. He was speechless too."

My heart, the muscle that belonged in my chest, leapt to my throat. "When you told who?"

"Jonathan Hess. I tried to call you earlier. When I couldn't get you, I called the Hess' home. Jonathan answered and I told him where the girls are."

My hands shook so much the phone receiver stuttered against my earring.

"Amy..." What had she done? God save me from good intentions. They really did pave the way to hell. "I have to go." I touched the receiver to the cradle before she could object, then I lifted it again and dialed the farm.

Mrs. Smith answered.

She barely had time to say hello. "You need to pack up the girls and get out of there. Donna's stepfather is on his way."

"But—"

"No buts. Just go. Now!"

"Are you su—"

"I'm positive. Please get the girls out of there."

She must have heard the urgency in my voice. She didn't argue or ask any more questions. "I'll do it now."

I hung up the phone with fingers rendered clumsy by too much adrenaline. Where was my purse? I had to go. I spotted it, yanked it off the counter, fished for keys and came up with a handful of loose change, the second set of keys to the car Grace left at the hunting cabin and a tampon. I dropped the lot on the counter, lowered my gaze to the handbag's depths and searched in earnest. "Damn. Damn, damn, damn."

Where the hell were they?

In the tote.

I tossed the purse onto the counter, reached for the tote bag and searched. The keys were in there. They had to be. I dug deeper. I opened it wide and peered into its depths. I stepped toward the door to the hallway and thumped into a solid chest jacketed in navy blue summer-weight wool.

"Watch out, Ellison."

I looked up into Hunter's face just as his hands closed around my upper arms.

"What are you doing here?" I asked.

"Aggie called. She told me you found the girls."

Aggie might be worth her weight in gold, but she had to stop sharing my secrets with Hunter Tafft. "Where is Aggie?"

"She's getting something out of her car. I offered to help but she sent me in to check on you."

I nodded—well, my chin stuttered. "I have to go."

His grip on my arms tightened. "Where?"

"The girls are in trouble."

"Aggie said they were safe."

"Old news. Thanks to Amy McCreary's big mouth, Jonathan Hess knows where they are."

In fairness, Grace's big mouth started the problem. She should know by now that we lived in the smallest of small towns hidden within a city. Secrets were hard to keep.

Hunter stiffened. "Where are they now?"

"Mrs. Smith is getting them away from the farm." The words came out in a rush, tumbling over each other.

"Taking them where?"

"I'm not sure." I tugged to loosen his grip on my arms. I had to go!

"So where exactly are you going?"

An excellent question. I didn't know where to go.

"Just wait a minute. Listen to me. There are some things you should know about Hess."

"What?" That he kept unsavory company? That I knew. "It doesn't matter. I have to go to the farm." From there I could find out where the Smiths had taken Grace.

"No, you don't."

"I do." I jerked free of his grasp and pushed through the door.

He followed me into the hallway.

"Ellison, wait."

"I have to go."

"Why? So you can have a confrontation with Hess? The Smiths will get Donna and Grace to a safe place. If you go up there, you'll make things worse. Please, Ellison, take a few deep breaths before you get in the car."

I drew one deep breath then another. Then a third. Every molecule of my being urged me to the car, to lead-foot it north, to fight for Grace.

But Hunter was right. The Smiths were well capable of hiding Grace and Donna. Between the two of them, the couple had a passel of sisters and brothers and cousins—all with homes Jonathan Hess would never find.

"I can't just sit here."

"The girls will be fine. If you go up there, you could run into Hess. That's the last thing anyone wants." Hunter's hand closed on my elbow and he halted my progress toward the front door. "I don't want you to put yourself in danger."

He admitted Hess was dangerous.

"I—"

"Adrenaline and emotion are doing your thinking for you. Please, Ellison, calm down."

Easy for him to say. It wasn't his daughter.

Again I pulled loose of Hunter's grip. I pushed through the front door.

Aggie stood on the other side with an enormous overnight bag looped over her arm.

Hunter smiled at her. "I asked Aggie to stay until Grace is safely home."

The righteous anger I should feel over Hunter's meddling in my life refused to get out of its comfy chair. Instead it sank lower and stuck its nose into a copy of *Jonathan Livingston Seagull*.

Maybe because I liked having Aggie around. She was as comfy as my righteous anger's chair. Maybe because I was more worried about my daughter than his interference.

"You shouldn't go," Hunter insisted. "Tell her, Aggie. Maybe she'll listen to you."

"What happened?" Aggie asked.

I quickly recounted Grace's phone call, then Amy's. I told her about Mrs. Smith's promise to get the girls away from the farm. I explained my need to be there.

Aggie shook her head. Her dangly earrings swung like a hangman's noose. "Mr. Tafft is right. You should stay here. There's nothing you can do until you hear from Mrs. Smith."

Aggie was a muumuu-wearing Judas. And she was probably right.

"I'll take you to dinner," said Hunter.

No way could I eat. I needed to sit by the phone and drum my fingers through a table waiting for a call from the Smiths. "I'm not hungry."

His lips quirked. "I am. You can watch me eat."

That sounded marginally better than staring at a silent phone knowing I was powerless to *do* anything.

He loaded me into his Mercedes and drove me to a restaurant paneled with dark wood. Its chairs were upholstered in hunter green wool. Its tables didn't need matchbooks to remain steady.

He ordered a martini.

I ordered a club soda. Hunter Tafft could lead me to a bar but he couldn't make me drink.

"I looked into Jonathan Hess." Hunter wore an I-know-something-you-don't-know expression—a superior lift of his left brow coupled with a knowing tilt of his strong chin. The expression was as annoying as hell.

"Oh?" My promise of silence to Anarchy chafed. Just once I'd like to prove to the high-handed man sitting across from me that I was capable of learning things without him.

"Hess is a bad guy."

Duh. "We knew that."

"He has a history."

"Of what?" Had he done something to his own daughter? Had he killed his first wife? Jonathan Hess seemed the type. "Did you find out anything about his first wife and child?"

Hunter raised a brow. "No. I found a Ponzi scheme."

Damn it. Hunter did know things I didn't.

"Back East?" Maybe that was why people were trying to run him down in the streets.

He shook his head. "Here."

"Here?" My voice was an octave or two too high.

"He's already talked some pretty smart people into investing." Hunter sipped his martini then popped an olive into his mouth.

"Who?"

"John Ballew, Howard Standish and John McCreary, for starters."

Lord love a duck.

I waved at the waiter.

He hurried to the table.

I pointed toward Hunter's drink. "I'll have one of those."

"How did you find out?" I asked.

"I was looking for malfeasance."

Malfeasance. A five-dollar attorney word that meant Jonathan

Hess was more than just a monster. He was a monster who defrauded investors. Where was my drink?

Hunter lifted his and sipped. "I thought you'd be happy."

"Happy?"

He nodded. "Jonathan Hess goes to jail for fraud. India divorces him. Donna is safe."

"That seems simple." Too simple. Things were never that easy.

The waiter put the martini in front of me. It barely touched the table before I lifted it to my lips. "I don't believe in simple."

TWENTY-THREE

Hunter saw me home. He closed his hand on my elbow and escorted me up the front steps. It was time to dig for keys. I dug. Peering into the depths of my bag seemed much safer than looking into Hunter's eyes. Safer than looking at the sky where the moon danced a rhumba, spinning romantic beams.

Aha! Success. I pulled my keys out of the depths and held them up.

"Ellison." His voice brushed against me, soft and warm and as full of promise as a breeze in springtime.

I dropped the damn keys.

I crouched and my fingers scrabbled on the bricks.

He crouched but his fingers didn't scrabble. They effortlessly found mine. Held them.

With his free hand, he brushed a stand of hair off my cheek.

My insides went all warm and melty. My lips might have parted.

He kissed me.

Warm lips. Firm lips. Delectable lips. They made me tingle.

Tingling was bad. Tingling led to bed. Bed led to marriage. Marriage led to infidelity.

I pulled away.

"Ellison." That voice again. It was too seductive.

"I should say goodnight." I snatched the keys off the bricks and stood.

Hunter stood as well. "If Henry weren't dead, I might kill him for what he did to you."

Hunter didn't see my retreat as a rejection. The damned man saw straight into my soul, saw my inability to trust, saw my fear.

I scowled. Hunter Tafft ought not peer into my hidden corners.

"Goodnight, Hunter. Thank you for dinner." I inserted the key in the lock, turned it, and slipped inside. I leaned against the closed door. My heart beat as if I'd just faced a lion.

I drew a shaky breath.

"Oh, good! You're home." Aggie emerged from the kitchen. "Mrs. Smith called. The girls are safe at her sister's house. She says not to worry."

"Thank you, Aggie."

"Did you have a nice dinner?" she asked.

I manufactured a smile, nodded, walked into the family room, and burrowed into the corner of the couch.

My gaze fixed on the flickering images on the television screen. My mind pinballed between Mrs. Smith's sister's house and the remembrance of Hunter's lips.

The Smiths told me I was not to worry about a thing. Yeah, right.

Brinng.

Again with the phone? I glanced at the clock on the bookshelf. A quarter after ten. Grace was under strict orders to contact no one. Not even me. It was too late for anyone else to call.

I didn't move. Whoever was on the other end of the line could call back tomorrow.

Brin—

Or Aggie could answer.

A moment later she poked her head into the family room.

My shoulders tensed and Max lifted his head. "Who was it?"

"My sister, Sophia."

My shoulders relaxed.

"My niece, Rosie, is in labor and Sophia asked if I'd go take care of Rosie's two year-old so she can go to the hospital."

"Go."

"You're sure?"

"I'm sure." It was nice having her around, but I'd managed for years without her. I lifted my hands and shooed. "Go be with your family."

"I could come back..."

"Don't be silly. Go."

I didn't have to tell her a third time.

I watched images flicker for another hour then I let Max out. He sniffed around the backyard, chased some small night creature through my hostas, ignored my scolding and finally agreed to come inside in exchange for a dog biscuit. I turned out the lights and climbed the stairs. My bed never looked so welcoming. I climbed in it, closed my eyes, and drifted to sleep.

Grrrrrr.

I opened one eye and squinted at the clock in the darkness. It was barely after midnight. Max couldn't possibly have to go out again already.

Grrrrrrrrr. Longer. Lower. More menacing.

I opened the second eye. Max stood at the closed door to the hallway. His growl rumbled in his throat. The sound gave me shivers. Was there someone in the house?

I reached into my bedside table, closed my fingers around the gun I kept there and swung my feet to the floor.

Across the room, Max paced.

I opened the bedroom door and Max crept into the hallway—a silent hunter.

I followed him down the stairs, through the front hall, and into the kitchen, where moonlight reflected off the broken glass from a pane in the back door.

My hand, the one holding the gun, slicked with sweat.

My nerve endings tingled. With my free hand, I fumbled for the phone.

A glove reached through the broken pane and closed around the doorknob.

My heart beat fast enough to explode. I tightened my grip on the gun and abandoned the phone. Instead, I stepped into the shadows and wished—fervently—I wasn't wearing a white nightgown. The damn thing seemed to glow. I raised the gun. I'd shoot as soon as the intruder crossed my threshold.

Max still lingered in the light. The hair on his back stood on end. Shards of light glinted off his bared teeth.

Bang!

I jumped. Gasped. My gaze flew to the unfired gun clenched in my hand. Someone else was shooting. In my backyard. The glove invading my kitchen jerked backward.

Bang!

Max barked. Deep warning barks that told whoever was pulling the trigger that there existed nearby a dog ready to tear out their throats.

His bark was the only sound I could hear in the silence lingering after the gun's retort. "Shhh."

He rolled his doggy eyes but quieted.

I listened. Heard nothing. An eternity passed—or maybe it was just a few seconds. I tiptoed through broken glass to a window that gave me a view of the backyard and peeked through the curtains.

A figure—a shadow, really—climbed the back fence. Had the shadow stuck its gloved hand into my kitchen? If so, who'd done the shooting?

I scanned the patio. Someone had been shooting at something—or someone. There! Legs protruded from my hostas.

Damn.

I stepped backward, sliced open my foot on a piece of glass and yelped. Drat! I lowered my chin to my chest, bit my lip until I tasted blood, counted to ten and called Anarchy Jones.

"There's a man in my hostas."

"Is he dead?"

"He's not moving."

Anarchy's silence lasted the length of a few heartbeats. "Does he have a pulse?" He seemed insultingly unsurprised that yet another man lay dead in my yard.

"I don't know," I admitted. "I didn't go outside."

That was met with a longer silence.

I swallowed the urge to fill the silence by offering my services as a prodder of potentially dead bodies. I didn't want the job.

I had a sneaking suspicion I knew who was lying in my hostas. Although the leaves hid the upper half of the body, the out-of-season madras pants looked all too familiar. I wanted nothing to do with him.

"Is someone on their way?" I asked.

"I am."

I wrapped my foot in a towel, gimped up the stairs and exchanged my nightgown for a pair of jeans and a t-shirt. The gun I kept.

Experience told me the police wouldn't take long to arrive. They knew the way. After all, it was just a few months ago they came to investigate Henry's death.

I'd been down this road before and I knew where it led—nowhere good. No way was I traveling it in a white lace negligee.

I limped to the kitchen and rested the weight of my exhausted self against the center island. Max rubbed his head against my leg.

I rubbed his ears then scratched under his chin. "You're a big, brave doggy."

He grinned.

Now I had to be brave. I sighed, picked up the phone, and dialed. "Mother, it's Ellison."

She mumbled something about time.

"Yes, I know what time it is."

Mother mumbled something slightly more coherent about Grace.

"She's fine."

"Then why are you calling? Is someone dead in your front yard?"

"Backyard."

"That joke is in poor taste, Ellison."

"Not a joke, Mother. I just called so you wouldn't hear about it from the neighbors first."

The muffled sounds of her waking up Daddy carried down the phone lines. “We’re on our way.”

“There’s no need for you to come. I’m fine. Grace is safe.”

“Are you sure?” Her doubts in my ability to handle the situation carried down the phone lines far more clearly than her attempts to wake up my father.

“Yes.” I was more than sure. I was adamant. Mother’s stony mien would only lend a sense of déjà vu to the proceedings. The comfort of Daddy’s arms might bring me to tears.

Mother sighed. My sigh had been resigned, the sigh of a man walking to the gallows. Mother’s sigh communicated deep disappointment, untold annoyance and the heavy weight of being mother to a daughter who found bodies in her hostas. “I suppose this means you’re missing the committee meeting tomorrow morning?”

“I imagine so.” I’d take my blessings where I could find them.

“I wanted you to be there. This gala is important to me.”

I had a body—another body—in my hostas. The importance of yet another committee meeting paled in comparison. What was on the agenda? The color of the napkins? Over-sauced beef or rubber chicken for dinner? “I’m sorry to disappoint you.”

She treated me to another sigh.

I promised to call if anything changed, closed an unhappy Max into the laundry room, then filled up Mr. Coffee and let him work his magic.

A moment later the doorbell rang. I took one last look out the back window. With the exception of those crushed by the body, my hostas had their leaves intact. Not for long.

I sent the first set of uniformed officers around the side of the house. And the second. And the third. Anarchy Jones I let through my front door.

“What happened?” he demanded.

I recounted Max’s growls, the broken glass, the gunshots and the shadow climbing the back fence.

He pushed past me into the kitchen. His brown eyes scanned

the broken glass, the blood on the floor, Mr. Coffee's full pot.

"You cut yourself on the glass," he said, as if it was a given. Idiot Ellison attracts a murderer and hurts herself. Again. "Are you badly hurt?"

"No."

He opened his mouth as if he meant to argue.

I narrowed my eyes.

He snapped his lips shut.

Smart man.

He inventoried the rest of me. The injured wrist. The messy hair. The gun stuck in the waistband of my jeans. His brows lifted.

"I didn't shoot it."

"It has to be tested anyway." He held out his hand.

I put the gun in his palm.

Our fingers brushed for an instant.

My breath caught and I looked up, away from the place where we'd touched.

Anarchy stared deep into my eyes, as if he could see my secrets—and desires.

He reached out and brushed a stray hair from my cheek.

He parted his lips and for a half-second I thought he meant to kiss me.

Voices from the backyard wafted through the broken window and he stepped away.

Of course he did. I was once again a person of interest in a murder investigation and it was probably against rules and regulations to kiss suspects. Anarchy always followed the rules.

He ran his fingers through his short hair. "They probably need me outside." Rather than open the back door, he pushed open the door to the front hall.

His disappearing steps rang out against the hardwoods.

Anarchy Jones nearly kissed me. My fool heart did a samba in my chest and my mouth dried. I poured myself a glass of water and drank deeply. What. Had. Happened?

There was a dead man in the backyard. I shouldn't be kissing—

almost kissing—anyone. But most especially I shouldn't be almost kissing the investigating officer.

I pulled the curtains back on the happenings in the yard, took a seat at the kitchen counter and watched.

The police flooded my backyard with light. They tromped up and down the driveway, up and down my hostas. They didn't tell me who they'd found.

I drummed my fingers on the counter. Didn't they realize a tired, stressed woman waited to hear what had happened in her backyard? No. They were too busy trampling my perennial border into pulp.

Was it too much to ask for them to keep me informed?

Apparently.

I deserved answers. I finished my coffee, put the mug in the dishwasher, exited my house from the front door and walked around the side yard.

A uniformed officer stopped me from stepping foot on my own patio.

I stood in the driveway and waited for Anarchy to see me. If he noticed I was there, he didn't acknowledge the fact. He focused solely on the body lying in the broken remains of my shrubbery.

I blew a strand of hair away from my face and waited.

And waited.

Nothing. The man had nearly kissed me not thirty minutes ago and now he pretended I didn't exist?

I marched back to the front of the house, through the front hall and into the kitchen. I took a deep breath, opened the back door and stepped onto the patio.

Everyone noticed me then.

They lifted their heads as one.

"You just disturbed a crime scene." Anarchy's voice was cool and professional.

"I opened my back door." I jerked my head toward the body. "Who is it?"

No one spoke.

"Who is it?" I asked again.

Anarchy, his lips thinned to nonexistence, spoke. "Jonathan Hess."

I'd been right. I nodded. "Thank you."

"What was he doing here?"

Lord love a duck. I should have stayed inside.

"Well?"

"He—"

"I found a casing!"

Anarchy turned away from me.

I snuck a deep breath.

Would the young officer pointing at the brass casing find it odd if I kissed him? He *had* saved me.

Anarchy's eyes can look as warm and melting as chocolate fondue or as cold and rigid as an oak tree in the depths of winter. My arrival on the patio had brought out the oak tree in him. Now wasn't the time to explain why Grace and Donna ran away. Nor was it the time to explain how I hid Donna from her parents. Not with Jonathan Hess' body lying ten feet away.

What had brought Jonathan to my patio? Had he really thought I'd bring Donna and Grace home? Since he'd never shown any great respect for my intellect, perhaps he'd believed just that.

I sidled to my right, toward the driveway. From there I could circle to the front of the house and re-enter without attracting any more attention.

Anarchy pinned me with his gaze.

"I'll just get out of your way."

"Why was he here, Mrs. Russell?"

Mrs. Russell? We'd returned to Mrs. Russell?

I straightened my shoulders. "I have no idea, Detective Jones."

He waited for me to scratch my nose.

I shoved my hands in my pockets and returned his cold stare with one of my own.

"Someone will be inside shortly to take your official statement."

Fine. Perfect. I went into the house the way I came—through the back. I closed the door with enough force to jar loose a piece of glass that had somehow remained in the pane. It shattered against the bricks.

Ding-dong.

Holy mother of midnight callers. Which neighbor was here to complain about the police this time? Hopefully not Mrs. Hamilton. The woman who lived just to the east got testy when activities at my house interrupted her nightly broom rides.

I shuffled toward the front door, mentally composing an artful apology.

Not that it would do any good. No matter what I said, Margaret Hamilton would delight in throwing an extra eye of newt into her bubbling cauldron, then she'd wait for the next full moon, dance a quick jig around a bonfire and hex me.

I opened the door to Mrs. Landingham, my neighbor to the west. A nicer woman was never born.

I breathed a sigh of relief.

It died on my lips when I saw who stood behind her.

"Frances called," said Hunter.

Of course she had.

"Are you all right, dear?" Mrs. Landingham asked.

"Fine," I assured her. "An intruder was shot breaking into my house. I apologize for the hullaballoo."

"You shot him?" Hunter asked.

"No."

"Then who did?"

I shook my head. "I only saw a shadow."

Mrs. Landingham's wrinkled hands fluttered near her throat. "You mean there's a murderer roaming the neighborhood?"

Hunter turned the full force of his mesmerizing gaze on my neighbor. Then he added one of his brilliant smiles. The woman's hands fluttered faster than a hummingbird's wings. "I'm sure," he told her, "that this is an isolated incident. May I see you safely home?" He extended an arm.

She glanced at me, her face a study in indecision.

"Hunter is an old family friend. He'll see you home and he'll check to make sure all your doors and windows are securely locked. He'll even check the closets." I gazed at her enormous house. Every light burned brightly. "If you like, I bet he'll check the basement and the attic too."

Hunter's pursed lips, gathered brows and rolled eyes might have meant annoyance. The expression was too fleeting for me to judge.

"Are you sure it would be no trouble?" she asked Hunter.

"No trouble at all," I assured her.

Hunter coughed but Mrs. Landingham still closed her hand around his arm.

They turned away.

"What are you doing here, Tafft?" If Anarchy's voice had been cold as January on the patio, it was positively arctic now.

Hunter glanced over his shoulder. Smirked. "Checking on Ellison."

"Did you call him?" Anarchy asked.

"Mother." Who knew four-letter words sometimes required six letters? I did now.

"Ellison is not a suspect." Anarchy crossed his arms over his chest and scowled. "You can leave."

Ellison? Anarchy and I were back on a first-name basis?

"How do you know Ellison didn't do it?"

Hunter was supposed to be on my side. Call me old-fashioned, but that included *not* suggesting me as a suspect.

Mrs. Landingham loosed her hold on Hunter's arm and turned back toward my house, presumably to see my reaction.

I scowled.

"You didn't tell him about Hess' problem back East?" Anarchy raised a brow. He must think that the same people who'd run Jonathan down had tracked him to my hosta beds and shot him.

I'd promised not to tell anyone about the attempted murder. I shifted my scowl to the detective. "I swore I wouldn't."

Anarchy smiled then—a delectable glimpse of the smile that matched his eyes. Warm. Swirly. Delicious.

Hunter cleared his throat.

Anarchy shifted his gaze back to the lawyer in the drive, and the warm smile disappeared, replaced by an expression colder and more biting than a blizzard.

Hunter's expression matched Anarchy's, snowflake for snowflake. "What didn't you tell me, Ellison?"

I glanced at Anarchy.

The detective shook his head.

"I can't tell you."

Hunter's eyes narrowed and he extended his arm. "Mrs. Landingham, may I see you home?"

She tittered and laid her hand on his arm.

They walked down the driveway. Not once did Hunter look back.

I turned on Anarchy. "Was that really necessary?"

"What?"

"That—that pissing match, or whatever it was."

His lips quirked. "I need to get back to work."

He disappeared down the hallway.

I longed for something heavy to throw at him.

Instead, I stepped outside, sat on the stoop and waited for Hunter.

And waited.

TWENTY-FOUR

Maybe I should have spent a sleepless night, tossing and turning and fretting. A man had died in my hostas. But his death meant that Donna and, by extension, Grace, were safe. I slept like a baby and woke to mid-morning sun. I yawned and stretched and moseyed to the kitchen for coffee.

Mr. Coffee was full of morning nectar. That meant Aggie's niece had her baby and Aggie was home. That and the stack of phone messages on the counter. I ignored those.

Instead, I poured myself a cup. Then, with Max at my heels, I went outside and surveyed the damage.

Damage suggested something that could be repaired—a dent in the car, a loose grip on a golf club, red paint on my front door. My hostas weren't damaged. They were destroyed.

I skirted the crime scene tape, sank into a wrought iron chair and clutched my mug. Max ignored the tape, sniffed at the shrubs, curled his doggy lips then collapsed in a patch of sunshine.

Libba found us there. She regarded the yellow tape and the remains of my border with one eye squinted. "Your mother said you had a rough night." She settled in the chair across from mine. "It had to be really awful for her to let you skip a committee meeting."

She'd obviously attended. Why else would she wear an Ungaro sweater in shades of red and beige and black, a matching swing skirt and black pumps? Her usual outfit was tennis clothes.

I sipped my coffee. "Mine was better than Jonathan Hess'." Somehow I couldn't work up too much sympathy for him. I stared at the sad remains of my hostas. "Do you think the garden club will kick me out?"

Libba gazed at the trampled leaves and the broken flowers. "They might."

I choked on my coffee.

"What?" She steepled her fingers and looked down her nose. "It's not like you spend much time with those women."

Those women. Spoken like a woman who didn't know the difference between a caladium and a zinnia.

I took a bracing sip of coffee. "I'll cut down what little is left and mulch the beds."

She settled herself in the chair across from mine. "Do you want to talk about it?"

"Not really. All I need is a pair of shears and some mulch."

"I meant having someone else murdered at your home."

I knew that. Hadn't Libba ever heard of avoidance? "Maybe I could put some pansies in. For color. Until the weather turns cold. Purple or yellow?"

"Ellison—"

"Maybe both."

"Ellison! You can't pretend this didn't happen."

I tore my gaze away from the shrubs. "It happened. There's nothing I can do about it...except plant pansies."

"This is exactly how you acted when Henry was killed."

"There was nothing I could do about that either."

"Grieve? You were married to the man for seventeen years."

I did my grieving when Henry was still alive. Every time he stood up Grace so he could play slap and tickle with some woman, my heart broke. Every time he publicly humiliated me, I wailed inside. But I couldn't *say* that. I shrugged.

Libba rolled her eyes. "People think you're cold."

"Maybe I am."

She blew a loose strand of hair away from her face. "I know better. I know this bothers you."

"This?"

"This." She waved her hand at my ruined perennials. "Having someone die right outside your door."

"The man was a monster. I'm more upset about my hostas."

"I don't believe you."

"Believe it."

She shook her head. "Still, it's so soon after Henry's death."

I snorted.

"You have to forgive him someday."

She couldn't mean Jonathan Hess. "Henry? Why?"

"Because holding onto your anger hurts you more than it hurts him. He's dead."

"I know he's dead. I ran over his body." Libba must have found a new therapist. Where else would she come up with this psychobabble?

"What about Grace? What if your anger is hurting Grace?"

Damn.

What if it was?

Aggie poked her red head out the back door. "Phone call for you, Mrs. Russell. It's Mr. Tafft."

"I'm indisposed."

She raised a penciled brow.

"On second thought, please tell Mr. Tafft I have company."

"Please?" Her voice held just the right amount of pleading. "I hate to keep him waiting."

We couldn't keep Mr. Tafft waiting. Not for a second. Waiting was the sole province of the fool woman who sat on her front stoop last night thinking Hunter might come back.

And Aggie. Aggie stood waiting in the doorway. She wouldn't move until I complied.

I stood, meandered inside, and picked up the phone from its resting place on the counter. "Hello."

"There was an attempt made on Hess' life earlier this week." Apparently we weren't bothering with pleasantries.

"I know."

Whatever answer Hunter was expecting, it wasn't that. He treated me to a moment's silence then cleared his throat. "That's what you promised not to tell me?"

"Yes."

"You gave Jones your word not to tell me?"

"Not to tell anyone."

On the other end of the line, he was probably shaking his head. "I'm your lawyer."

"I don't need a lawyer. I'm not a suspect. And when he told me, Hess was still alive."

"You didn't think it might have any bearing on Donna and Grace's disappearance?"

"No. By the time he told me, I already knew why Donna ran away. It had nothing to do with someone back East wanting him dead."

"What did Hess do?"

"No idea."

"You didn't ask?"

"Anarchy didn't tell me."

"Ridiculous."

"Pardon me?"

"His name. It's ridiculous. Who names their kid Anarchy?"

"A professor at Berkeley and his artist wife."

Hunter snorted.

I twisted the phone cord around my fingers. I'd left my sunny patio for this?

"Ellison, about last night...why don't I take you to dinner this evening?" It was probably as close as Hunter ever came to an apology.

"Grace is coming home."

"Bring her."

"I mean, I think Grace and I need some mother/daughter time. Perhaps another night?"

I bit my tongue. Hard. What the hell was I thinking? I should have just told him no.

"When do you expect her?"

I glanced at the clock. The morning had disappeared. "Soon. I called the Smiths last night—I mean, early this morning." They'd been incredibly gracious about a two a.m. phone call. "She should be on her way home now."

"And Donna?"

"Donna too." I picked up the stack of messages and flipped through them.

"What does India Hess have to say about all of this?"

"I haven't spoken with her." Three messages from India. One from CeCe Lowell. Four from Mother. Two from Hunter Tafft.

"You didn't call her?" The judgment in his voice made my fingers itch to end our conversation the easy way.

Hanging up on Hunter would be rude. Rather like leaving someone sitting on a stoop in the middle of the night. "India didn't believe me when I told her about her husband and Donna. She loved him. What was I supposed to do? Call and say now that Jonathan's dead in my hostas I thought I'd let you know I've been hiding your daughter?"

"The woman must be beside herself with worry."

"Presumably Hess told her where they were before he got himself murdered. He knew they weren't out on the streets."

"What if he didn't tell her?" Hunter asked. "What if he just drove up there?"

I hadn't thought of that. Damn. I dropped the messages back onto the countertop. "I'll call her now."

"Ellison, I—"

"You're absolutely right, Hunter. I should call India. Now. Goodbye." I hung up the phone.

The blasted man with his reasoned arguments and half-assed apologies. I'd had enough.

I studied one of the messages, written in Aggie's exuberant script, and dialed.

India answered with a quaver in her voice. I probably should have told her how sorry I was about her husband, but I'd lied to her enough already. Instead I told her Donna was on her way home.

"Thank God." She sounded so relieved that the guilt Hunter dredged up raised its finger and poked me in the solar plexus.

Then she made it worse. "She's with Grace? They're both all right?"

Poke? Ha. More like a breath-stealing jab. "Fine."

"How did you find them?"

Hess hadn't told her. I swallowed. Twice. "They were at my parents' farm. In Daddy's hunting cabin."

A full moment of silence ticked by. I tracked each second on the clock. Five seconds into minute number two I said, "India?" Had she fainted? Put the phone down and gone to pour a martini?

"You knew the whole time?" Her voice was faint.

"No."

"You knew when you met me at the café?"

"Yes."

"I see." More silence. "People say your mother is a force of nature, that the worst thing anyone could do in this city is get on her bad side."

I didn't argue. Instead I cleared my throat.

"You're worse."

I raised my hand to my cheek as if she'd slapped me. Her words stung. "I was protecting Donna."

"Not. Your. Job."

India wasn't the only mother who'd worried. "You're right," I snapped. "That's your job. Only you weren't doing it."

She exhaled. The expulsion of breath from her lungs carried down the phone lines. A simple breath that told a complicated story. She'd paced. She'd worried. She'd sobbed until she'd run out of tears. She was the victim. I should feel guilty.

I gritted my teeth. She could try to make me feel guilty. She could even enlist Ma Bell's aid in delivering poor, poor, pitiful me sighs. Didn't matter. Donna was the victim and I'd protect Donna again in a minute. India had failed her daughter in myriad ways. "I'll bring her home as soon as I can."

"Thank you."

"You're welcome."

She hung up without so much as a goodbye. I stared at the

receiver in my hand. Slowly, I put it back in the cradle.

I poured myself another cup of coffee and peeked out the window at Libba. She'd put her feet up on my empty chair and tilted her face toward the sun. She was wrong about me. I was cold.

If nothing else, Frances had given me the ability to compartmentalize. Infidelity? Stick it in a box, lock said box and store it on a back shelf of my brain. Dead husband? Another box, another lock, another shelf. Dead man in the backyard? Box. Lock. Shelf. Those boxes stayed locked on their shelves unless I stood in front of a canvas with a paintbrush in my hand. It was a fabulous system. For me, it worked like a charm—until it didn't. Until my unwillingness to feel hurt Grace.

Unbridled emotion made me squirm. There'd never been any on display during my childhood. If Mother and Daddy disagreed—even slightly—she treated Marjorie to a day of shopping and Daddy and I played a round of golf. They'd both come home happy.

Some of my best talks with Daddy happened on the golf course. Driving down the cart path, our eyes on the hole ahead, freed us to say things we'd never utter across a table. Perhaps Grace and I should play. It was Thursday. Women were allowed to book tee times. We might as well take advantage.

I turned away from the window, picked up the phone, dialed the club and reserved a time for later in the afternoon.

"You're still on the phone?" Libba asked. She refilled her coffee cup. Apparently Mr. Coffee had charms my sunny patio did not.

I dropped the receiver into the cradle. "Hunter suggested I call India." I didn't tell Libba about the tee time. She might reassess her opinions of my coldness if she knew I planned on playing golf less than twenty-four hours after a man died in my backyard. As a dedicated tennis player, she didn't understand golf as therapy.

Outside on the patio, Max barked then stood, his stubby tail wagging madly.

"Grace is home." A heretofore undetected constriction near my heart loosened.

"How do you know?" Libba asked.

“Just look at Max.”

“Yeah, right.” Spoken like a cat lover, one who couldn’t discern the difference between a warning, feed-me-now, and I-can’t-wait-to-lick-your-face bark.

Max scratched at the back door and whined softly.

The phone rang.

“Would you please get that and let Max in?” I pushed open the door to the front hall.

Grace stood in the foyer.

I rushed to her, wrapped her in my arms, inhaled the scent of her hair. “Thank God you’re home safe.” The words were banal. The tone was fierce.

She hugged me back.

We didn’t move. A moment caught in amber. A mother. A daughter. Forgiveness.

Max bounded down the hallway and sniffed Grace’s bottom.

We laughed. Shaky at first, as if we feared the sound might destroy the moment. Max sniffed again, added a headbutt then somehow squeezed himself between her legs and mine for a hug that included him.

We laughed harder and Grace released me, dropped to her knees and wrapped her arms around Max’s neck.

He rubbed his head on her shoulder.

“We’re both glad to see you home.”

“I’m glad to be here. I missed you, Mom.”

My throat swelled. My jaw ached. I blinked back a tear. “Where’s Donna?”

“I dropped her at her house.”

“Grace.” Libba’s heels clicked on the hardwoods. “It’s good to have you home.” She too claimed a hug.

Libba turned to me. “That was CeCe Lowell on the phone.” She swiveled her head from side to side as if she feared eavesdroppers. “CeCe was going through Bobby’s things and found something she says you ought to see.”

TWENTY-FIVE

Libba really ought to move to Hollywood and become a starlet in B movies. My foyer certainly wasn't big enough for her emoting. She delivered her line with all the subtlety of an actress in a slasher film.

Grace and I gawked. Even Max shifted his adoring amber gaze away from Grace.

"And?" I asked.

"And she's coming over."

Oh dear Lord. "When?"

"She's on her way."

My runaway daughter was safely home. I wanted some time with her. "No." As if my saying it could actually stop CeCe from arriving.

"Yes. The woman lost her son. What would you do if Grace hadn't come back?"

She *had* come back. And I wanted a chance to process that before I had to deal with CeCe's revelation. I wagged a mental finger in my own face. The woman had lost her son. The least I could do was see her when she needed me. I'd hardly thought of CeCe or Bobby when Grace was missing. "Fine."

Grace stared at her feet and mumbled.

"What?"

She raised her gaze. "I'm going to go shower." She gave me a quick, fierce hug then climbed the front steps. Max followed her.

I glared at Libba. She deserved it.

"What?" She held out her hands, palms upturned, innocent expression on her guilty face. "Don't shoot the messenger."

"The messenger shouldn't have said yes."

"You are cranky as hell today." She lifted her nose. "The messenger is leaving."

"I thought you'd want to wait around for the big revelation."

She grinned. "You'll tell me later."

I hate it when she's right.

I closed the front door behind my so-called friend, glanced at my watch, walked into the study and called Mother, safe in the knowledge she played bridge at the club over lunchtime on Thursdays.

She answered the phone.

Damn.

"You're home." The words slipped out before I could stop them.

"You were expecting Flora?"

Mother and Daddy's long-suffering housekeeper hadn't scolded me yet. "Don't be silly, I'm delighted to catch you." Liar, liar, pants on fire. I scratched my nose. "I just wanted to let you know that Grace is home."

"Well, that's a relief. What about the other girl, the one who caused this whole mess?"

Mother still blamed Donna for Grace's disappearance.

Donna had every reason in the world to leave home. Grace had made the decision to go with her. Donna couldn't be blamed for Grace's poor decision-making. But it wasn't worth the attempt to explain. Mother saw the world through the Walford colored glasses. "Grace dropped her off."

"You really ought to do a better job helping Grace pick her friends."

That I answered with silence.

"Are you there, Ellison?"

My fingers hovered over the button that would end our call. Instead, I extended an olive branch. "I talked to Libba. She said you had a good meeting." Extending an olive branch never hurt anyone.

"It makes me look bad when my daughter can't get herself to my meetings."

"Dead man in the hostas. Remember?"

"So sordid."

I didn't argue. She'd already put my olive branch through a chipper.

"I presume this means that policeman will be hanging around again?"

"He's investigating a murder."

"I don't like him. He's too familiar and he looks at you as if you're a piece of candy and he's a man desperate for something sweet."

"Don't be ridiculous." I wrapped the phone cord around my ring finger. Candy?

"Does he ever actually catch anyone?"

"He has several leads."

"I bet they all lead to your door."

I wasn't having this conversation. I closed my eyes and tightened my fingers around the receiver. "Please let Daddy know Grace is home. I don't want him to worry."

"We were never worried. Grace will always land on her feet."

That was too much. "You just got done telling me Grace needs help picking her friends. You thought she'd be okay on the streets?"

"She wasn't on the streets. If you'd given it a half-second's thought you'd have realized that immediately."

My grip on the phone tightened until my hand hurt. "Hindsight is twenty-twenty, isn't it?"

Mother sniffed.

I'd had enough. "CeCe Lowell is on her way over. I have to go."

"I need to tell you what we assigned to you."

"Not now."

"But, Ellison—"

"I'm not doing any committee work today."

Another sniff.

"Goodbye, Mother."

I waited for her response.

She answered with silence, using my own trick against me.

Wow, was that annoying. "Goodbye." I hung up the phone.

Just as well. The doorbell rang.

I hurried back to the foyer and opened the door to CeCe Lowell.

Poor CeCe. Never a large woman, she seemed to have lost half her weight since Bobby's death. Bones covered with skin. Her clothes hung on her. Her hair—well, nothing says defeat like a flattened bouffant.

Any annoyance I had over missing time with Grace dissipated. "Come in."

I gave her an awkward hug. "Would you like some coffee? Maybe a cookie? I could make lunch. I think there's some leftover quiche in the fridge."

"No, thank you. I couldn't eat. I just came to give you this." She held out a wad of paper. Someone had folded a sheet of loose leaf until it was roughly the size of a golf ball. CeCe put it in my hand slowly, reluctantly, as if letting go of one sheet of paper was the same as letting go of her son.

"What is it?"

"A note."

That much I'd guessed. I unfolded it and read.

No one can know.

We have to tell.

We can't!!! He'll kill me...or you.

I won't let him hurt you.

Please! Don't tell anyone.

This can't go on.

I stared at the paper in my hand—dog-eared, worn at the seams—and knew. Jonathan Hess killed Bobby Lowell. I knew it with the same certainty I knew my own name.

He'd shot Bobby and left him for dead. If ever a man deserved to die in a perennial border, it was Jonathan.

I'd been the fly in his ointment. Bobby hadn't died right away and I found him. Talked to him. No wonder Jonathan Hess asked so many questions the morning he picked up Donna from sleeping over.

CeCe cleared her throat then looked at me as if she expected an explanation. "Have you found the girl?"

Had I ever. I swallowed. If I told CeCe about Donna, she'd want to know who the potential killer in the note was. I'd have to tell her about the abuse. Donna or India needed to tell her about that. Not me.

"Not yet." A blatant, painful lie.

CeCe's face crumpled. "I just can't believe he's gone." Tears waterfalled down her cheeks.

"Let me get you a tissue." Of all the stupid, useless things I've ever said, offering a tissue to a woman disintegrating over the death of her son ranked high.

She wrapped her arms around her body as if they could somehow hold her together.

I forgot about the tissue. Poor woman. I draped my arm around her shoulders, led her to the kitchen and perched her on a stool at the counter. "I'll make some tea."

"No, thank you." She drew a wet breath. "That tissue would be nice."

I handed her the box.

She daubed beneath her eyes, blew her nose and clutched the wadded tissue as if it was the only thing keeping her going. "I'm sorry. I don't mean to make a scene."

"If anyone is allowed to make a scene, it's you. Is your sister still here?"

CeCe nodded. "She won't leave."

There was a reason for that. If my sister looked as bad as CeCe, I wouldn't leave her either.

"If only I knew why. I lie awake at night wondering." She

pulled a fresh Kleenex from the box and wadded it too. "Why is my son dead?"

Bobby was dead because he interfered with Jonathan's plans for Donna. I ought to just tell CeCe. Except it wasn't my secret. Besides, the man who'd killed her son lay dead. He couldn't go to prison for what he'd done. Justice wasn't possible. I reached across the counter and patted her free hand. "I can't imagine what you're going through."

CeCe lifted her fisted hand, Kleenex and all, to her face and covered her mouth. "Alice was madly in love with him."

"She was."

"Do you think she killed him?"

"No."

"She could have. She could have stabbed him in a fit of jealousy."

I didn't argue.

"You must think I'm a complete fool."

"Absolutely not."

She shook her head. "Other women have lost their sons and they don't fall apart. Think of all the women who sent sons to Vietnam. They're not sobbing in your kitchen." She stared at the painting of the salad, the same one Donna liked. "He'll never get married."

"He'll never deal with infidelity."

She shifted her gaze from the painting and offered me the bitter smile that all wives with cheating husbands master.

I smiled the same smile.

She unlatched her purse, stuffed the dirty Kleenex inside, and stood. "I won't keep you."

"You're welcome to stay."

"I...I can't. I can't seem to stay in any one place too long." She used her fingers to wipe her red-rimmed eyes. "If you find anything..."

What kind of woman was I? CeCe deserved the truth. The sordid, nasty, gut-wrenching truth. "If I find her and if revealing her identity would hurt her, do you think Bobby would want me to tell?"

CeCe Lowell stood in my kitchen clutching her pocketbook. Her hair was askew. The hem of her rumpled dress hung at a jakey angle. Grief had devastated her pretty face. Yet she still possessed a certain dignity. She even managed a sad smile. "Bobby loved his secrets, and I'm sure he'd want to shield her, but I'd still like to know."

Perfect. Now what should I do?

Grace and I teed off at three o'clock. The course looked like an emerald carpet dotted with citrines instead of sandtraps. Despite the approaching line of fluffy white clouds, the sun warmed my shoulders. My tee shot landed in the center of the fairway.

Grace's did too.

She climbed into the golf cart and stared straight ahead at the lovely expanse of verdant grass. "Are you mad at me?"

I drove down the cart path towards our balls. "No."

"You look angry."

I did? I'd been trying hard not to. "We need to talk."

She got out of the cart, pulled a seven iron from her bag and knocked her ball onto the green. It landed within feet of the cup.

I too hit a seven iron but my ball landed in the fringe. I swallowed a lump as big as my golf ball and said, "I think you're angry too. Angry at me. Why?"

Grace rolled her eyes.

"I mean it, Grace. We need to talk about this."

She shoved her club back in its bag and completed a second roll of her eyes. "You don't get it, Mom."

"Explain it to me."

"Dad's dead."

I nodded. I was with her so far.

"And you're not even sad."

Oh. Damn. I drove us to the putting green. "I mourned your

father long before he died. I've already spent my grief."

She considered that for a moment then got out of the cart. "I'm sad."

"You should be. He was your father and he loved you."

"What happened? Between you?"

There was a question I didn't want to answer. "We grew apart."

That earned me another eyeroll. Rightly so.

"What did he do to make you stop loving him?"

I wasn't about to tell Henry's daughter, a girl who still loved him, about the women or the whips or the foul things he'd done for money. "Your father didn't like my painting. He asked me to give it up."

"But that's part of who you are!" She nodded to my ball caught in the fringe. "You're away."

I putted. The ball stopped on the lip of the hole, poised but unwilling to drop. "I know. I couldn't stop just because he wanted me to. After that, things just fell apart." I tapped in for a bogey.

Grace lined up her putt, her upper lip caught in her teeth. "He was a bad husband."

"He was a good father," I replied.

Grace putted in for a par then bent to pick up our balls. "I'm sorry, Mom." She stood and handed me my ball. Tears stood in her eyes. "I love you."

No tears in my eyes. They were too busy running down my face. "I love you too."

TWENTY-SIX

Grace and I finished our round accompanied by the first few drops of a soaking rain. We hurried inside the club for dinner—to the grill since we wore golf clothes. With its pecan paneling, tartan upholstered chairs and sideboard boasting an enormous arrangement of yellow and red spider mums, it felt familiar, comfortable, just what we needed to reestablish normalcy.

We ordered familiar, comfortable dinners from a familiar, comfortable waiter.

Buoyed by my eagle on the fifteenth hole, I'd somehow forgotten morbid curiosity. That too was familiar, but it wasn't comfortable. Members circled us like vultures, picking at the still warm bones of Jonathan Hess' murder. Then they picked at the cold bones of Henry's demise.

I couldn't really blame them.

Two men killed at my house in less than four months. That had to be some kind of record.

I beckoned the waiter, ordered a scotch and soda, and scared away Audrey Miles with a look I borrowed from Mother.

Prudence Davies wasn't as easily cowed. "I hear you had some trouble." Her smile might look sympathetic but it didn't reach her eyes. Those held all the warmth of an early morning in late mid-winter.

I shrugged.

Grace looked pained.

"If you're not careful, you'll get a reputation as a black widow."

I lifted the scotch to my lips and drank. "There are worse reputations to have."

Prudence flushed.

Prudence and my late husband had something of a…relationship. When I was feeling petty—and even when I wasn't feeling petty—I dreamed of sharing the details of that relationship. But, lucky for Prudence, shielding Grace from Henry's misdeeds was more important than dragging Prudence through the muck. Besides, given Prudence's predilections, she might enjoy the muck—or at least being dragged.

"Amy McCreary is talking about you as if you're some kind of heroine." Prudence lifted the corner of her too-thin upper lip. "Florence Nightingale reincarnated."

"I called an ambulance."

Prudence wrinkled her nose. "She'd be better off without him."

Grace choked on her Tab.

Prudence gifted us another unpleasant smile, displaying her horsey teeth. "Everyone will know by tomorrow. The man who died in your backyard was some kind of con artist. John invested heavily. Lost everything." She rubbed her hands together. Some clever German coined the word *Schadenfreude* with Prudence Davies in mind. She looked positively gleeful at the McCrearys' misfortune. "Amy would be better off if he'd died. At least she'd have his life insurance."

Henry once called Prudence a horse-faced, bony-assed harpy. That description was far too kind.

The waiter put a Cobb salad in front of me and a hamburger in front of Grace.

It's a rule, if you're table talking and food is served, you leave. Prudence didn't budge.

I offered her a smile as warm as the one she'd given me. "Please give my regards to Kitty."

She sucked in her cheeks, but stood firm. Why, when Mother offered her regards, did people disappear? When I offered the same, they seemed to linger longer.

"What do you want, Prudence?"

Her eyes widened at the direct question.

She wanted gossip, the coin of the realm. Prudence wasn't the sharpest pencil in the bag. That I knew. She'd taken up with Henry. Admittedly, I married him—but at least I can blame the starry-eyed ignorance of youth. In ten million light years, why would Prudence think I'd tell her anything?

I swirled the ice cubes in my glass and waited for an answer.

"I'm keeping you from your dinners." She said it as if she'd just noticed the plates sitting in front of us. "Toodles."

She toodled, taking her bony ass into the hallway.

"She's a real bitch," said Grace.

Good parenting demanded I respond with outrage. Children were supposed to respect their elders. I lifted my gaze to the ceiling. "You got that right."

Grace squeezed a second slice of lime into her Tab. "Did you really save Jack's dad?"

"Not really. I called for help then I drove Jack and Betty to the hospital."

"Jack didn't tell me that."

There was probably a lot Jack didn't tell her. "It sounds as if he's got a lot on his mind."

"Yeah." Grace bit into her burger. Chewed. "His mom left last night."

"Left?"

Grace squirted ketchup onto her plate. "She and his dad had a big argument. She was gone for hours and hours. Jack was worried she might not come home."

"How do you know?"

"He didn't go to school today. We talked."

My fork speared avocado, chicken and blue cheese, the trifecta of a perfect bite.

"You don't think—" Grace's brow furrowed.

"What?"

"You don't think Mrs. McCreary killed Mr. Hess?"

Oh. Dear. Lord.

I put down my loaded fork.

"I mean, she has a reason and no alibi."

This called for another sip of scotch. I caught the waiter's eye and pointed at my glass. "She could have been at her sister's."

"Nope." Grace shook her head. "Jack called there. What I think is..." Her face paled.

I glanced over my shoulder. The Standish family. All of them glared at us.

Alice Anne stepped forward—steamed forward—like some turn of the century ocean liner. Lord knows she had the same heft. She cut through the grill like a steamship cut through waves, unconcerned with wind or water or gossip. She even looked the part. Her prow, a proud nose. Her top deck, the perfectly shaped, perfectly white bouffant that sat atop her head.

"Mother, wait." Howard followed in her wake for a step or two.

She paid him as much attention as a ship's captain pays a gull. She docked at our table.

There are scads of rules. Don't wear white shoes—or madras—after Labor Day. Do wear black to a funeral. And, when a grande dame—or old battle axe—deigns approach your table, stand.

I stood. So did Grace.

Alice Anne could have stopped us with a murmured *please don't get up*. She could have sent us back to our chairs with a pleasant *please, sit down. I insist*. She didn't.

"How nice to see you, Mrs. Standish." A polite, expected lie. My nose didn't bother itching.

"You got the check?" Alice Anne murmured; her lips barely moved.

I'd half-expected the stentorian tones of a foghorn. Alice Anne's whispered question surprised me. I blinked, thought about checks then remembered the one Alice gave me. "I did. Thank you."

From her vantage point in the entry, Alice looked furious. Howard looked green. Kizzi looked for a waiter, probably to order a gin martini.

"My family has had a difficult week."

As had mine.

“I appreciate your discretion, Ellison.” She cast a warning glance at Grace. “And yours, young lady.”

If Alice Anne was so blasted grateful, why didn’t she let us sit down and eat? Grace’s hamburger would be stone cold by the time she ate it.

“The man...” She bit her lips so tightly it looked as if she didn’t have any. “The man in your yard, why was he there?”

“I don’t know.” Coming up with a better answer probably ought to top my priority list. People might think that Jonathan and I were having an affair. An occurrence even less likely than me scoring an eagle on all eighteen holes. Plus—yuck.

“Awful man.”

I didn’t argue. Instead my gaze lingered on Grace’s cooling dinner. Not exactly a subtle hint.

A hint Alice Anne ignored. She lowered her voice further. “He and Howard had some business dealings.”

So I’d heard. “Oh? Grace, sit down and eat your dinner while it’s hot.”

Grace hesitated.

Alice Anne offered the slightest of nods. A grande dame’s version of permission. Me, she kept standing.

Grace sat.

Alice Anne twisted the enormous diamond on her left hand. Nerves? From Alice Anne Standish?

I waited.

“You knew him well.”

“I knew him slightly,” I corrected.

“I saw his wife last evening.”

“Oh?”

“I stopped by their home.”

At this rate, I’d be standing next to our table ’til breakfast. At least Grace got to eat. She dragged a fry through a pool of ketchup. My daughter might look as if her sole focus was the food in front of her. I knew better. She was as impatient for Alice Anne to make her point as I was.

"I believe you know her from school."

"To be honest, I didn't remember her until a friend reminded me."

"Well," another twist of her ring, "she categorically denied that her husband would steal."

"Steal?" I raised my brows.

She drew a deep breath. One that expanded her substantial chest. "Howard's investment is gone."

"What a shame." Not exactly empathetic, but given the words painted on my door and car, I didn't much care about the Standish fortunes.

Howard, Alice and Kizzi followed Elaine, the hostess, to a table as far as humanly possible from mine. Alice still looked furious. Howard still looked green. Kizzi looked happier. She carried a glass of clear liquid with ice cubes and a lime floating in it.

"It was a large investment."

What in the name of sweet Jesus did the woman want? Was she telling me the check for repainting my door would bounce? "What a pity."

She scowled. With her broad forehead, assertive nose and strong chin, the expression was fearsome. "Since his wife refused to tell me where he'd stashed the money, I thought you could."

"I could what?"

She offered up a still more fearsome expression. "Tell me where Jonathan Hess hid Howard's money."

Grace froze with her Tab on her lips.

"Why would I know?"

"He was seen leaving your house early one morning."

I swallowed.

"You had a public argument with his wife."

My jaw dropped.

"He was murdered at your house in the middle of the night."

Grace, God love her to little pieces, laughed. Unfortunately, the laugh was coupled with a sip of her drink. Tab erupted from her nose and sprayed the table.

Rules be damned—I sat. And I picked up my drink. “Just so I’m clear, you think I was having an affair with Jonathan Hess and that I know where he stashed Howard’s investment.”

Alice Anne looked down her considerable nose and nodded.

Next she’d be accusing me of causing John McCreary’s heart attack. This rumor had to be stopped. Now. There is no one more unwelcome or unpopular than a woman who sleeps with other women’s husbands. “No.”

She drew her shoulders straight. “Pardon me?”

I took a bracing sip of scotch. “I barely know the Hesses. The only reason he was at my house in the morning was to pick up his stepdaughter, Donna. India and I argued over art lessons for Donna. I suggested them, and since India wants Donna to concentrate on her studies, she told me it was none of my concern.”

“He died at your house.”

“I have no idea what he was doing there.” I tightened my grip on the old-fashioned glass to keep my fingers away from the end of my itchy nose.

Alice Anne stared at me with narrowed eyes, taking my measure, waiting for me to break. “I don’t believe you. Where there’s smoke there’s fire.”

I glanced at Grace. She looked from me to Alice Anne and back again. “Mom’s dating Hunter Tafft.”

Also not true. But as rumors went, it was infinitely preferable to my carrying on a torrid affair with Jonathan Hess.

I smiled at the waiter who put a fresh drink in front of me, waited until he walked away, then said, “I don’t know anything about Howard’s investment. But if I were you, I’d be a bit more discreet. Someone murdered Jonathan Hess and money is a powerful motive.”

Alice Anne’s ruddy complexion turned as white as her hair.

“How dare you suggest such a thing!”

She’d suggested I was an adulteress. Tit for tat.

“My Howard would never—”

“Your Howard does all sorts of things.”

She gasped, and her face turned the exact same shade of green as Howard's, a saturated celadon hue—maybe with a slight touch of moss.

Across the room Howard pushed away from his table.

Around us, other diners stared.

Howard strode.

Alice Anne opened and shut her mouth. Repeatedly.

"What's going on here?" Howard pitched his voice low enough for privacy.

I waited for Alice Anne to explain.

Her lips were too busy with calisthenics.

"Your mother accused me of adultery."

"She didn't."

"She did," said Grace.

Helpful, but I shot her a not-another-word look. There would be fallout from this dinner and I didn't want any of it landing on my daughter.

Alice Anne pointed at me. "She accused you of murder."

Howard looked as if he might throw up.

"I didn't." I hadn't. Suggesting motive wasn't the same thing as an accusation. Besides, Alice Anne should be more concerned with Howard's *other* secret. The one I'd never tell. If Howard wanted to borrow Kizzi's mink stole and parade around in an evening gown, it was no one's concern but Howard's. And Kizzi's. And Alice's.

And I thought Grace and I had problems.

Alice Anne scowled at me. "You did."

"Technically, she..." Grace's voice died. I guess when I really need to, I can channel Mother. Lord knows the look I gave Grace was straight out of Mother's repertoire, a classic shut-the-hell-up-or-else expression.

I looked up at the green-faced Standishes. "This is hardly the time or the place..." My gaze encompassed five or six tables of rapt diners who'd abandoned watching us discreetly. They all gawked.

"I hardly knew the man," said Howard.

"That's not what your mother says."

His skin tone transitioned from celadon to split-pea.

"I didn't kill him." Howard spoke too loudly. Jaws at nearby tables dropped.

I might have believed him, but he scratched his nose.

TWENTY-SEVEN

Grace and I drove home. Slowly. The slick streets glistened with reflected light. The darkness outside pushed against the car's rain-streaked windows.

So much darkness, so many secrets—abuse and murder and deep water running through shallow families.

"Why didn't you tell me Bobby and Donna were together?" I asked.

"When you first asked I didn't know. Then..."

She'd stopped talking to me. Stopped trusting me.

"Did you tell Donna what Bobby said? That he loved her?"

"I did, but I think she appreciated hearing it from you. I mean...you were there."

I couldn't argue with that. "Did Bobby know about her stepfather?"

Grace stared out the window but her chin bobbed.

I slowed for a red light. Stopped. Thought. Amy's worries about John were just worries. Alice Standish, with her ribbons and paint, was nothing but an overwrought teenager. And Howard? He could hardly stand up to his daughter; there was no way he had the gumption to kill. "I know who killed Bobby."

She whipped her head in my direction. "What?"

"Jonathan Hess did it."

"How do you know?"

The light turned green and I pushed the accelerator. "CeCe showed me a note. Donna was worried for Bobby."

Grace crossed her arms over her chest and stared out the window. "Poor Donna."

If I were my mother, I'd point out that Donna left chaos in her wake. "Poor Bobby."

"What do you think happened?"

"I think Hess lured Bobby under the bleachers with a note then shot him."

"I can't believe no one heard the gun."

"Do you have any idea how loud it was in those stands? People were stomping and yelling and clapping. It's a wonder we're not all half-deaf."

"He could have shot you."

We pondered that possibility for a block or two, then I reached across the seat and took Grace's hand in mine.

"He didn't shoot me."

Grace squeezed my hand until the bones hurt. It felt fabulous.

"So, are you going to tell Detective Jones?"

"If I tell Anar—Detective Jones that Jonathan killed Bobby, he'll want to know why." I tilted my head and looked at the roof of the car as if an answer might be written there. It wasn't. I shifted my gaze to the road ahead. It was straight. The exact opposite of my thoughts. Those twisted and turned like a mountain road.

If I shared my theory—my certainty—Anarchy would investigate.

No matter how discreet he was, everyone we knew would speculate as to why Jonathan Hess killed Bobby. Some vicious someone would guess why. Donna's secret would be known to all and Grace would blame me. The bridge we'd rebuilt would crumble faster than a potato-chip cookie.

Jonathan was dead. He couldn't go to trial or prison. Donna—and India—had to live in Kansas City.

"I can't tell him."

"What about Mrs. Lowell?"

What about CeCe Lowell? She deserved closure.

Oh, hell.

The light ahead glowed green and the road remained straight. My thoughts, not so much.

"I don't know. What would you do?"

Grace grinned at me. "You're the adult here."

Screeeeeech. The sound of brakes failing on wet pavement.

Light. It flooded our car. Too bright. Too close.

Then came the horrendous, stomach-twisting sound of metal crunching, collapsing.

An annoying beep punctuated the white noise and the sharp scent of iodine tickled my nose. I slitted my eyes to antiseptic beige.

I lay there, obviously in the hospital. Every muscle, every bone ached. A tear-inducing ache. How had I ended up there? I struggled to remember.

Golf.

Dinner.

Grace.

Grace! My heart stopped and my lungs lost their ability to inflate. I levitated off the hospital bed. "Grace!" One word—a prayer, a plea, my life.

My gaze flew around the room. No Grace.

Anarchy Jones sat in the armchair next to my bed; his elbows rested on his knees and he wore a solemn expression.

He was going to tell me...

"The traffic officer found my card in your wallet. He called."

"Grace?" The question used the last of my oxygen. Complete and utter terror will do that for you—empty your lungs, still your heart, create a buzzing in your ears louder than a chainsaw.

"Broken arm and a concussion." Anarchy spoke slowly. He looked into my eyes. "She's going to be fine. Your parents are with her."

My lungs filled and I held the air inside, savoring the overlooked blessing of breathing. "What happened?"

"Someone blew through a red light and hit you."

"I have to see her."

"Nope." He shook his head.

"No?" I raised my brows and wished I hadn't. Someone had whacked my forehead with a croquet mallet while I wasn't looking. I lifted my hand to my forehead and felt gauze.

"You hit your head on the steering wheel." He offered me a wry grin. "You won't scar. Your mother pulled the hospital's best plastic surgeon away from his anniversary dinner. You'll be as pretty as ever."

Pretty as ever? I stashed that in one of my mental compartments for later consideration. "Who set Grace's arm?"

"The best orthopedic." Anarchy didn't add *of course*. He didn't have to. Mother being the chairman of the hospital board was quite handy. "A neurologist is monitoring you both."

Slowly, with every molecule in my body screaming its displeasure, I pushed myself to sitting. "I have to see her."

"Just rest."

He didn't understand. If I'd lost Grace...my heart stuttered again just thinking about it. "Who hit us?" I needed the name of the driver who could have stolen my daughter from me.

"He died, Ellison."

I waited for a surge of sympathy for the man who'd lost his life. It didn't come. Perhaps I could blame my appalling lack of empathy on dizziness. The room seemed to be spinning and maintaining my current upright position grew more difficult with each passing second. "Would you please raise the mattress? I'd like to sit."

Anarchy adjusted the mattress and I leaned back against its questionable comfort and closed my eyes. I'd almost lost Grace.

How must CeCe Lowell feel? She'd lost her son. The mere thought deflated my lungs with a whoosh. A few tears snuck past my eyelids' defenses. They rolled down my cheeks.

The rough pad of a man's finger wiped them away.

"It's going to be all right, Ellison." Anarchy's voice was as gentle as his fingers. "Grace will be fine."

I wasn't crying for Grace. I was crying for CeCe Lowell and for Bobby.

I opened my eyes.

Anarchy still stared at me.

His brown eyes looked as warm and delectable as the morning's first cup of coffee. I ought to tell him everything. Instead, I closed my eyes and asked, "When can I see Grace?"

"In a few hours. Last I heard, she was sleeping."

"What time is it?"

"Three in the morning."

Three in the morning and he was sitting at my bedside? My abused heart skipped a beat. "Don't you have work tomorrow?"

I heard his smile. "You're becoming my full-time job."

"Is she awake?" Mother's stage whisper saved me from responding.

I opened my eyes.

She stood in the doorway. "Thank God you're all right."

"How's Grace?" I asked.

"She'll be fine." Mother crossed the room, stood next to my bed, raised her hand as if she meant to stroke my hair, but let it fall to her side. "Worrying about you is going to give me gray hair."

This was a worry I hadn't caused. I could hardly be blamed for other people running traffic lights. Besides, Mother's hair was already snow white. Monsieur Claude kept it teased in a perfect helmet.

"So stop worrying."

She smiled as if I'd told a joke. "I'll do that as soon as you stop worrying about Grace." She reached for my hand and squeezed until the bones hurt. It felt wonderful.

She loosed my fingers. "You should sleep. Thank you, Detective Jones, for sitting with her. You must be very tired."

Subtle is not a word used to describe Mother.

Anarchy's lips twitched. "Goodnight, Ellison. I'll stop by tomorrow."

Mother scowled her disapproval of regular visits from police detectives. "Have you found out who killed the man in Ellison's backyard?" Obviously he should be hunting a killer, not visiting her daughter's hospital room.

"Not yet." He glanced at me. "Trouble may have followed him from Connecticut."

That was infinitely preferable to John McCreary being a murderer. It was even preferable to Howard Standish.

Anarchy raised a brow. "We'd still like to know what he was doing there."

Mother snorted. "I imagine he was looking for his no-count stepdaughter."

Anarchy's fondue gaze hardened to chocolate chips. Chips that had been stored in the freezer. "She was still missing when Mr. Hess was shot."

"Maybe he thought Ellison was hiding her."

"Why would Ellison do that?"

Mother stood straighter. Nice to have good posture when you've jumped down a rabbit hole.

I moaned, a low, pitiful sound, and they both shifted their gazes to me. "I'm very tired. I'd like to sleep."

"Of course you would, darling." Mother leaned over as if to kiss me but stopped and wrinkled her nose. "We'll get you some shampoo in the morning." She directed a dragon gaze at Anarchy. Her meaning was crystal clear. She wanted Anarchy out of my room. Now.

With a small wave and a smaller smile, he complied.

"Why was Jonathan Hess at your house?" Mother asked.

"I assume he was looking for Donna."

Mother drew herself up to her full disapproving height. "People will think—"

"I know."

She planted her hands on her hips. "You can't let them—"

"I know."

"What are you going to do?"

I didn't know.

What had Grace said? *You're the adult here.* Maybe I should act like it.

TWENTY-EIGHT

Whoever said things will be brighter in the morning didn't wake up in the hospital.

The light—far too bright—wasn't doing my aching head any favors. I oozed out of the hospital bed, limped to the bathroom and squinted in the mirror.

Blood caked my hair. A bandage traversed my forehead. A bruise the exact color of nightshade blossomed on my cheek. The rest of my skin looked gray. And that was just my head.

No wonder Mother wrinkled her nose rather than kiss me. I couldn't go to Grace's room looking like a cast member from *Night of the Living Dead.*

I turned on the shower, stepped inside and let warm water wash the blood from my body. Raising my arms to wash my hair hurt like hell. I did it anyway. I slid down the wall. There's no rule I knew of against sitting while you shower, and if there was—well, the shower police could give me a ticket.

After a few minutes of sitting, I climbed out of the tiny stall and dried off with a towel only slightly larger than a postage stamp.

I glanced at the blood-stained hospital gown. I wasn't putting that back on. There had to be something in the room I could wear.

I opened the door and froze.

Hunter froze too.

We stared at each other. Hunter—suave, debonair and a walking lesson in sartorial perfection. Me—wet, bruised and naked.

My muzzy brain made the connection between thought and

action. I stepped back into the bathroom and slammed the door. "What are you doing here?" My tone mirrored an outraged screech owl.

"Aggie thought you might want...clothes." The last word sounded strangled. "I brought a bag."

Did he expect me to open the door and thank him? "Leave it," screeched the owl.

I waited for the sound of a door opening and closing, then I cracked my own door. A small suitcase sat on the floor. The room was empty.

Hunter Tafft had seen me naked. At least he hadn't yawned. He'd looked...stunned. Probably he'd never seen so many bruises on one body before.

I dashed—a relative term given my aching body—into the hospital room, grabbed the bag and retreated to the bathroom. Aggie had packed me a toothbrush and a tube of toothpaste. God bless her. She'd also packed clean underwear, a silk nightgown, peignoir and slippers. I dug into the bag, desperate for real clothes. There weren't any. Just a brush, a bag of makeup, deodorant...

Damn it.

I donned the nightgown, slipped my arms into the robe and jammed my feet into the slippers. I didn't have time to worry about my lack of actual clothes. I had to see Grace.

I scuffed my way to the nurses' station and asked for Grace's room number. One of the nurses, probably out of school for all of five minutes, had the temerity to suggest I should be in bed. I gave her my best Frances Walford don't-you-dare-cross-me look.

The girl paled. "Room four-thirteen."

I thanked her and shuffled to the elevator. It would have been too easy, too convenient, for Grace and me to have rooms on the same floor. Instead, I had to wander an entire hospital in nightclothes. At least I wore shell pink Dior and not a standard issue gown that gaped in the back.

I rode the elevator to the fourth floor, stepped out, and leaned against the wall. Since when did riding an elevator make me tired?

I waited 'til my legs felt strong enough to put together a string of steps then walked down the hall.

I paused again when I reached Grace's door. There was no need for her to see me looking as if I might pass out from the effort of walking. I closed my eyes and borrowed uprightness from the wall.

A voice from inside the room snuck into the hallway.

"Of course we came. Donna insisted." India Hess was visiting my daughter. "You've been a good friend to her.

Donna murmured something I didn't catch.

"Still, I know this must be a very difficult time for you. Thank you for coming and for the flowers. They're lovely." Grace's voice sounded strong. And polite. The latter would make her grandmother ecstatically happy. It was Grace's strength that pleased me—she didn't sound as if she was suffering.

I pushed away from the wall but a wave of dizziness washed over me. I leaned again. One more minute and I'd go in.

"These are for your mother."

"She'll love them. She's really into flowers and gardening."

"I thought so. That zebra plant in your living room is gorgeous, and so hard to grow. I've never had one I didn't kill. And her hostas are fabulous."

Were fabulous. My hostas were now compost, and the blame for that lay clearly with India's husband.

I pushed away again—slower this time—then crossed the threshold into Grace's hospital room.

"Mom! Oh my God, you should sit."

That sounded like an excellent idea.

Donna vacated the chair next to Grace's bed and I collapsed into it.

"Should I call for help?"

"I'll be fine. Just let me sit for a moment."

"Let me push the button for the nur—"

"Don't. I just need a moment's rest." That and I needed to see with my own two eyes that Grace was whole. Her face was bruised, her arm was in a cast, but her skin was the color of skin, whereas mine looked like wet newspaper.

"We'll let you two visit." India pulled on Donna's elbow. "Let's go, dear."

"Call me," Grace said. She even mimed talking into a phone with her unbroken arm.

Donna nodded. "Okay." The girl looked subdued. I would have expected dancing munchkin happiness. The monster was dead. But Donna looked as if...she looked as if her best friend had nearly died in a car crash.

"Thank you for coming," I said.

"Let us know if you need anything," said India. Kind of her to offer given what she had on her plate.

They disappeared into the hallway and I leaned back in the chair and drank in the sight of Grace. "You're all right."

She lifted her arm and made a scrunchy face. "I will be. What about you? You don't look as if you..."

"She looks as if she should be in bed." Hunter stood in the doorway looking far better than any man had a right to. "I went back to your room and you were gone. I figured I'd find you here."

"Hi, Mr. Tafft." Grace sounded almost chipper.

"Call me Hunter."

Grace grinned.

Oh dear Lord. It was there, burning in my daughter's eyes—the light of a matchmaking flame. I'd seen that exact expression often enough in Mother's eyes.

"Thank you for bringing my bag." That sounded more civil than asking why the hell he'd entered my hospital room without knocking first. I really ought to mention the skimpiness of the towels to Mother. She'd have the problem fixed in hours flat.

"That nightgown suits you."

I scowled at him.

"The nurses on your floor are fluttering around like demented hummingbirds." Hunter picked an invisible speck of dust off his immaculate sleeve. "You're not supposed to be out of bed."

I crossed my arms. “No one was prepared to stop me.”

He chuckled. “No one is prepared to come get you either.”

What do you know? Channeling Mother had an upside. I’d fill out the discharge paperwork from where I sat.

“They sent me to get you.”

Liar. I bet he offered.

Grace’s gaze bounced between us as if we were rallying a tennis ball.

“I have no intention of returning to my room.”

“There’s a neurologist who wants to shine a light in your eyes. He’s waiting.”

“Hmmph.”

“I’ll help you get up.” He stepped toward me, apparently unaffected by the scathing look I sent his way.

“I’m not going anywhere.”

“Go, Mom. See the doctor. You can come back later.”

Et tu, Grace? I’d raised a Judas.

“Or I can come see you,” she offered.

Hunter cleared his throat.

“You’re very bossy.” I gave up on glaring; my scowls seemed only to amuse him. Instead I crossed my arms over my chest, donned a neutral expression and stared at Grace’s hospital bed.

“And you’re a terrible patient.”

So what if I was? I faked a yawn.

“The hospital has rules about injured patients wandering the halls.”

Rules? That was rich coming from a man who made his living finding legal ways to circumvent rules. “Since when do you care about rules?” I *might* have sounded petulant.

“Since this one seems designed to guard your welfare. Come on, Ellison.” He held out his hand.

“You look as if you need to lie down,” said the teenage Judas.

Grudgingly, I took Hunter’s hand.

He pulled me to my feet. “There’s a chair waiting in the corridor.”

A chair? I got rest stops? Then it dawned on me. Hunter had a wheelchair waiting in the hall. "I'm walking to my room."

"Fine. You walk out of Grace's room on your own and we'll forget the chair."

I bent, kissed my sweet Judas on her forehead, stroked her hair and ignored the sudden tilt of the room.

I made it to the end of Grace's bed. Three lousy steps, then I grabbed the bottom of her mattress for balance.

Hunter didn't smirk. If anything, he looked concerned. "Ellison, you've got to let someone help you."

No I didn't.

I took three more steps before my knees gave out. Hunter caught me, his arms circling me, warm and strong.

"Get in the chair, Mom. Please." Worry pitched Grace's voice too high.

Fine. I'd ride in his damned chair. For Grace. But I wouldn't like it.

He pushed me down the corridor in silence. Lord knows I wasn't saying anything. I broke one silly rule and the hospital sent a high-power attorney after me. What would they do if I stole a Band-Aid? I grumbled.

"Did you say something?" he asked.

"No."

"Are you sure? I thought I heard you say something."

"Nope."

He stopped the wheelchair in front of the elevators. "You don't want to talk about it?"

"Talk about what?"

"Whatever is bothering you."

How did he know something was bothering me? I grumbled again.

"Give me a dollar."

"I don't have a dollar." In case he hadn't noticed, I was wearing a nightgown and robe. No handbag in sight.

The whisper of fine cloth rustled past my ears, then Hunter

came into view, wallet in hand. He withdrew a dollar and handed it to me. "Give me a dollar."

I gave him the bill. Had he lost his mind, or forgotten that I was the one with the head injury?

"Perfect. I'm officially your lawyer. Anything you say to me is privileged."

The elevator doors opened.

"What makes you think I want to tell anyone anything?"

Rather than push me inside, he crouched next to the wheelchair and looked into my eyes. "Because I know you. You're stuck in a hospital so you can't paint your problems away. Something is eating you. Tell me about it. I can help."

"I need coffee."

Hunter stared at me for a few more seconds then resumed his post at the back of my chair. He pushed me into the elevator, leaned past me and pushed the G button instead of three.

"Where are we going?" I asked.

"Coffee shop." He's not all bad.

He pushed me past India and Donna, both eating slices of coconut cream pie. We nodded, the uncomfortable nods of people who've already said goodbye and don't want to begin another conversation.

Hunter, bless him, never slowed. He wheeled me to a corner table, ordered two coffees, folded his hands together and waited.

I glanced around the near-empty coffee shop. No one could hear us. "Privileged?"

"Yes."

"Jonathan Hess killed Bobby Lowell," I whispered.

He wore his lawyer's expression, which meant no reaction.

"If I tell Anar—" A scowl flitted across Hunter's face. "Detective Jones, he'll want to know why. Everything Donna's been through could become common knowledge. She's been through enough."

The waitress delivered our coffee and I lifted a steaming cup to my lips.

"At the time of the murder, you told him everything?"

I nodded. A mistake. The movement of my chin conjured an ice pick in my brain.

"Don't tell him. Hess is past justice." Hunter Tafft, problem solver.

"Doesn't CeCe deserve to know who killed her son?"

"Tell CeCe."

"And if she ruins Donna?" I glanced across the coffee shop at the girl whose life I might destroy.

"Then *she* ruins Donna. You can't claim problems that aren't yours." He took a sip of his coffee. "I bet CeCe keeps it quiet. After all, Bobby loved the girl."

"He did."

"Problem solved." Hunter leaned back in his chair and exhaled. "I thought you knew who killed Jonathan Hess."

Holy damn. I put my cup down on the table with enough force to slosh coffee over its rim. I did know.

TWENTY-NINE

Hunter's lips moved but I didn't hear a word he said. The buzzing in my ears left no room for other sounds.

"Ellison. Ellison! Ellie!"

Every diner in the shop turned and gawped at us, including India and Donna.

I blinked.

Hunter leaned forward and lowered his voice. "You know?"

I nodded.

"Not a mysterious assassin from the east coast?"

"If only." Life was never that simple or neat. At least not in my experience.

"Who?"

"Privileged?"

Hunter answered with a curt nod of his chiseled chin.

I too leaned forward. "It was—"

"You're supposed to be in your room." Anarchy Jones frowned at me as if not following the nurses' directions was akin to murder. Rules are rules. Break a small one and the path toward perdition opens at your feet.

Hunter reached across the table and claimed my hand. Anarchy's expression darkened further.

I pulled against Hunter's grasp but he held firm. My muscles hurt too much to fight him. If he wanted to hold my hand, let him.

Mother charged up to the table. Well, why not? When you've just figured out who murdered the man in your backyard, the more the merrier. She ignored both men, her sights set on me alone.

"Ellison Walford Russell, what are you doing here? Dr. Parker gave up waiting for you. He's a busy—" She noticed my hand in Hunter's and the thundercloud on her face gave way to bright sunshine. "Hunter, how nice to see you."

A smirk from Hunter. A scowl from Anarchy. And a better-than-Christmas-morning grin from Mother.

I stared across the shop at Donna and India and my stomach churned. "Mother, as long as you're here, why don't you see me back to my room?"

Her gaze lingered on the table, on Hunter's and my hands. "Don't be silly, dear. As long as I'm here, I want pie."

Pie? Mother? The woman ate grapefruit for breakfast every day. Pie was an anathema.

Hunter let go of my hand, stood and pulled out a chair for her.

She sat. The matchmaking gleam in her eyes didn't burn. It blazed.

Oh dear Lord. I looked up at Anarchy. "Please, join us." Why not? It was rude to leave him standing.

Mother's lips thinned but she recovered quickly. "Isn't that India Hess and her daughter?" Her stage whisper was loud enough to fill a coliseum.

Both India and Donna looked up from their pie.

"They came to see Grace." My voice sounded as if I'd been sniffing helium. I drew a breath. "They brought her flowers." That at least sounded passably normal.

"The whole town is talking about her late husband. He was some kind of con artist."

Anarchy turned in his chair. "What have you heard, Mrs. Walford?"

For the first time ever, Mother favored Anarchy with a smile. "He scammed any number of people—smart people." Her gaze shifted from Anarchy to me. "Ellison found him pushy."

Anarchy's brows rose. "Oh?"

I'd also found him dead. "It hardly matters." Now my voice sounded gritty, dry, brittle.

"What kind of pie, Frances?" Hunter, bless him, waved at the waitress. "Coconut cream? Ellison, pie? How about you, Detective Jones?"

"I couldn't eat a bite." Truer words were never spoken. My stomach pirouetted like Pavlova and those few sips of coffee threatened a grand jeté. I stared across the room at India and Donna. What was I going to do?

"Ellison." Mother's voice was so sharp that everyone in the restaurant swiveled to look at us, including India Hess.

From across the room, our gazes caught. She paled.

She'd complimented Grace on my hostas. The hostas in the front yard were long since cut and covered with mulch. They shared earth with impatiens. No one would ever guess a perennial border lurked beneath the rioting annuals. India had been to my house once. At night. In the living room at the front of the house. She'd never seen my backyard, so how did she know I had fabulous hostas?

There was no one on earth with more reason to kill Jonathan Hess. If someone hurt Grace the way her husband had hurt Donna, I'd be a murderess too.

I dropped my gaze to the table. "Is murder ever justified?"

Anarchy's eyes narrowed. "Never." Of course he'd say that. Rules are rules. Absolutes.

"It depends." Hunter caught the tip of his chin between his thumb and index finger and pondered. For Hunter, rules were fungible and could be molded to suit his purposes.

Mother rolled her eyes. "Why would you ask such a thing?" Her meaning was also clear. *Stop worrying about abstract ideas and snag Hunter Tafft.*

"Hunter?" My voice was hardly more than a whisper.

He looked at me expectantly.

"You know that dollar you gave me?"

He nodded.

"I have a friend who might need it."

His gaze traveled to India and Donna's table and his face took on a lawyerly look that was frighteningly similar to Anarchy's cop look. No nonsense. All business. Wheels turning. "I can't make you any promises on the results."

"Ellison, what *are* you talking about?" Mother's displeasure with me manifested itself in flared nostrils and an even straighter spine. "I think we'd better track down that neurologist."

Anarchy pinned me with his gaze. "What do you know, Ellison?" No nonsense. All business. Wheels turning.

Rules are rules.

Rules are bendable.

Rules are secondary to finding a husband.

If I discounted Mother's opinion, I was still left with two impossible choices. Take Donna's mother away from her or let a murderess walk free.

Everyone at the table stared at me.

India stared at me.

Even Donna stared at me.

Waiting.

My skin prickled and the adrenaline coursing through me dried my mouth and thickened my tongue.

Did I believe in rules as absolutes? Murder was wrong. India committed murder. India had to face justice.

Those absolutes didn't take into account a teenage girl who'd already suffered far too much.

I reached for the tiny glass full of crushed ice and water next to my coffee cup and sipped. The ice hit me in the nose.

Anarchy Jones could find Jonathan Hess' murderer without my help. That was an absolute I could believe in.

I smiled round the table. "The only thing I know is that I've changed my mind. I do want pie."

Despite cajoling, threatening and tears, the neurologist decided to keep me in the hospital for observation. Maybe he was just scared of Mother. She'd decided I needed *a few days' rest*.

There's no place less restful than a hospital.

I was lying in bed with a sketchpad and a bad attitude when India Hess knocked on the open door to my room.

"How are you feeling?" she asked.

I picked at the bandage circling my wrist. The one I'd worn since Bobby's murder. "Fine, thank you."

With that, we ran out of conversation.

She fiddled with the handle of her purse.

I put the pad down on my lap.

"What are you working on?" Her voice was new penny bright.

I turned the pad and showed her a drawing of blooming hostas.

"Oh." The word slipped through her lips like a whoosh of air.

She sat in the ugly armchair next to the bed.

I fingered the nurse's call button.

We both stared at the institutional beige walls. It was easier than looking at each other.

"You know?" she asked.

"I know."

"What are you going to do?" The skin on India's face looked stretched, too tight, hardly up to the task of covering her skull.

"I don't know."

She folded her hands in her lap. "I should turn myself in."

"What about Donna?"

"She's the reason I haven't." India shifted her gaze to the ceiling. "I got home that afternoon and I was so furious. Jonathan was nowhere to be found." She patted the dark circles beneath her eyes. "I went through his drawers and I found..." She shuddered. "I should have confronted him when he got home but he was so, so angry. He scared me. He said you were hiding Donna and then he left." She lowered her gaze and looked directly at me. "I followed him to your house and..."

He deserved it. The words struggled to escape my lips. I swallowed them.

"When we first met, I thought he was interested in my money.

I told him that everything was held in trusts." She shook her head. "Donna and I get a generous allowance, but major expenditures must be approved by a trustee. Despite the house and the cars, marrying me wouldn't make him a rich man. He kept calling. I thought he wanted me. I never dreamed he wanted Donna."

"Of course not."

"I was..." She covered her eyes with a shaking hand. "I was a fool. But he seemed so *nice*."

Donna had said the same thing—well, about his seeming nice.

We resumed our study of the beige walls.

"What should I do?" Her words barely qualified as a whisper.

A tap on the door saved me from telling her I had no earthly idea. "Come in."

At first I saw only an enormous Swedish ivy. Then I saw who carried it.

CeCe Lowell deposited the plant on the window sill, offered India a polite smile, and said, "Ellison, how are you?"

I'd been in a car accident. I was bruised and battered and a trip to the bathroom required a follow-up nap. I still looked better than either of my visitors. "Have you two met?"

"I don't believe so," replied India.

"India, this is CeCe Lowell." Unbelievably, the skin on India's face tightened further. I waited until CeCe claimed the second chair, then said, "CeCe, this is India Hess. Bobby was in love with her daughter, Donna."

The two women stared at each other across the expanse of my hospital bed.

Finally, CeCe spoke. "She made him very happy."

I bit my lip. *Tell her. You have to tell her.*

Somehow, India heard me. "There's something you should know." She told CeCe everything—about Jonathan and Donna, about her refusal to believe, about shooting him.

When she was done, we all stared at the walls.

Minutes passed. Hospital minutes—which means each one felt like an hour.

"Your husband killed Bobby?" CeCe's voice was quiet, strangled, dry.

"Yes."

"And you killed your husband?"

"Yes."

"Then justice has been served."

I exhaled a breath I didn't know I was holding.

Tears welled in India's eyes, overflowed, then ran down her cheeks. "Thank you."

"I'd like to meet Donna." Now tears ran down CeCe's cheeks as well.

I *might* have brushed some wetness from my own face as well.

They stayed for a few more minutes, but we had too much to say to actually talk.

I breathed a sigh of relief when they left.

A moment later, Mother and Grace walked in.

Grace grinned. "You look better."

"That thing I was worried about...It took care of itself."

"So you don't have to lie to Detective Jones?"

Mother looked suitably scandalized. "You were lying to the police?"

She would have done the same—to protect me, or Marjorie, or Grace. "I wasn't exactly lying. I just didn't tell him everything."

She looked slightly mollified. "I have exciting news."

"Oh?"

"You're being discharged."

That was exciting.

"And Hunter Tafft is coming to dinner."

I guess mothers never stop trying to fix their daughters' lives. Thing was, I didn't blame her. Not one bit. I even managed a smile. "Thank you, Mother. That sounds lovely."

Then I scratched my nose.

JULIE MULHERN

Julie Mulhern is a Kansas City native who grew up on a steady diet of Agatha Christie. She spends her spare time whipping up gourmet meals for her family, working out at the gym and finding new ways to keep her house spotlessly clean—and she's got an active imagination. Truth is—she's an expert at calling for take-out, she grumbles about walking the dog and the dust bunnies under the bed have grown into dust lions. She was a 2014 Golden Heart® Finalist.

In case you missed the 1st in the series

THE DEEP END

Julie Mulhern

The Country Club Murders (#1)

Swimming into the lifeless body of her husband's mistress tends to ruin a woman's day, but becoming a murder suspect can ruin her whole life.

It's 1974 and Ellison Russell's life revolves around her daughter and her art. She's long since stopped caring about her cheating husband, Henry, and the women with whom he entertains himself. That is, until she becomes a suspect in Madeline Harper's death. The murder forces Ellison to confront her husband's proclivities and his crimes—kinky sex, petty cruelties and blackmail.

As the body count approaches par on the seventh hole, Ellison knows she has to catch a killer. But with an interfering mother, an adoring father, a teenage daughter, and a cadre of well-meaning friends demanding her attention, can Ellison find the killer before he finds her?

Henery Press Mystery Books

And finally, before you go...
Here are a few other mysteries
you might enjoy:

PILLOW STALK

Diane Vallere

A Madison Night Mystery (#1)

Interior Decorator Madison Night might look like a throwback to the sixties, but as business owner and landlord, she proves that independent women can have it all. But when a killer targets women dressed in her signature style—estate sale vintage to play up her resemblance to fave actress Doris Day—what makes her unique might make her dead.

The local detective connects the new crime to a twenty-year old cold case, and Madison's long-trusted contractor emerges as the leading suspect. As the body count piles up, Madison uncovers a Soviet spy, a campaign to destroy all Doris Day movies, and six minutes of film that will change her life forever.

FINDING SKY

Susan O'Brien

A Nicki Valentine Mystery

Suburban widow and P.I. in training Nicki Valentine can barely keep track of her two kids, never mind anyone else. But when her best friend's adoption plan is jeopardized by the young birth mother's disappearance, Nicki is persuaded to help. Nearly everyone else believes the teenager ran away, but Nicki trusts her BFF's judgment, and the feeling is mutual.

The case leads where few moms go (teen parties, gang shootings) and places they can't avoid (preschool parties, OB-GYNs' offices). Nicki has everything to lose and much to gain – including the attention of her unnervingly hot P.I. instructor. Thankfully, Nicki is armed with her pesky conscience, occasional babysitters, a fully stocked minivan, and nature's best defense system: women's intuition.

ARTIFACT

Gigi Pandian

A Jaya Jones Treasure Hunt Mystery (#1)

Historian Jaya Jones discovers the secrets of a lost Indian treasure may be hidden in a Scottish legend from the days of the British Raj. But she's not the only one on the trail...

From San Francisco to London to the Highlands of Scotland, Jaya must evade a shadowy stalker as she follows hints from the hastily scrawled note of her dead lover to a remote archaeological dig. Helping her decipher the cryptic clues are her magician best friend, a devastatingly handsome art historian with something to hide, and a charming archaeologist running for his life.

DINERS, DIVES & DEAD ENDS

Terri L. Austin

A Rose Strickland Mystery (#1)

As a struggling waitress and part-time college student, Rose Strickland's life is stalled in the slow lane. But when her close friend, Axton, disappears, Rose suddenly finds herself serving up more than hot coffee and flapjacks. Now she's hashing it out with sexy bad guys and scrambling to find clues in a race to save Axton before his time runs out.

With her anime-loving bestie, her septuagenarian boss, and a pair of IT wise men along for the ride, Rose discovers political corruption, illegal gambling, and shady corporations. She's gone from zero to sixty and quickly learns when you're speeding down the fast lane, it's easy to crash and burn.

PRACTICAL SINS FOR COLD CLIMATES

Shelley Costa

A Mystery

When Val Cameron, a Senior Editor with a New York publishing company, is sent to the Canadian Northwoods to sign a reclusive bestselling author to a contract, she soon discovers she is definitely out of her element. Val is convinced she can persuade the author of that blockbuster, The Nebula Covenant, to sign with her, but first she has to find him.

Aided by a float plane pilot whose wife was murdered two years ago in a case gone cold, Val's hunt for the recluse takes on new meaning: can she clear him of suspicion in that murder before she links her own professional fortunes to the publication of his new book?

When she finds herself thrown into a wilderness lake community where livelihoods collide, Val wonders whether the prospect of running into a bear might be the least of her problems.